"Hatcher's entertaining story uses biblical principles to show how 'real' people can survive, and truly recover from, the devastation of adultery. The book contains wisdom and enough heart to make it worthwhile reading for every woman, including those who've experienced or caused adultery's pain."

—CBA MARKETPLACE

"GOLD MEDAL–4 1/2 STARS. Popular historical author Robin Lee Hatcher debuts on the inspirational scene with an amazing book—clearly blazing her own way and setting her own fine standards with a life-changing book that readers will read over and over again."

—ROMANTIC TIMES

"Robin Lee Hatcher has opened her heart in this book, and her devoted fans will find a treasure beyond imagining within these pages."

—ANGELA ELWELL HUNT, BEST-SELLING AUTHOR

"A story of hope in the darkest hour, of betrayal and healing, of destruction and building, this book will make you evaluate your life and your relationship with God."

—BEAVER HERALD-DEMOCRAT

"Powerful…anointed…a riveting look at broken relationships and how lives can be brought to refinement by the hand and the heart of the Father."

—DEBORAH BEDFORD, BEST-SELLING AUTHOR

"*The Forgiving Hour's* subtitle, 'A Searing Tale of Love, Betrayal and Forgiveness,' describes the depth and meaning with which Hatcher writes."

—CHRISTIAN RETAILING

WHISPERS from YESTERDAY

ROBIN LEE HATCHER

WATERBROOK
PRESS

WHISPERS FROM YESTERDAY
PUBLISHED BY WATERBROOK PRESS
5446 North Academy Boulevard, Suite 200
Colorado Springs, Colorado 80918
A division of Random House, Inc.

Scriptures are taken from the *New American Standard Bible®* (NASB). © Copyright
The Lockman Foundation 1960, 1962, 1963, 1968, 1971, 1972, 1973, 1975, 1977, 1995.
Used by permission. Scripture quotations are also taken from the *King James Version* of
the Bible and *The Holy Bible, New Living Translation,* copyright © 1996. Used by permission of Tyndale House Publishers, Inc., Wheaton, Illinois 60189. All rights reserved.

The characters and events in this book are fictional, and any resemblance
to actual persons or events is coincidental.

ISBN 0-7394-0741-4

Printed in the United States of America

To my friend LaDonna Thomas,
who has touched countless lives because of her servant's heart.
Thank you, LaDonna, for being
an example of His light wherever you go.

For we are His workmanship,
created in Christ Jesus for good works,
which God prepared beforehand
so that we would walk in them.

Ephesians 2:10

Acknowledgments

....

No book arrives in a reader's hands without the efforts of many. I'd like to thank a few of them.

Thanks to Lisa Bergren, Traci DePree, and Carol Bartley for sharing my vision of the stories I want to tell, then helping me make them even better.

Thanks to Dan Rich and Rebecca Price for making me a part of the WaterBrook family. You believed in me before I believed in myself.

Thanks to Liz Duckworth, Don Pape, and Cynde Pettit, who have answered countless e-mails, phone calls, and faxes from me. You've helped make my WaterBrook experience a refreshing one, indeed.

Finally, thanks most of all to my beloved husband, Jerry Neu, who tolerates all the "weirdness" that comes hand in hand with being married to a novelist, including but not limited to the odd hours I keep, talking to myself (and sometimes to people who aren't there), spoiling movies by guessing how the plot will end and then telling him, and tolerating the dust bunnies under furniture and all the other household chores that are left undone as deadlines approach. Thanks for sharing my love for our Lord Jesus Christ and for joining me on this earthly journey.

FEBRUARY 14

LOS ANGELES, CALIFORNIA

Karen opened her eyes to the sterile brightness of a hospital room. MacKenzie Gleason, her father's attorney and longtime Butler family friend—about the only one that was left—stood at the bedside, staring down at her with a look of exhaustion and concern.

"You found me," she whispered. "I lived." If she'd had the strength, she would have cursed him.

"Karen—"

She closed her eyes. "Why didn't you let me die, Mac?"

"Suicide isn't the answer."

"It was Daddy's answer."

His hand alighted on her shoulder. "But Randolph was wrong. He was very, very wrong."

Tears welled behind her eyelids, but she refused to let them fall. She had cried for days after her father's death, but no more. She wasn't going to cry anymore. Not for him. Not for herself. Not for anyone. Not ever again.

"Everything is gone," she said after a moment. She looked at him again. "And so has everyone. Why have *you* bothered to stick around?"

"I guess I'm as stubborn as you are, Miss Butler. And I'm your lawyer. I'm hoping to collect my usual, inflated fee."

Despite herself, she smiled at his stupid joke—but it was a smile without humor.

"Things will look better tomorrow, Karen. You'll see."

Mac was mistaken. About life. About death. About tomorrow.

He should have let her die.

Saturday, February 14, 1931

Dear Diary,

My name is Esther Ruth Thompson, and today is my twelfth birthday. Because I am always writing stories on whatever paper I can find, Mama and Papa gave me this journal to keep my thoughts in. So today, I begin writing the story of my life.

Mine is not a very exciting life, living on this farm in Oregon. I go to school in a one-room schoolhouse on the edge of town, several miles from here. I have one sister, Sophia. She turned thirteen yesterday. She is my dearest and best friend, and I love her more than anyone in the world, except for Mama and Papa.

I don't know what I want to be or what I want to do. Maybe I will become a great writer. But I doubt that. Miss Godwin, my teacher, says I have an average mind and that it will take great discipline for me to amount to anything.

I think that was a horrid thing for a teacher to say to her student. Don't you?

Esther

Thursday, August 6, 1931

Dear Diary,

I could hardly wait for family prayers to be over this evening so I could hurry upstairs to my desk. I wanted to write down what happened today.

First, Goldie had puppies. A litter of six. They are the cutest little things I've ever seen. Well, maybe they do look more like rats than dogs, as Papa says, but before you know it, their eyes will open and their coats will get long and silky like Goldie's. Mama says I must find homes for all of them, that we have more than enough pets around the farm. I almost cried at the thought. I wish I could keep them all. But then I saw her holding and petting one of them, and I think maybe we'll be able to keep at least one.

I was so excited and wanted to share the news with Sophia. So I went looking for her. She was supposed to be returning Mrs. Sprague's butter churn. Which I guess she did. Only I found her behind the barn with Earl Sprague. And he was _kissing_ her!

They both blushed the brightest reds when they saw me. Sophia was furious, and she grabbed my arm so hard I thought I would have bruises to show for her anger. She made me swear

I would never tell a soul. And I promised. But I never said I would not write it in my journal.

I wonder if any boy will ever want to kiss me. I cannot imagine even wanting one to. It seems a lot of nonsense to me.

Esther

One

JUNE 10

OWYHEE COUNTY, SOUTHWESTERN IDAHO

A hot, dry wind swept across the high Idaho desert, driving eddies of dust ahead of it. The sun glared down upon the side of the house, bleaching what remained of the yellow paint that had once made it a bright spot in a bleak setting.

Not that this land of sagebrush and rattlesnakes, jack rabbits and coyotes, wild horses and range cattle didn't have its own unique beauty. It had plenty. And Sophia Taylor couldn't imagine living anywhere else. Not in the dead of winter with snowdrifts piling against the front door nor in the blistering heat of summer when water holes went dry and each day seemed a full week long.

Seated in her rocking chair on the front porch, Sophia closed her eyes, her thoughts drifting backward in time. Through the years. Over the decades. Back to the first time Bradley had brought her to the Golden T Ranch.

Ranch? Hardly. There'd been nothing but land and wildlife. No house. No barn. No fences. No cattle or horses. But her husband had been full of dreams for the future. Their future. They'd worked hard, the two of them, to make those dreams come true.

"And we did it, Bradley," she whispered. "We made them come true. And now it's even more than we dreamed."

He'd been gone nearly thirty-two years, her Bradley, but there were times Sophia expected to turn and see him sitting beside her on this porch that he'd built with his own two hands. Times she thought she could feel his arm around her shoulders as she watched the setting sun, splashes of orange, purple, and pink spilling across wispy clouds on the horizon. When she closed her eyes, she could see him and their daughter, Maggie, and Lucky Sam, the hired hand. She could see the cattle and the cowpokes, the dogs and the horses. They were all there in her memories, almost real enough to touch.

Funny how the older she got, the closer she felt to the past than the present. Maybe her time to leave this earth was near at last.

I'm ready whenever You say, Lord. It's been a good life, and You've blessed me in abundance.

Yet, even as her silent prayer drifted through her mind, she knew with a certainty it wasn't yet time. There was something still to be done. Something unfinished. She didn't know what, but God would reveal it to her in His time.

"Miss Sophie!"

She opened her eyes and watched as twelve-year-old Billy Slader galloped an ugly, Roman-nosed horse into the yard. It was nothing short of a miracle the boy didn't fall and break his neck, the way his arms and legs flopped around.

"Miss Sophie!"

She rose from the rocker. "What is it, Billy?"

"You shoulda seen me. I roped a calf. I did it. I really did it."

"That's wonderful." She looked up the canyon, knowing Dusty and the other boys couldn't be far behind.

But before the riders came into view, Sophia's attention was drawn toward the highway by the sound of a car coming up the long narrow drive. She didn't recognize the automobile as belonging to anyone she knew, and this county wasn't exactly a hot tourist attraction.

"Who is it?" Billy asked.

"I don't know."

The car stopped. The engine was silenced. Sophia squinted against the glare of sunlight, trying to see who was behind the wheel. At last, the door opened. When the driver stepped into view, Sophia gasped.

"Maggie," she whispered, her hand over her heart.

But even as she said the name, she knew it couldn't be her daughter. Margaret Taylor Butler had died four years before—and had left clear instructions that her mother wasn't welcome at the funeral.

The young woman shaded her eyes with one hand. "Is this the Golden T?" She walked toward the house.

"Yes."

The resemblance was remarkable, Sophia thought. The young woman had the same glorious blond hair as Margaret had when she was a girl, the same intense blue eyes. She was tall and slender, and she moved with the grace and confidence of a model on a fashion-show runway.

Could it possibly be—?

"Are you Sophia Taylor?"

"Yes." Her pulse was racing. Her mouth was dry. It had to be her. It had to be—

"I'm Karen Butler." She hesitated a moment, then added, "Your granddaughter."

Sophia swallowed a lump in her throat and blinked away the sudden tears that blurred her vision. "Yes, I know who you are." She smiled sadly. "For just a moment, I thought you were your mother."

Karen didn't reply to that nor did she return Sophia's smile. Instead, her gaze flicked toward the house, her expression disdainful.

That, too, was very much like her mother.

"Come sit in the shade." Sophia motioned toward the chairs on the porch. "It's too hot to stand in the sun, and you must be tired. You've come a long way."

With obvious reluctance, Karen did as she was bid.

"Billy, would you pour us some lemonade? The pitcher's on the top shelf of the refrigerator."

"Sure, Miss Sophie. Be right back." The boy disappeared into the house.

Questions swirled in Karen's eyes as her gaze followed Billy, but she didn't voice them.

Softly Sophia said, "I'd almost given up hope of ever meeting you. I've often prayed the Lord would grant me this desire of my heart."

"You *wanted* to meet me?"

Her granddaughter's question nearly broke her heart. "Always."

Before she could say more, Dusty and the three other boys rode into the yard. Noah and Ted immediately called out to Sophia in excitement after their first full day on the range. Hal, the eldest of the boys, remained sullenly silent. As usual.

Only Dusty seemed to notice they had a visitor. "You boys put up the horses," he said as he dismounted, then handed the reins to Ted.

He strode toward the porch, his long legs eating up the distance in short order. He moved with that rolling gait common among tall, lean cowboys. Despite it being only June, the sun had bronzed his handsome face, exaggerating the tiny lines at the corners of his eyes and mouth. When he reached the bottom step, he removed his Stetson and raked the fingers of one hand through his thick brown hair. "Afternoon," he said, his gaze once again on Karen.

"Dusty, this is my granddaughter, Karen Butler. Karen, this is Dusty Stoddard."

"Pleasure to meet you, Miss Butler." He climbed the three steps to the porch. "I'd shake your hand, but I'm a bit dirty."

"That's quite all right," Karen replied in a chilled tone.

Dusty glanced toward Sophia, his expression inscrutable. Then he slapped his Stetson back on his head as he said, "Where's Billy?"

"In the house, getting us some lemonade."

"Well, send him out to the barn when he's done. We've still got chores to do before supper."

"I'll tell him." Sophia watched Dusty walk across the yard toward the barn, all the while wondering what had brought her granddaughter to Idaho for the first time in her twenty-seven years.

Karen was wondering much the same thing as she stared at the sun-bleached outbuildings, the rotting corral fences, and the dusty barnyard. What on earth had possessed her to listen to Mac Gleason's advice? There must have been some other option than this.

Only there hadn't been. Karen had nowhere to go but here. She was at the end of her rope. And from the look of this ranch, she'd finally hit bottom. It couldn't get any worse than this.

"Will you be able to stay long?" her grandmother asked.

She turned toward the old woman. She had envisioned Sophia Taylor as something other than the frail-looking, white-haired person who sat across from her. Based upon what little her mother had told her, Karen had expected to find a glowering, meanspirited witch at best. At worst, she'd expected to be tossed out on her ear.

"Can you stay long?" Sophia asked again. "Can you stay here with me at the ranch?"

After another moment's hesitation, she answered, "Yes, I can stay. If you'll allow it."

"Allow it? I *want* you to stay. Very much. More than I can say. We've a great deal to catch up on, you and I. Twenty-seven years in all."

Karen drew in a deep breath, then let it out. "You might as well know the truth," she began, sitting up straight, her hands

12

clenched in her lap. "I only came because I have no place else to go."

"No place else?" Sophia shook her head. "I'm afraid I don't understand."

"I'm penniless, and I'm homeless."

"But your father is a wealthy—"

"My father lost everything he had because of some illegal business practices. He was probably going to serve time in jail, if the IRS had their way. So he killed himself rather than face the shame of it."

Sophia covered her mouth with her hand. "Oh, you dear girl. I hadn't heard."

Karen jumped up from her chair and walked to the porch railing. She gripped it, determined not to shed one single tear. Not for herself or for her father.

She stared at the yard, the outbuildings, and the surrounding land a second time while she fought for control of her emotions. She'd thought cattle ranches had acres and acres of green pastures. She'd thought they had big houses made of logs or bricks, and sleek horses cantering in white-fenced paddocks, and lots of great-looking cowboys working the place. None of that was true of the Golden T. This wasn't at all what she'd imagined.

I never should have left Los Angeles. What am I going to do now? I can't live like this!

"Here's the lemonade, Miss Sophie."

Karen didn't turn around at Billy's announcement. She heard the old woman speaking softly to him and knew the boy was being sent to the barn as that cowboy had instructed.

She frowned to herself. Who was Dusty Stoddard anyway? Who were all those boys? What were they doing in this forsaken part of the world, on her grandmother's ranch—if that's what one called this ramshackle place?

She rubbed her temples with her fingertips. Her head was beginning to throb—before long, she was going to have a full-fledged migraine. She knew all the signs.

"Are you all right, Karen?"

She turned toward the old woman. "Just a headache."

"Maybe I should take you to your room." Sophia rose from her chair. "We can talk later."

"Perhaps that would be best."

What am I doing here? I don't know her. She doesn't know me. This is crazy. I should leave. Tomorrow I'll leave. I'll go back to L.A.

Only there was nothing to go back to, no place else to turn. This was it.

From just inside the barn, Dusty watched as Sophia and her granddaughter disappeared into the house.

What had brought Karen Butler to Idaho? he wondered. It couldn't be for any good reason. One look at her was all it took to know that. Vain. Rich. Spoiled. Those were just a few of the adjectives he would use to describe her, and he'd bet his last dollar he wasn't wrong about a single one of them.

If she hurt Sophia...

"Can you give me a hand, Junkman?"

Dusty glanced over his shoulder in time to see Billy Slader struggling to lift a saddle onto the saddle tree. Hal Junker, known as Junkman to his peers, went to Billy's aid, giving the younger boy the help he'd asked for.

Dusty frowned as he observed them. Of the four boys staying at the ranch this summer, Hal would be the greatest challenge. He had one of the toughest facades Dusty had seen in all his years of working with at-risk kids. The boy had been abandoned as a toddler by both of his parents, raised in poverty, shuffled between members of an extended family, never wanted by any of them. Even his nickname said he was a throwaway, a kid without worth. Just junk. Unfortunately, that was how Hal saw himself too.

Somehow Dusty had to help the boy discover the truth. That he had great value, especially in the eyes of God. But how could he break through Hal's tough exterior? That was the hard part. Breaking through. It was always the hard part. And he only had three months each summer to do it in.

"Hey, Dusty," Noah called as he tossed hay into a stall. "Who was the lady with Miss Sophie?"

Ted looked out of the tack room. "Some looker, huh?"

It was Billy who answered Noah's question. "That's Miss Sophie's granddaughter. I heard her say so."

"That right?" Hal helped Billy toss the last of the saddle blankets over the railing.

"Yes," Dusty answered. "Seems she'll be staying awhile."

"Things just might be lookin' up, fellas." Hal's laugh was suggestive.

Dusty shook his head in a silent warning. The rules were strict at the Golden T. The boys were required to use polite language at all times. Especially when it came to women.

But there was no denying that Karen Butler was a looker, just as Ted had said. Whether or not her presence at the ranch meant things were looking up was still in question.

He hoped so, for Sophia's sake. The elderly woman deserved good things to happen to her in her sunset years.

❧

"You holler if you need anything," Sophia said as she backed out of the bedroom, closing the door after her.

Alone at last, Karen sank onto the bed. "I understand now. No wonder Mother got out of here as fast as she could."

The bedroom was small, barely enough space for the double bed and an ancient four-drawer bureau. The wooden floor was hidden beneath an old rag rug, and the wallpaper looked to be as old as the house, judging by the faded design and curling edges.

It was impossible for Karen to picture Margaret Butler living in this place. Impossible? No. It was laughable.

She lay down, draped an arm over her eyes, and wished for sleep so she could escape the reality of her situation.

Mac isn't around to save you now. Killing yourself would be a lot easier. You could go park that piece of junk you're driving in the middle of the desert and nobody would find you for weeks, maybe years.

"Like father, like daughter."

That was what had kept her from another suicide attempt. Not wanting to be like Randolph Butler was what had helped her fight her way back from the pit of depression. It was probably the only thing that could have done it. That and Mac's unflagging support.

Mac had paid her hospital bills out of his own pocket. He and his wife had taken Karen into their home for several months. And finally, he'd provided the means for her to come to Idaho.

She moaned softly. Based upon the things her mother had said years before, she hadn't expected this to be a picnic, but she'd had no idea how bad it would be. They were miles and miles from a town of any size. She'd rarely seen so much emptiness, apart from the desert around Las Vegas—and who noticed the desert when one went to Vegas? This entire house was smaller than the living room of the Butlers' L.A. residence.

Correction. *Former* L.A. residence.

It would kill Mother to see me here. Maybe knowing that would remove some of the sting.

Margaret Butler had hated this ranch as much as she'd despised her mother. She'd never tried to hide either fact from Karen.

"Your grandmother is a hateful, despicable woman," Margaret had said once. "I was lucky to escape her and that dreadful ranch. Never ask me about her again. As far as I'm concerned, she's dead."

But that *despicable* woman had welcomed Karen into her home without question. Her eyes had been kind, her words tender. Was it all an act? Or was it because she was old? Sometimes the elderly changed when they faced eternity—or so she'd been told. Was her grandmother ill, perhaps facing death?

She winced at the thought.

Before leaving Los Angeles, she'd figured the one bright spot about going to Idaho was that her grandmother was over eighty years old. If she played her cards right, Karen had thought she might inherit the ranch once the old woman kicked off. Then she could sell it and return to Los Angeles with the necessary funds to resume the lifestyle to which she was both accustomed and suited.

But inherit this place? What a joke! The Golden T couldn't be worth much more than the thirty-year-old car Mac had given to her.

And why should she be surprised? Nothing else in her life had gone right lately. Why should this be any different?

....

Christmas Day, 1933

Dear Diary,

I write this by candlelight. The house is silent. Everyone else is asleep. Except for me. I am still too excited, for I love this day beyond any other of the year. It isn't the presents. We have never had many of those. It isn't the dinner, for Mama's food is always delicious. I suppose it must be the love we all have for one another.

Of course, there were some presents. Mama made Sophia and me each a new dress. Mine is buttercup yellow. Sophia's is sky blue. And both are pretty with lace collars. Mama must have worked many hours in secret. We wore our new dresses to church this morning.

I saved my money from thinning apples last summer. I bought Papa a new watch chain because he lost the one Grandpa gave him. He was very pleased. I bought Mama a new straw hat. She says it's the loveliest she has ever owned. It isn't, but I liked her saying it was so.

I bought something very special for Sophia. She's been admiring a comb for her hair for many months now. When it disappeared from the shop window, she was disappointed. She had no idea I bought it for her. She was so surprised, and she says she will wear it because I am both her best friend and her beloved sister.

I thought it the best Christmas ever.

Esther

Wednesday, February 14, 1934

Dear Diary,

I am fifteen today, and this is my first entry in my fourth
journal. I know now that Mama will give me a new book for my
thoughts every year for my birthday. Although I cannot say my
writing will ever be of much interest to anyone. Not even to me.

What will this next year bring? I wonder. Fifteen is nearly
grown, after all. Some girls marry at sixteen, although I cannot
imagine wanting to do so.

Sophia tells me I will change my mind when the right boy
comes along. She says love will make me forget my tomboyish
ways. I wonder if that is true. Perhaps. Sophia knows much
more than I. She's been kissed, while I never have.

Sophia's the pretty one. Am I jealous?

Esther

Karen fell asleep in her clothes. It was the smell of frying bacon that brought her around in the morning.

When she sat up, she found that someone had brought in her suitcases from the car and had placed them at the foot of the bed. Her cosmetic case was on top of the bureau. She went to it immediately, desperate for her toothbrush and toothpaste, a brush for her hair, and her roll-on deodorant.

Half an hour later, she emerged from the bathroom, feeling more human, and went to the kitchen.

Dirty dishes were stacked on the counter next to the sink, and two of the boys she'd seen yesterday were washing and drying them. Sophia sat at the table in the middle of the room, sipping a hot beverage from a delicate china cup.

Her grandmother's eyes brightened when she saw Karen. "My dear, you must be famished." She rose from her chair. "You slept right through supper last night."

The boys stopped what they were doing and turned to stare. Karen glared back at them.

Sophia didn't seem to notice the exchange. "Sit down and I'll scramble you some eggs. And we have bacon and grapefruit, too."

"I'd be happy with a cup of coffee and some dry toast," Karen answered, feeling uncomfortable. She was used to being waited on. But by servants, not old women. "Just show me where things are, and I'll get them myself."

"Don't be silly. You're my guest." Sophia motioned toward the chair opposite her. "Sit down. Please."

Karen didn't know what else to do but oblige.

"I've asked Dusty to show you around the ranch this evening after it cools off. If you're up to it. Do you ride?"

"Yes." Lessons at boarding school had seen to that, she could have added.

"Good." Sophia dropped two pieces of white bread into a four-slot toaster, then pushed down on the knob. "I think you'll enjoy getting out once you're rested."

Getting out is exactly what I'd like to do. Out of here.

Her grandmother poured coffee into a china cup similar to the one on the table. "As soon as Ted and Noah finish their chores, you and I can sit in the parlor and get better acquainted." To the boys, she said, "Hurry up, you two. Quit your dawdling."

"Sure thing, Miss Sophie."

"We ain't dawdling."

"Says who?" She swatted the shorter of the two boys on the backside with a dishtowel, smiling at him with affection. "And say hello to my granddaughter, Karen Butler."

"Hi, Miss Butler. I'm Noah."

She nodded. "Hello, Noah."

"And I'm Ted Haney. Nice to have you here. Where you from?"

"California. Los Angeles. And you?"

"From around here," Ted answered with a shrug. Then he turned toward the sink and continued washing and rinsing while Noah dried and stacked.

What were these boys to Sophia? Karen wondered again. Relatives of some kind? Sophia's great-grandchildren? Did Margaret Butler have a brother or sister she hadn't bothered to tell Karen about?

Nothing would surprise her. It seemed there were a great many things her mother hadn't bothered to tell her.

"Karen?"

She glanced up to find Sophia standing directly across the table from her.

"Don't be too hard on your mother."

"I don't know what you mean."

"Maybe not yet. But you will in time."

"So how's it going?" Grant Ludwig asked as he and Dusty followed the four boys up the draw.

The six of them were headed toward the foothills that formed the southern border of the ranch. It would be a long day, but it was the sort Dusty liked best. He enjoyed being on horseback. Gave a man time to think, to talk to God, to work things out. Surrounded by nature and little else, it was a good object lesson on a person's dependence upon the Creator of the universe.

"Okay," Dusty said in reply to Grant's question. "They've settled in."

Grant Ludwig worked part-time for the Golden T Youth Camp, his small stipend paid by the four area churches that helped support the camp. He'd volunteered his services nearly five years ago, right after Sophia gave Dusty the use of her ranch for his work.

"The four of them seem to be getting along with each other," Grant commented.

Dusty shrugged. Both men knew that appearances could be deceiving. Boys were sent to the Golden T when options were running out. Usually by their parents, occasionally by a judge who believed in the work Dusty was doing. This was the place boys came, in the hopes they could be turned around before they got into serious trouble with the law.

Sometimes it worked. Sometimes it didn't.

The times that it didn't were the ones that kept Dusty awake at night, wondering what he might have done differently.

"Miss Sophie have company? Or did you get another car?"

"No. It's her granddaughter's."

"Do tell?" Grant's eyes widened in surprise. "I didn't know she had any family left."

"I don't think Miss Butler's here 'cause she wants to be."

"What do you mean?"

Dusty frowned. "I don't know. Just a gut feeling. You'll see for yourself when you meet her." He gave his head a slight shake. "I'm afraid it'll break Sophia's heart when she leaves. You should've seen the way she looked last night. I swear, it took ten years off her, having Karen sleeping in Margaret's old room."

"Well, it isn't like Sophia couldn't use some help around the place. That'll be nice for her."

Dusty didn't comment. From the looks of Karen Butler, he'd guess she hadn't lifted a finger to do anything for herself from the moment she was born with that silver spoon in her mouth. From the tips of her manicured nails to the toes of her designer shoes, she had big money written all over her. The suitcases he'd brought in last night would have supported everybody on the ranch for a couple of months, minimum. Probably longer. The only thing that didn't fit was the rattletrap car she was driving.

He bet that was killing her.

ARE YOU JUDGING HER, MY SON?

With a nod, he acknowledged the gentle question spoken to his heart.

But he *still* believed Karen's presence at the ranch could only mean disappointment for Sophia.

⁂

Karen looked at the framed photographs covering the top of the upright piano in the parlor. Photos of her mother when she was a girl. Photos of her mother's father, Bradley Taylor. Photos of the three of them as a family.

"Do you play?" her grandmother asked from behind Karen.

She turned around. "Pardon?"

"Do you play the piano?"

"Yes." More exclusive boarding-school lessons, she could have added.

"I taught your mother on that piano."

"Really?" Another surprise. "I didn't even know she could play."

Sophia's expression turned sorrowful as she sat down in the nearby chair. "Because of me, I suppose. She learned to hate anything I loved. Except for Bradley. We both loved her father."

"Tell me about Mother when she was young." Karen glanced over her shoulder again. "I never saw any photos of her as a child. I assumed you hadn't taken any."

"Oh, we took lots of photographs. She was beautiful, our Maggie. She was very much like her father."

Karen leaned closer to the piano, squinting at one snapshot of father and daughter together. "Do you think so? It looks to me like my grandfather had dark hair and eyes. Nothing at all like Mother."

Sophia remained silent.

"No," Karen continued as she perused more of the photos, "it doesn't seem like Mother resembled either one of you."

"She was devoted to Bradley. If he'd lived, perhaps the rift would have healed between her and me, given enough time. He was the peacemaker in our family."

Karen faced the older woman a second time. "What happened between you and Mother?" She settled onto the piano bench. "I'd like to understand."

"It was never just one thing." Sophia looked beyond Karen, beyond the piano, beyond the present, and into the past. "She and I were like oil and water, almost from the very beginning."

"Why didn't you love her?" She hadn't meant to sound so harsh, but that was the way the words came out.

"That's what she thought—that I didn't love her. But it wasn't true. I loved Maggie more than I could express. So much more." Her eyes refocused on Karen. "Our relationship was complicated, your mother's and mine. I caused her great hurt. It was because of my inability to overcome feelings from my past, things she'd had no part in. But I *did* love Maggie. From the first moment I laid eyes on her, I thought the sun rose and set with her."

"Then I guess it runs in the family."

"What does?"

"The inability to show love even when one feels it." Karen was immediately sorry that she'd spoken. Her words revealed too much, far more than she wanted her grandmother to know.

"I'm sorry." Sophia's eyes fluttered closed and her voice dropped to a whisper. "The sins of the fathers are visited upon the next generation and the next. Forgive me, Lord. I'm so sorry I couldn't learn that lesson in time."

Karen felt like an eavesdropper. Was the woman actually praying?

Sophia opened her eyes. "Whatever else might be said, Maggie did raise a beautiful daughter."

"Mother didn't raise me." Karen stood up, suddenly restless.

"That was left to paid employees and the staff at fancy boarding schools." She headed for the door. "I need some air. I'm going for a walk."

❧

As the door swung closed behind Karen, Sophia closed her eyes a second time.

O Father, now I know what is still undone. Use me as You will, but heal this girl's heart. Don't let her go through life, as Maggie did, believing herself unloved.

She released a sigh as her thoughts began to drift, back to the day Margaret Rose had arrived. It had been in the spring of 1946. The war in Europe had been over nearly a year by the time the four-year-old girl stepped off the train in Nampa, Idaho, clutching the rag doll Esther had made. Sophia would never forget the way her heart had twisted in her chest, torn in two directions from the first moment she laid eyes on her sister's orphaned child.

Her sister's child…

And Mikkel's child.

So many regrets, Lord. So many regrets.

I WILL MAKE UP TO YOU FOR THE YEARS THAT THE SWARMING LOCUST HAS EATEN. YOU SHALL PRAISE THE NAME OF THE LORD YOUR GOD, WHO HAS DEALT WONDROUSLY WITH YOU.

The words brought immediate comfort, for she knew the Scriptures were true. Sophia couldn't change the past, but God, in His mercy, could make up for the years her anger, resentment, and jealousy—her personal swarming locust—had eaten.

"Well then," she said aloud. "How do we begin, Jesus?"

And the answer came: GIVE HER ESTHER'S DIARIES.

Give them away? But, Lord, they brought me to You. They're all I have of left of—

ESTHER'S DIARIES.

It took a few moments, but then she understood. The diaries would tell Karen the truth. The truth about Esther, Karen's real grandmother. The truth about Karen's heritage of faith. The truth about love.

And it would be better if she learned all of this from Esther. In her own words.

Sophia sighed. "I'm a stubborn old woman, Father. Stubborn as the day is long." She pushed herself up from the chair. "But I'm trying to overcome it, because I want more than anything to do Your will."

Then she walked toward her bedroom at the rear of the house.

....

Sunday, July 19, 1936

Dear Diary,

The most incredible thing has happened. Our little church has a new minister. Pastor Mikkel Christiansen is his name. Christiansen. What a perfect name for a pastor. Don't you think so?

He is not at all what I expected. Nor what the congregation expected either. He is much younger than our previous pastor. Papa thinks no more than 25 or 26. (I suppose I would seem a mere child to him, being only 17.) He is ever so handsome. Tall as an oak with hair the color of straw and eyes a piercing blue. God forgive me, I did not hear a word of his sermon, for all I was looking at was him.

Sophia was no better than me. I could tell by the expression on her face. And she blushed three shades of red when she shook his hand at the end of service. Tonight, she pulled out the dress patterns. She wants to have something new to wear to church next Sunday.

But something tells me (maybe only wishful thinking) that it was me whom he noticed. My heart nearly stopped beating when he shook my hand. Such a strong grip and yet so gentle at the same time. He looked directly into my eyes, and it was like he could see straight through to my heart. No one has ever made me feel that way before.

Oh, I ramble. I don't know what to write tonight. All I can think about is Pastor Mikkel Christiansen.

Esther

Thursday, July 23, 1936

Dear Diary,

Pastor Christiansen came to call on our family today. Only a brief visit. An introductory call, as he put it. Just a few minutes to acquaint himself with members of his new congregation. He sat right here in our tiny parlor, in Papa's favorite chair, and I was on the sofa across from him. Nervous as you please.

He is even more handsome than I remembered. Sophia was not yet home from her job in town when he came, and she was pea green with envy when she found out she had missed him.

At supper tonight, Papa said he was mightily impressed by the young pastor. He doesn't have to convince me. My friends at school would call him snazzy, although I'm sure that isn't a very reverent description for a minister.

Never before have I heard anyone talk about God the way he does. As if God were his closest friend, not someone far away. I think I could sit and listen to him talk for hours and hours and hours.

I cannot tell Sophia how I feel, because I am afraid she feels the very same way herself. What will happen if I'm right? We've been so close, the two of us, able to share our deepest secrets, the ones we can tell nobody else. Papa says we couldn't be more alike if we'd been twins. It bothers me to think of something coming between us, and yet, I cannot help wanting him to notice me rather than Sophia.

Maybe he won't notice either of us. But if that's true, my heart might break right in two.

Esther

Horses belonging to the Randolph Butlers had been boarded in stables nearly as pristine and spacious as one of the Butler homes. The floors in those exclusive stables had been covered with sawdust or straw, the grounds carefully raked and perfectly manicured. There had been stableboys to clean the saddles and other tack and to groom the sleek, purebred animals when Karen and her friends were finished riding.

The barn at the Golden T was nothing like that.

This rickety building smelled of dirt, manure, and old leather, and it looked as if it were ready to collapse. The only horse in sight was a sorry-looking rack of bones that would have been better off sent to a glue factory.

Mac wouldn't believe this if I told him, she thought as she looked around. If he'd known, he wouldn't have suggested she come to Idaho. If he'd known, he would have—

Would have what? Kept on supporting her? Kept on paying her bills? Let her live in his house while people she used to call friends looked at her with pity in their eyes and whispered behind her back. *Poor Karen Butler. Did you know about her father?*

Karen set her jaw. She wasn't going to think about that. She was going to find some way to get back the things her father had lost. She wasn't going to let this beat her. She would show them. She would show them all.

Restless and agitated, she left the barn and headed toward the largest of the other outbuildings. Opening the door, she found one long room with several bunk beds set against the back wall, a wood-burning cookstove, a table with a couple of benches on either side, and a few other pieces of furniture. A second, smaller room to the right of the door held a single bed, a desk cluttered with books, papers, and ledgers, an old office chair with worn upholstery, and an antique wardrobe.

So this was where that cowboy and those boys lived. But why on earth would anyone hire kids to help run a ranch? Even *she* knew that didn't make sense. Maybe her grandmother was senile, although the old lady didn't seem so. Or maybe that cowboy was some sort of con artist. Maybe he was stealing from Sophia Taylor.

Karen was tempted to look through the things on the desk, then decided against it. What did it matter who they were or what they were up to? This ranch was nothing to her. For that matter, the old woman was nothing to her. This was a temporary stop.

"And I've got to get out of here soon," she muttered. "I've got to get back to California where I belong." She turned to leave.

But her way was blocked. Dusty Stoddard stood in the doorway, watching her with disapproving eyes.

"Find what you were looking for?" he asked after a lengthy silence.

"No...I mean, yes...I mean, I wasn't—" She stopped abruptly. She didn't have to explain anything to the hired man. "Excuse me," she said brusquely. Then she walked toward him, expecting him to move out of the way.

He didn't.

She had to stop. Reluctantly, she lifted her gaze to meet his again.

"What is it you want, Miss Butler? What are you doing at the Golden T?"

"I don't believe that's any of your business."

"Maybe not." He jerked his head toward the house. "But Miss Sophie *is* my business. She's a good woman with a good heart. She's prepared to love you, if you let her. No. She *already* loved you, before you ever came. So don't hurt her. Whatever brought you here, it better not end up hurting her."

"*You* are presumptuous." She lifted her chin. "Now kindly get out of my way."

He had the audacity to grin as he stepped back, giving her room to pass. "Don't go breaking one of those pretty nails on your way back to California, princess."

⁂

Did she deserve that? Dusty wondered as Karen swept past him in a huff. *No, probably not.* He let out a deep sigh. *Definitely not.*

He wasn't proud of himself for the way he'd treated her. Not when he knew how much Sophia loved the girl and wanted her to stay.

But I'm not sorry for what I said either.

He'd seen the way Karen looked at him, at the boys, at Sophia's ranch, and he didn't like it. It set his teeth on edge, having people act as if they were his betters. He'd always been determined to prove them wrong.

And where did that get you?

No place but trouble.

He turned around in time to see Karen walking toward the draw, following Bonnet Creek. Muttering to himself, he hurried after her.

"Miss Butler!" he called as he approached her. "Wait."

She glanced over her shoulder but kept going.

He quickened his stride. "Wait."

She must have realized she couldn't outrun him, because she stopped, hesitated, then turned.

"Look, I'm sorry." He stopped too. "I shouldn't have said what I did."

She didn't appear mollified by his apology. Her light blue eyes were like ice, and she looked at him as if he were a bug she should step on.

A number of comments popped into his head, none of which would have been a proper witness to Christ's redeeming love. He had to take a deep breath and silently count to ten before he trusted himself to speak.

"Look, Miss Butler, I was out of line, and I'm sorry. Sophia is my friend. I've known her a long time. I know how glad she is to have you here. I just...I just care about her. That's all."

Her expression didn't change. "How *long* have you known my grandmother?"

"Almost fifteen years."

His answer obviously surprised her. "Fifteen?" she repeated, her eyes widening.

"Ever since I came to Idaho. I lived with Jock and Merline Carter." He pointed toward the river. "The Carter spread was over there. Sophia was a good friend of theirs, and she sort of became the grandma I never had. Kind of like she is to the boys you met."

"Speaking of those boys, just who are they? What are they doing here? Don't tell me they're the hired hands, because I can't believe it." She made a sweeping motion in the direction of the house and barn. "And if you *are* the hired help, it doesn't look like you do anything around here to earn your pay." That snooty tone was back in her voice.

"The ranch needs plenty of work, I'll grant you that. But it's because there isn't enough money to go around."

"So why *are* you here?" she challenged.

He lost control of his temper again, his disdain matching hers. "Because this could be the last chance for these kids, and Sophia cares enough to give them a home *and* a chance." He leaned closer. "It may not look like much to you, but it's a whole lot better than juvenile hall or prison or a plot in some cemetery, which could be their other options unless somebody steps in to help turn things around."

"They're *delinquents?*"

"That's an ugly label to hang on a kid."

"But you said—"

"I'll make you a deal, princess. You stay out of our way, and we'll stay out of yours. Then we'll all get along fine."

He spun on his heel and strode away, heading straight for his horse. He swung up into the saddle and rode out, completely forgetting what had brought him back to the ranch in the first place.

Sophia was old, but she could still see pretty good and her hearing was excellent—when she wanted it to be. From where she sat on the front porch, she didn't miss the altercation between Karen and Dusty.

It reminded her a little of Bradley and her when they'd been about the same age. Goodness, how the sparks had flown. That was more than fifty years ago, but it was fresh in her mind.

My, how we could get under each other's skin.

She glanced down at the old diaries, some in her lap, more on the porch floor.

Esther would have liked my Bradley.

There were thirteen diaries in all, the cloth covers showing signs of age. At one time, their pages had been white and fresh and empty, but they'd eventually been filled with the script of a young woman telling the story of her life as it unfolded each day.

Dearest Esther, pouring out her heart into these books, year after year.

Sophia ran a hand slowly over the cover of the top diary, wishing she could go back in time and change the role she'd played in Esther's life. She wished she hadn't parted with her sister on such bad terms. She wished she'd answered just one of Esther's letters. She wished…

But, of course, she couldn't change what had gone before.

She glanced toward the draw, saw Karen strolling slowly back to the house, an aura of futility hovering over her.

No, Sophia couldn't change what had happened in the past, but she could change what would be in the future, as far as it was up to her. She could change it by her obedience to the Father's will. Esther had learned that truth at an early age. It had taken Sophia a great deal longer.

Perhaps Karen had inherited Esther's wisdom and would see the truth sooner rather than later.

Karen stopped when she reached the porch and saw her grandmother there. She was uncertain what she should do or say. She wondered if Sophia had overheard the angry exchange with Dusty Stoddard.

"I haven't lost my senses," the elderly woman said. "Dusty and his boys are on the ranch because I want them here. I'm glad if God can put to use whatever I have. He's given so much to me."

God again. It was all Karen could do to keep from rolling her eyes.

"Come." Sophia patted the seat of the chair across from her. "Join me. I have something for you."

Seeing no gracious way to avoid doing her grandmother's bidding, Karen crossed the porch and sat in the proffered chair.

Sophia lifted some clothbound books toward her. "These were my sister's. Esther was her name. I thought you might like to have them." She motioned toward her feet where there was a stack of similar-looking books. "And those, too."

Karen took those that her grandmother was offering, placed them in her lap, then opened the top one. She was surprised to find handwritten entries rather than typeset print. "It's a diary." She checked the others, finding the same neat script in them all, then glanced up. "Why would you want me to have these?"

"I want you to read them. I think they'll help you to know and understand your family. I suspect your mother said as little as possible about me." She closed her eyes. "And she didn't remember Esther."

Karen didn't know what to say. She couldn't imagine why anyone would want to read old diaries, especially those of a poor farmer's daughter.

Sophia looked at her. "Esther and I grew up in eastern Oregon. Then she married and moved away. I never got to see her again. After her death, her journals were sent to me. From them, I learned what an extraordinary woman she became. A woman with a remarkable faith in God and tremendous courage. I think you might discover the same."

"All right. I'll keep them in my room while I'm here at the Golden T."

That was noncommittal enough to get her off the hook, in case she never opened one of these book covers again.

And, if it was in her power, she wasn't going to be at the Golden T long enough to read anything.

Saturday, August 22, 1936

Oh, Diary,

I just returned from the Draker barn dance. I danced and danced and danced and danced. Best of all were the times I danced with Pastor Mikkel Christiansen.

Mikkel.

Oh, Mama would wash my mouth out with soap if she knew I was thinking of him by his given name, let alone writing it down that way. She wouldn't care that I am seventeen and not a child any longer. She would still punish me.

But I cannot help it. It is how I think of him all the time now.

Mikkel.

He danced with me twice, and he gave me the most dazzling smile afterward. Both times.

Sophia did not even speak to me during the drive home. Mikkel only danced with her once, and I know she is jealous. But I didn't care that she didn't want to talk. The old Ford is too noisy anyway.

And why would I want to talk to her when I could close my eyes and think about Mikkel?

Esther

Monday, August 31, 1936

Dear Diary,

Sophia and I had a horrible argument this afternoon. We were picking tomatoes in the garden for Mama, just the two of us. All of a sudden, Sophia accused me of flirting with Mikkel. She said I should be ashamed for throwing myself at Pastor Christiansen the way I've been doing ever since he came to our church.

But I have not been flirting. I have not thrown myself at him. I am quite sure I have not done anything of the kind. I go to his Sunday school class, and he speaks to me after services every week. But I have done nothing to be ashamed of. Mama and Papa would let me know if I had, and I told Sophia so. She said they are blind to what I am doing because I am their favorite daughter.

But that is not true either. Sophia has always been the apple of Papa's eye. She is much smarter than I am, even though she is only a year and a day older. She was the most popular girl in the class, all through high school, and Bobby Kingston asked her to marry him before they graduated. She refused because she was not in love with him. So it is her own fault if she does not have a boyfriend.

But how did she know if she loved Bobby or not?

I have never been in love. Is that what I am feeling for Mikkel Christiansen? Is it possible to fall in love with a man without ever being alone with him?

Oh, I am confused and most dreadfully vexed. Yesterday, Mikkel's sermon was about taking all hopes and dreams to the Lord, no matter how big or how small. He said God cares about us so much, He wants to be involved in all matters of our lives. Even the smallest of details. I never thought about God caring for little everyday things.

I wonder if it would be all right to ask God to make Mikkel love me.

Esther

Four

All her life, Karen had lived according to certain rules.

She'd attended the right schools. She'd lived in the right exclusive neighborhoods and driven the right make and model of expensive cars. She'd belonged to the right social and philanthropic organizations. She'd played golf and tennis at the right country clubs and vacationed at the right resorts around the world. She'd been surrounded with the right friends, and she'd dated the right men. Her calendar had been filled weeks and months in advance, making certain she was seen where she should be seen—at the right charity functions, at the right parties, even at the right political rallies.

But there was nothing on her calendar now. There weren't any friends to call or parties to attend. Everything familiar to her was gone, stripped from her, first by her father's foolish ambition and then by his selfish cowardice.

She was pondering the futility and emptiness of her life when her grandmother rapped on her bedroom door, about an hour after they'd finished eating an early supper, just the two of them.

"Karen?"

"Yes."

The door opened. "Are you ready to go for that ride?" Sophia stepped into the room. "Dusty is here with the horses."

"Ride?"

"Remember. I told you this morning that I'd asked him to take you out on horseback and show you around."

"But I thought after—"

"Dusty is a man of his word."

Inwardly Karen winced. He'd promised Sophia, and so, no matter how he personally felt about Karen, he was here to keep that promise. Maybe he considered her a challenge, like one of those delinquent boys of his.

"Do this for me, will you, dear?" Sophia asked softly. "There is so much more about this ranch than what you see on the surface. I think you'll fall in love with it too, if you give it a chance."

Karen doubted that. Still, she couldn't refuse her grandmother's request. She was, after all, a charity case.

"All right," she answered. "Give me a few minutes to change."

"I'll tell Dusty." The elderly woman smiled. "Give him a

chance too. You'll find him a very nice young man." As she spoke, she took a step backward, then closed the door after her.

"Oh, right," Karen answered to the empty bedroom. "A real peach of a guy."

Dusty wasn't surprised that he had to wait. A princess had to make a tardy entrance in order to be properly noticed. If it wasn't for the promise he'd made...

"Ah, here she is," Sophia said, drawing his attention to the front door.

He couldn't deny that Karen looked spectacular in her designer jeans and boots, her silky blond hair tucked beneath a short-brimmed baseball cap—designer variety, of course. Only a dead man wouldn't have noticed how pretty she was.

But that didn't change the way he felt about her. She didn't belong at the Golden T, and in his humble opinion, the sooner she went back to California the better for all of them.

"Dusty, take her up to the bluff overlooking the gorge so she can get a good view."

"Will do," he answered Sophia.

Karen came down the steps, moving with the same reluctance Dusty felt. Her gaze flicked between the two horses, then shifted to him. "Which one is for me?"

"This one." He handed her the reins to the paint. "Need a hand up?"

"No, thanks."

She spoke the truth. She mounted the horse without difficulty.

Dusty swung into the saddle, gathered the reins, then said, "This way."

He nudged the gelding with his boot heels, and they set out. They rode without speaking for a good thirty minutes, the horses following a well-worn trail.

It was Karen who broke the silence. "How much of the land belongs to my grandmother?"

"Not much anymore." He glanced at her. "Sophia's had to sell off a lot as she got older. The Taylors weren't ever rich, from what she's told me. They never would have mixed with your crowd."

She stopped her horse.

He did the same.

Their gazes clashed.

"Why do you dislike me?" she asked.

It was a fair question. He decided to give it an honest answer. "I suppose because of the way you look down that pretty nose of yours at everything and everyone."

"But I don't—"

"Yes, you do."

She looked away, releasing a sigh.

"This country isn't for the idle or the pampered, Miss Butler. Your grandmother's worked hard for everything she has. That may not be much, materially speaking, but Sophia Taylor is a rich woman in all the things that count."

Karen continued to stare at the rolling, sagebrush-covered valley.

"So why'd you leave California if you didn't want to be here?" he asked. "And it's plenty obvious you don't."

That drew her gaze to him. "She didn't tell you why?"

"No."

"Because I had nowhere else to go after my father...died."

For just an instant, her superior, aristocratic facade crumbled, exposing the raw vulnerability beneath.

"I'm sorry," Dusty said, meaning it. "I didn't know you'd lost your father."

She looked away again, her cool demeanor returning. "I'd rather not talk about it. Can we go on now?"

"Sure." He clucked to his horse. "Follow me."

❧

Silence returned.

Neither of them spoke while they finished the ride to their destination—a ridge with a spectacular view of the river plain and the dramatic bluffs to the north of them. At their backs, the Owyhee Mountains rose toward the sky, the peak of War Bonnet Mountain still covered in snow.

They dismounted, then left the horses with reins trailing the ground.

"The Birds of Prey Reserve is over that way." Dusty pointed with an outstretched arm as they walked on a bit farther. "I'll be taking the boys there this month. Maybe you'd like to come along."

She looked at him, surprised by the invitation.

"I think you'd enjoy it," he added.

Was he asking her because of another promise to her grandmother?

"And up that dirt road"—he turned around and pointed in the opposite direction—"is Silver City. It's a ghost town now, but in its heyday, it was quite the place. We'll take the boys there, too. Probably in August. It takes about an hour, even though it's only twenty miles. The road climbs more than six thousand feet in elevation. It's mighty steep and windy in places. Worth it though. I think you'd enjoy seeing it. Silver City's a real slice of Idaho history."

Karen didn't want a history lesson. Nor did she want to be some cowboy's good deed for the day. She didn't need him. She didn't need anybody.

That was a lie, and the minute she thought it, she knew it.

I'm pathetic. I wish I were dead.

A glaze of unshed tears blurred her vision. She had to turn quickly, before he noticed them.

"Karen..."

"What?"

"I lost my dad when I was sixteen. It was hard, especially since I was such a disappointment to him. I ran with a tough crowd and got into lots of trouble. Bad trouble." He paused a moment, as if remembering something he'd rather forget. Then he continued, "After Dad died, I left Chicago. Hitch-hiked my way west. Wound up in Idaho about a year later."

"Chicago?" She turned around to stare at him in disbelief. "*You're* from Chicago?" Her gaze traveled the length of him, from the brim of his dusty Stetson to the tips of his well-worn boots.

"Yeah. Guess there isn't much of a city kid about me any longer."

"Not much."

He grinned, apparently amused by her surprise.

She didn't think it was funny. "That's why you run this place for those boys, isn't it? Because you were in trouble once your-self?"

His expression sobered. "Partly, yes. I want to help if I can."

There was something about his eyes, something about the way he looked at her—was that compassion? It made her feel exposed and vulnerable again. She didn't like it. And she certainly didn't want to like him.

She returned to her horse. "It's time to go back," she said as she slipped her foot into the stirrup and stepped up, swinging her right leg over the saddle. Without looking to see if he followed, she started down the trail.

Running away. These days, it seemed, she was always running away from something.

Sunday, September 27, 1936

Dear Diary,

I love Indian summer. The days are warm and golden, and the nights are crisp. The leaves crunch beneath my feet when I go for walks, and flocks of ducks and geese fly overhead in enormous V formations, honking and quacking.

Papa invited Mikkel to join us for a picnic after church today, and he accepted. We went to the Snake River where we spread blankets in the shade of some huge old trees. Sophia looked stunning in the rose pink dress Mama made for her. I am certain Mikkel will pay her a call soon. I am doing my best not to be disappointed and to accept it as God's will.

I have learned much on that subject since Mikkel came to pastor our church, but not nearly enough to fully understand what God expects of me.

I suppose I should write his name as Pastor Christiansen in these pages. I have no right to be so familiar, even in this most secret and private place. Especially since it appears we shall never be more than friends.

And I do feel he has become a dear friend. He was very relaxed today, and I think we were privileged to get a glimpse of the real Mikkel Christiansen. Not at all reserved and stuffy as some ministers can be nor so heavenly minded as to be no earthly good, as I have heard Papa say before.

Mikkel visited with Mama and Papa, answering lots of questions about himself. His parents were born in Denmark and came to America as newlyweds. They settled in Wisconsin, which is where Mikkel was born and raised. His paternal grandfather is a Lutheran minister in Copenhagen. Mikkel has three younger sisters, and they all speak Danish and can write it a little too. He says the family prays in Danish in the evening and in English in the morning.

Mikkel asked Sophia and me if we spoke a foreign language. Neither of us do. He offered to teach us a little Danish if we were interested. We both said yes, we would like to learn. But I am afraid I will be a great disappointment to him. I do not have a good head for that sort of thing.

Esther

Tuesday, October 6, 1936

Dear Diary,

I am so pleased. ~~Mikkel~~ Pastor Christiansen asked me if I would teach the children's Sunday school class because Mrs. Filbert has taken ill. I said I did not know if I could do it. I am not a teacher. But he said he would help me prepare the classwork and would answer any questions I had. He believes I can do it, which makes me happy.

Esther

Five

....

Mornings were Sophia's favorite time of day. That hadn't always been so. In her younger years, when resentment had twisted her heart, she had preferred to sleep late. But no more. Now she was eager to welcome each day the Lord gave her.

In the summer she often went to her garden where she could sit on the wrought-iron park bench beneath a tall globe willow Bradley had planted their first summer in this house. There, under those wide-spreading branches, she would watch the sun rise.

Early on this Saturday morning in June, lacy clouds in the east were tinged with lavender, while the morning star winked in a sky trapped between pewter and blue.

As was so often the case, praise welled up in her chest, and she had to let it burst forth in song. It mattered not that her voice in this, her eighty-second year, was only a frail reminder of what it once had been. She merely assumed that was why God had seen fit to have the psalmist write about making a joyful noise. The good Lord didn't want anyone to keep silent because of the quality of his or her voice.

Her song finished, she leaned against the support at her back and closed her eyes. "It's a beautiful day, Lord. Thank You for it. All good things are from above, and You pour them out upon us, the just and the unjust."

She hugged her large-print Bible to her chest.

"I lift Dusty before You, Lord. He's still hanging on to those rags of guilt, isn't he? He's not letting go. I don't know how to help him, except to love him and to pray. So that's what I'm doing. Be his guide and let him know Your peace, Father."

Leaves rustled over her head, and the gentle morning breeze kissed Sophia's cheek.

"Bless our boys, Hal and Noah and Ted and Billy." She pictured each one of them as she spoke their names. She knew God saw them too. Saw *them*—saw their needs—and knew the answers for their lives. "Only Billy has come to know You, Jesus, as Savior. Speak to the hearts of the other boys. And help us to plant the seeds of truth. Let them see You in me and in Dusty and in Grant."

The song of a meadowlark could be heard in the distance.

"And Karen... O God, I know You've brought her here because of Your great love for her. Reveal that love, Lord. And let her know my love too. Help me to undo the wrongs I've committed toward her because of the wrongs I did her mother."

She released a deep sigh.

"Poor Maggie. My poor, poor Maggie."

Regrets.

She had so many regrets.

❦

Sophia stood beside the bed, staring down at the little girl. The pale lamplight revealed tear tracks on the child's cheeks, and even in sleep she clutched the rag doll to her chest as though her life depended upon it.

Margaret Rose Christiansen. Esther's daughter.

Mikkel's daughter.

Esther called her Rose, the letter from Hannah Abrams had said.

"I'll call you Maggie," Sophia whispered.

Maggie looked like her father. She had his pale gold hair, baby fine and curly. She had his eyes, too. Maggie's father had been able to silence a crowd with a mere glance from his piercing blue eyes. Eyes like Maggie's.

If Mikkel had married Sophia instead of Esther, it would have been Sophia's child who looked like Mikkel. It would have been her child who had glorious blond hair and beautiful blue eyes.

"Sophie?" Bradley said softly from the doorway. "Is she all right?"

Guiltily, she glanced over her shoulder at her husband. "She's asleep."

"Poor little tyke." He came to stand beside Sophia. "She must wonder what's become of her world."

"We're Maggie's family now. We'll make a better world for her."

"Maggie? But I thought—"

"It's what I want to call her. It fits her better than Rose. It's short for Margaret. That's her first name. That's what she should be called. And as you said, it's a new family and a new world."

Bradley was silent a moment. Then his arm went around her shoulders, and he kissed her cheek. "If that's what you want."

"It's what Mikkel would have called her, I think, if it had been up to him instead of Esther. Esther was never very practical."

Her husband didn't respond.

She turned toward him. Bradley had lost his right eye while serving in the Pacific, and that side of his face was scarred. But she thought it a wonderful face all the same.

Bradley loved her, and she loved him. Truly, she did. Theirs was a good marriage. He was going to make a wonderful father. Someday, she would give him a son. She hoped it would be soon.

In the meantime, there was Mikkel's little girl for her to tend to. Mikkel's...

And Esther's.

❦

Karen leaned her shoulder against the window frame.

She'd heard her grandmother singing. That's what had brought her fully awake, then had drawn her from her bed to the window. Once there, she'd heard the elderly woman talking softly to herself, too softly for Karen to make out what she said. Now Sophia appeared to be asleep in the chair, her eyes closed, her head resting against the tree trunk at her back, her arms clutching a book to her chest.

Sophia Taylor was a bit peculiar, in Karen's opinion. For one thing, she didn't seem to mind her bleak existence. She didn't seem to miss having lots of people around, places to go, things to do. And there was the way she talked to herself...and to *God!* Now that was the strangest of all.

Outside of a formal church setting, Karen had never before seen nor heard anyone do such a thing. As if the Almighty were really listening to an old woman in this desolate place. But then, maybe this place was *why* Sophia was a little odd.

"It would drive anyone mad," she whispered. Then she gave a humorless laugh. "It's already happened. Listen to me. *I'm* talking to myself."

She turned from the window. She should go back to bed. She couldn't remember the last time she'd awakened from a full night's sleep to see the sun rise. Maybe because it had never happened before.

Yes, she could crawl back into bed, but she knew she wouldn't sleep. She was wide awake now.

With a sigh of resignation, she grabbed some clean clothes and headed for the bathroom. She took a quick shower, then used the blow dryer on her shoulder-length hair, scrunching the natural curl to give it body. She applied her usual makeup, paying particular attention to her eyes—her best feature, she'd been told by her mother.

"If you know how to use those eyes," Margaret Butler had said, "you'll have any man you want at your beck and call."

The memory caused Karen to pause.

Any man I want, she thought as she stared at her reflection. *Except Alan Ivie.*

Suddenly chilled, she stepped back from the sink, turning from the mirror. She didn't want to remember Alan's rejection...or the reasons for it.

She left the bathroom in a hurry. It wasn't until she was out the front door and standing on the porch that she realized she had nowhere to run. She couldn't escape this ranch, her circumstances, or her thoughts. She had no committee work to take her mind off her problems. She had no friends to run away with, off to the Caribbean or to Hawaii or to the French Riviera. She didn't even have enough money to put gas in that old car and drive to the nearest town.

At that precise moment, Dusty strode out of the barn, headed toward the house. He'd covered about half the distance between them before he looked up and noticed her. His stride shortened, slowing his approach. His gaze never wavered from hers.

"Morning," he said.

"Good morning."

She wondered if her grandfather had been anything like Dusty. Bradley Taylor had been a cowboy too. From what little she knew, he'd built this ranch from nothing.

Dusty reached the porch steps and stopped. "You look mighty pretty at this hour of the day, Miss Butler." He smiled, revealing a small dimple in his left cheek.

He was only being friendly, offering an olive branch of sorts. Not flirting. But Karen's mother wouldn't have seen it that way. She would never have stood for him saying such a thing to her daughter. He was, after all, only a common workman. Blue collar. A cowboy. Not the proper company for a Butler.

Perhaps that was why Karen returned his smile, to defy her mother's memory, to defy the woman she'd spent a lifetime trying to please, without ever succeeding.

"Is Sophia up yet?" he asked.

"I think she's in the garden."

He bumped his hat brim with his knuckles, pushing it higher on his forehead. "I won't bother her then. It's where she goes to pray in the morning."

Praying. Of course. Karen should have realized.

And, no doubt, I'm the subject of her prayers. "Please, God, help poor Karen."

That thought made her uncomfortable, so she quickly sought another topic of conversation. "Did you know my grandfather?"

"No. He died more than thirty years ago."

"Mother never spoke about either of them. I thought I had no grandparents, that they were deceased." She stared into the distance. "I never would have known about Sophia if I hadn't found one of her letters to my mother. Mother was furious when I confronted her about it."

Your grandmother is a hateful, despicable woman. I was lucky to escape her and that dreadful ranch. Never ask me about her again. As far as I'm concerned, she's dead.

"She forbade me to ask about her," Karen continued in a low voice. "And I never did. Not about her or my grandfather or anything else from her past." She felt a sudden shame. "To be honest, I didn't care."

"It's not too late. Maybe that's why you're here."

"I'm here because I had nowhere else to go. I'm broke. I have a college degree, but I've never had a job. I don't know how to manage money. I've never done anything but enjoy myself. I'm basically a worthless human being."

"No one is worthless," he said softly. "You were created with love. You have great worth to God. Your circumstances might be His way of drawing you to Him."

His words made her instantly angry. Who was he to judge her? "Is that what you tell those"—she almost called them *delinquents* again, but stopped herself in time—"*kids* you've got staying here? That God loves and values them?"

"It's one of the things I tell them."

"And they buy into the fantasy?"

He didn't answer. Only looked at her. And it seemed as if he could see straight into her heart.

She hated it. She didn't want anyone to see inside her. She didn't want anyone to know the real Karen Jo Butler.

This cowboy had said she had great worth to God. But if he saw inside her, he would surely see he was wrong.

Monday, October 19, 1936

Godaften, Diary,

   That means "Good evening, Diary" in Danish. It isn't so much, but ~~Mikkel~~ Pastor Christiansen seems pleased with the few words I have learned and says I am making progress.

   He seemed even more pleased with the cake Sophia baked for him.

   Sometimes I have hope. Other days I have none.

   I am not certain falling in love is a good thing. I am wretchedly unhappy.

                                          Esther

Tuesday, November 3, 1936

Dear Diary,

Dutch Tallman asked me to go to the movie with him this coming Friday evening. Delphia Plum and Hap Gifford will be with us. I like Dutch and have decided to accept his invitation, if Mama and Papa say it is all right for me to go. We will have the use of Mr. Tallman's Fordor Sedan, so it will not matter that it is cold after dark.

Of course, I would much rather go to the movies with Mikkel Christiansen, but I have despaired of him thinking to ask me to go to a movie or anywhere else. Maybe he does not go to movies. I know many ministers do not, although our community church is not so strict about such things. And Mikkel did join in the dancing last summer.

Oh, that seems such a long time ago. What I would not give to have him hold me in his arms and waltz me around a barn again. Sometimes I cannot hear his lessons at Sunday school or during worship services because I am daydreaming about that. I am sure that is a horrible sin for which I will have to repent one day.

I am not always daydreaming, of course. I have learned much

from his preaching and teaching. And I find there are times when I am so hungry to know more, to understand more, to _feel_ more about God. I think I should like to love God as Mikkel loves Him, but I cannot say that I do.

Teaching the children's class has been wonderful, but my time doing so is nearly over. Mrs. Filbert has received permission from the doctor in Boise to resume her normal activities, and she has said she will return to the class the first Sunday in December. In time to arrange for the Christmas pageant. I will be truly sad when this happens, because then I will not have any reason for even a few minutes alone with Mikkel.

Oh, why can I not feel this same way about Dutch? He thinks I am pretty and would like to kiss me. Mikkel thinks I am just a child.

Esther

....

Six

"What are you doing with my car?" Karen demanded as she approached the Mustang.

The hood was up, and one of Dusty's boys was looking at the engine. Without straightening, he glanced over his shoulder but didn't answer.

"I asked what you're doing," she said again.

"Just seein' what sort of shape it's in."

Karen stopped a few feet away. "I did *not* give permission for you to touch my things."

"Why?" He straightened and turned toward her. His gaze was sullen, his tone defiant. "Afraid I'm gonna contaminate it or something?"

She winced. That was precisely what she'd felt, even if she hadn't put it into words.

"I know my way around cars, lady. I'm not gonna hurt nothing."

And how many automobiles have you stolen, you young hoodlum?

For several moments, they glared at each other.

Finally, the boy turned back toward the automobile. "This car's a classic. If you fixed it up, it'd be worth a lot of money."

"You're joking."

"No, I'm not."

She stepped closer. "How *much* money?"

"I don't know." He shrugged, then leaned over the engine again. "If it was done right, could be worth twenty, thirty thousand. Maybe more."

"Twenty thousand *dollars?*" She took another step forward. "That much? For this old car?"

"Maybe. It's a classic. Lots of people want to own an old Mustang."

Twenty thousand. That would be enough to get her out of Nowheresville, Idaho. She could return to California. It would be enough to support her for a little while. Not for long, but perhaps long enough. A few months anyway.

"What would it take?" she asked the boy. "And could you do the work?"

He met her gaze again. "You askin' me to help you?" The defiance was gone from his voice, replaced by surprise.

"Yes." She didn't suppose he was any more surprised than she was. "What would it cost to fix it up, get it ready to sell?"

"I'd have to do some figurin'. Look through some catalogs. Make some phone calls."

"Will you do that?" Of course, she'd have to come up with some creative way to pay for all this.

His eyes narrowed suspiciously. "And what's in it for me?"

"I...I would share a percentage of the profits with you. Naturally."

"You serious?"

She hesitated a moment, wondering how little of a percentage she could offer him and still have him accept, then held out her hand. "Yes."

He looked at her hand, as if not knowing what to do with it.

"I'm quite serious," she said. "I'm sorry. I can't remember your name."

"The guys call me Junkman." He still didn't shake her hand. "But my name's Hal Junker." His expression hardened. "I'll have to ask Dusty if it's okay before I can agree to do the work for you. We don't get a lot of time to ourselves around this place."

Of course. In her excitement, she'd forgotten what Hal Junker was doing at the Golden T.

Karen recalled her exchange with Dusty earlier that morning. He'd told her she looked pretty. He'd said she was of worth to God. Apparently he was starting to like her. She could think of no reason why he might deny her this opportunity to escape. Not if she handled him correctly.

"Maybe I'd better be the one to speak to Dusty," she said. "I'm sure he'll agree once he understands what a help it would be to me."

Confidence blossomed within her, the first she'd felt in many months. After all, her one real skill was knowing how to get what she wanted from men. Dusty Stoddard wouldn't stand a chance once she turned on her charms.

❧

Dusty stared at the notations in the ledger and shook his head. It was always a test of faith when he sat down to pay the bills of the Golden T Youth Camp.

Four churches in Canyon County supported the camp as part of their missions outreach, but their donations only went so far. And parents or guardians paid fees—*if* they could afford it; no boy was turned away from the camp for lack of funds. The boys earned wages by working for a couple of the area farmers during haying season. They got to keep a portion for themselves, but most of their earnings went for room and board.

On the surface, there never seemed to be enough to see them

through another month. But somehow they were able to pay the bills and usually have a little left over besides.

Dusty leaned back in his desk chair, the springs creaking as he did so. He covered his face with his hands and rubbed his eyes.

"Well, Lord, here we are again. Faith is believing in what we can't see, and I sure can't see how I'm going to make things stretch until the first of the month."

He swiveled toward the window. Through the dust-covered glass, he saw Karen and Hal talking as they stood next to her car. He rose from his chair.

Now, what could those two have to talk about?

He saw them shake hands, and he felt a knot of concern form in his belly.

What are they up to?

He wondered if he should go find out.

Hal leaned under the hood of the automobile. Karen soon joined him—being careful, Dusty noted, not to get her clothes or hands dirty. He gave his head a slow shake. He couldn't figure her out.

Spoiled? Certainly.

Vain? Probably.

Hurting? Definitely.

And pretty as the day was long.

Hal was sixteen. Boys his age had been known to fall hard

for women in their twenties. If that were to happen, if Hal was to get the wrong idea about Karen...

Dusty turned on his heel and headed for the door.

Karen must have heard the door close behind him as he left the bunkhouse, for she immediately straightened and looked in his direction.

"Car trouble?" Dusty asked as he drew near.

"No. Junkman thinks he might be able to fix up my car." She smiled, a look of sweet invitation.

If she'd looked at Hal that same way, Dusty was already too late.

"But," she continued, "he says he'll need your permission to do the work."

"What sort of work?"

Without looking up, Hal answered, "Everything. Overhaul the engine. Paint job. You name it, this needs it if it's going to sell for top dollar."

Dusty heard the underlying tone of excitement in the teenager's response, excitement the boy was trying hard to disguise. It was the first sign of enthusiasm Hal had shown since arriving at the Golden T. Dusty wasn't about to deny the kid a chance to succeed at something.

He looked at Karen. "You plan to sell it?"

"Yes." Her smile faded. "I need the money."

"You'd be without a car the whole time Hal's working on it, and there's no guarantee it'll get top dollar when he's finished with it."

"I realize that."

Dusty nodded, then looked at the boy. "You'd have to do it in your spare time. You've got your chores to do, just like everybody else, plus your studies. You won't get to shirk them to work on this car."

Hal scowled at Dusty but nodded that he understood.

"Then I don't have any objections. I'll ask Miss Sophie if you can use the shed to work in. I'm sure she won't mind."

"Wonderful!" Karen's smile returned, bright as the noonday sun.

Dusty suspected she was already mentally packing her suitcases. And it would be a relief once she was gone, he told himself.

Liar, his heart immediately replied.

"Karen's hurting and she's afraid," Sophia told Dusty. "She needs the Lord.

"You can lead a horse to water…" He let the old adage drift into silence.

Sophia knew what he said was true. Still, she didn't want her granddaughter leaving the Golden T yet. There was so much left undone. So much still unsaid.

Father, what is it I'm to do?

"It'll take Hal the rest of the summer to do the work," Dusty said.

"It will?" She released a silent sigh, suddenly at peace. Many things could happen in three months. She would simply have to trust the Lord's timing.

"Yeah, and even then I'm not sure the car will be worth much. Depends on how good Hal is."

"You're good with cars. You can help him."

Dusty shook his head, and he frowned. "I never tried to restore one. I was better at hot-wiring them, then selling them for parts and scrap metal."

"That's in your past, Dusty." Her voice softened. "Why is it you're so forgiving of others but you can't forgive yourself?"

He didn't answer. She hadn't expected him to. In the years Sophia had known Dusty, he'd shared many things about his past. But there was something that remained unspoken. Something he hadn't turned over to God. A guilt-laden secret that haunted him still.

She reached out and patted the back of Dusty's hand where it lay atop the table. "You tell Hal to put the car in the shed. He can start making calls to the junkyards on Monday."

"Thanks. He'll be glad to hear that." He rose from his chair. "I think this'll be good for him."

Sophia nodded. "Maybe you can get Karen to help. It might be good for her, too."

"I doubt it. She'd have to get her hands dirty."

"The worlds you came from are very different, Dusty, but that doesn't mean her heartaches are any less real than yours or any of our boys."

He looked chagrined. "I know. I'm sorry. I shouldn't have said that." He set his hat on his head. "I'll go tell them your decision." He turned and left.

Sophia closed her eyes. *What now, Lord? What do You have in store for us now?*

I WILL LEAD THE BLIND BY A WAY THEY DO NOT KNOW, IN PATHS THEY DO NOT KNOW I WILL GUIDE THEM. I WILL MAKE DARKNESS INTO LIGHT BEFORE THEM AND RUGGED PLACES INTO PLAINS.

She smiled as God spoke to her heart through the familiar Scripture.

Over the years, the Lord had led her along many paths she didn't know, making rugged places into plains, turning darkness into light. Whatever lay ahead that she couldn't as yet see, blind as she was, she knew God wouldn't leave them undone. He would see her—and all of those at the Golden T—through to the end.

Friday, November 6, 1936

Dear Diary,

The most extraordinary thing happened tonight. Dutch and Delphia and Hap and I went to see <u>Anna Karenina</u> at the Rialto Theater. Greta Garbo was fabulous as the tragic heroine, and Basil Rathbone was superb as the cold Russian nobleman she's married to.

In the movie, Garbo's Anna destroys her own life in order to run away with Fredric March, the handsome cavalry officer. Freddie Bartholomew played Anna Karenina's son, whom she loses because of what she does.

Both Delphia and I cried. Hap and Dutch thought we were ninnies and teased us unmercifully, but it did not make us stop. We were still drying our eyes with our handkerchiefs as we left the theater.

And there, in the lobby, we ran into Mikkel Christiansen. He was all alone, and I will never forget the way I felt when our eyes met. Both happy and sad at the same time. Happy to see him, and sad because I was with Dutch instead of him. He greeted us all and asked how we liked the movie. I am certain I made a fool of myself by gushing my opinion.

He walked outside with us, right next to me. I could almost pretend he was my date. And what did we find? A blizzard. Snow blowing so thick we couldn't even see the cars parked on the street.

Mikkel insisted that we could not drive home in it, so we went to the Penny Diner on the corner. We all called our parents, and Mikkel spoke to them too, assuring them that he would see we got home all right, no matter how late it was.

The storm began to let up by ten o'clock, and we set out for home. We had to drive very slowly. The roads were slick, and I could tell Dutch was nervous. It took us over an hour to reach Delphia's farm. Mikkel followed us in his own car the entire way. He even went up to the door to say a few words to Mr. and Mrs. Plum.

Then we went on to Hap's. That took us at least another twenty minutes or so. After Mikkel went up to speak to Mr. and Mrs. Gifford, he came to Dutch's car and suggested, since it was approaching midnight and our place was beyond Dutch's farm but before the church and parsonage, that he drive me the rest of the way home.

I don't think Dutch was too happy about the pastor abruptly interrupting our date. I think he was counting on a good-night kiss from me. He would not have gotten one, but that is what he wanted, all the same. Still, he couldn't argue with Pastor Christiansen, and so he agreed.

I would have moved over to Mikkel's automobile right then if he had asked, only he said I could do so after we reached the Tallman farm. So I stayed in the front seat of Dutch's Ford for another fifteen minutes. They were long and silent minutes too. Dutch must have sensed what I was feeling. I do not think he is likely to ask me out again.

After Mikkel spoke to the Tallmans, he walked me to his car. I was so nervous I was shaking as I got in. I nearly tore my handkerchief, I was twisting it so hard between my hands. But I was glad to be there. I even wished our farm was farther away from the Tallman farm than it is, so I could be with Mikkel longer.

As he drove me home, Mikkel and I talked about the movie some more. He said he was interested in what I thought of the story on a deeper level than merely great entertainment. He asked me a number of questions, and he listened to my answers as if what I had to say was important. Then he talked of reaping what we sow, and the heartache that awaits mankind when we seek our own way rather than God's.

And yet, even when he was talking about sin, he never sounded like he was preaching at me. It was like he was talking to God rather than me, carrying on a discussion and working things through in his own mind and heart.

When we arrived at our farm and he stopped his automobile, he took my arm and walked me to the front door. Just as if he was my escort for the evening. Unlike Dutch, I would have let Mikkel kiss me if he had tried. He did not, of course. But before Papa opened the door, he said, "Maybe next time we do this, Miss Thompson, it won't be so cold."

Next time. He said, next time. And he called me Miss Thompson. As if I were a woman.

I am deliriously happy.

Esther

Karen didn't want to go to church with Sophia and the others, but at the last moment, she decided anything was better than being stuck at the ranch for another day. Since arriving at the Golden T, she'd had enough inactivity to last her a lifetime.

In Los Angeles, she and her parents had attended a large, prestigious church where one went to see and be seen. Listening to the sermons was optional. Her father had been a master at pressing the flesh, making the acquaintance of people who could be helpful in his business ventures. Her mother had shown an equal expertise at speaking only to those who were socially acceptable, especially mothers of marriageable sons.

It was at that church where Karen had been introduced to Alan Ivie.

Handsome and intelligent, from a good family, a successful attorney with aspirations for political office, Alan was everything Margaret Butler could have wanted in a husband for her daughter. Knowing that, Karen had been prepared to dislike him. But she hadn't. She'd found they enjoyed many of the same things. Better still, he hadn't been in a rush to marry, even after they'd become officially engaged. Neither had ever proclaimed their undying love, but in this day and age, who expected that?

Still, it had hurt when Alan broke their engagement shortly after the news leaked about Randolph Butler's legal troubles.

"It's a skeleton I can't afford. Not if I want to run for office," Alan had told her. "My wife can't have a criminal for a father. Not even a dead one."

Prior to leaving California, Karen had heard that Alan was engaged again.

It didn't take him long to replace me. Only a matter of months.

She closed her eyes, trying to hold off the familiar feeling of despair. She was tired of it. It showed a weakness of character that she despised.

"Here we are," Sophia announced, drawing Karen's attention to the present.

She looked out the van window as Dusty turned into the parking lot. Her gaze swept over the church building. It was old and slightly shabby in appearance, although the front was brightened by a border of red and yellow flowers.

What am I doing here?

She considered asking if she could take the van to the nearest mall and return to pick them up when church let out.

Sophia glanced over her shoulder and said, "I'm so glad to have you with us, my dear."

Karen suppressed a sigh and forced herself to smile at her grandmother. "I'm glad I came too." Would God strike her dead for lying? she wondered.

Dusty parked the van, then got out and hurried around to help Sophia. The four boys followed. From the look on Hal's face, he wasn't happy to be there. Karen couldn't tell about the others. Except for Billy. He was grinning from ear to ear.

Sophia looped arms with Karen, and they walked toward the front doors of the church. "What a joy and privilege to be able to introduce you to my friends."

Once in the narthex, her grandmother proceeded to drag Karen from one person to the next, proudly announcing that Karen was her granddaughter, visiting from California, and wasn't she pretty and other such things. Karen did her best to smile, say "Nice to meet you," and sound as if she meant it.

She didn't, of course. Not really. She had nothing in common with any of these people. In ordinary circumstances, their paths never would have crossed.

The Randolph Butlers had sat in the next to the last pew of their large church. Sophia led Karen to the second row from the front. Dusty and the boys were already seated there.

"I like to be up front where the action is," Sophia said as she sat down beside Billy, leaving room for Karen next to the center aisle.

I never should have come. Oh, why did I agree to come?

❦

Dusty leaned forward, just enough to catch a surreptitious glimpse of Karen. If she'd looked any more stiff, he'd be afraid rigor mortis had set in. He couldn't help feeling a bit sorry for her. She was obviously miserable.

He recalled Sophia's words from yesterday: *The worlds you came from are very different, Dusty, but that doesn't mean her heartaches are any less real than yours or any of our boys.*

Sophia could have said a whole lot more to him. She could have pointed out that he wasn't giving Karen the same consideration Jock had given him or that Dusty, in turn, gave to the boys who came to the Golden T. She could have chastised him for not responding to Karen in a loving, Christian manner. She hadn't.

Okay, Lord. I see there's a lesson here for me. Open my eyes so I can see it.

At that moment, Pastor Rollins invited the congregation to stand while he gave the opening prayer. Then the worship team stepped to the microphones, and voices lifted in praise to God filled the sanctuary.

For a time, Dusty forgot everything except the joy he felt in the presence of the Lord.

⁂

Karen had never been more uncomfortable in her life than in the past hour and a half. She'd never seen people in church lifting their hands or clapping as they sang song after song after song. She'd never heard anyone say "Amen" as the minister gave his sermon, but several had done so in this service. She'd never been to a church where people welcomed and hugged each other during a time of greeting, their voices raised in laughter.

What did they have to be so happy about anyway?

She felt as if she were being smothered, sitting there in that pew.

It was with enormous relief that she stepped through the doors of the church and into the midday sunshine. Thankfully, her grandmother didn't seem inclined to linger and visit, despite the many friends who tried to detain her.

"I thought we could have lunch before returning to the ranch," Sophia said as Dusty helped her into the van. "My treat."

"Are you sure, Miss Sophie?"

"I'm sure. I've still got my mad money for the month."

Karen hugged herself. *Mad money.* She wondered how much

that constituted. Ten dollars? Twenty? Maybe even fifty? Of course, however much it was, it was still more than she possessed.

"Let's go to that little restaurant down the street," Sophia continued. "That one with the blue sign. I can't think of the name, but you know which one I mean. They have the best chicken-fried steak in town."

"Yeah, I know which one."

"Good." Sophia glanced over her shoulder at Karen. "You'll enjoy the food, dear, and no one will have to wash dishes. Won't that be nice, boys?"

A chorus of yeses erupted from the back of the van.

"Miss Butler?" Billy tapped Karen on the arm to get her attention. "Mind if I sit next to you at lunch?"

She shrugged. "If you'd like."

He grinned.

She felt an odd flutter in her chest as she met his gaze. He had such an eager look about him, and her reaction to it was totally unexpected. Why should she care if this boy liked her or not? He was nothing to her.

"Lucky for us, church let out early," Sophia said. "Looks like we're ahead of all the other Sunday diners. The parking lot is still half-empty."

Or maybe it's because the food is lousy, Karen thought. But she kept her suspicions to herself.

In actuality, the menu had enough variety to please everyone, even Karen. The atmosphere was pleasant with soft music playing in the background and pretty bouquets of fresh-cut flowers on the tables.

Engaged by Billy in conversation while they waited for their food to be brought to the table, Karen forgot to be upset by her circumstances and actually began to enjoy herself. Then a short, balding man marched up to their table. His fists were clenched by his sides, his face mottled with rage.

"Are you Stoddard?" he demanded, his voice carrying throughout the restaurant. "Is that your van outside?"

Dusty frowned. "Yes. What may I—?"

The man looked around the table. "And is that Junkman?" He pointed at Hal.

"Excuse me, but—"

"You keep that sleazeball away from my daughter, or I'll have him thrown in jail."

"I don't know what you're—"

"You heard me, Stoddard. Keep him away from her." With that, the man turned and left the now-silent restaurant.

Dusty looked at Hal. The boy met his gaze with a cool, defiant one of his own.

"Want to tell me what that was about?" Dusty asked.

"I ain't got a clue. He must be crazy."

Karen looked from Hal to Dusty and back again. There was

a split second when she wanted to reach out, take the boy's hand, and give it a squeeze of encouragement and understanding. She didn't.

"We'll talk about it when we return to the ranch," Dusty said softly.

"There ain't nothing to talk about."

"Yes, there is, Hal. But we'll do it at the ranch."

Karen wondered what sort of punishment Dusty would dish out. Then she reminded herself it wasn't any of her business what he did with these kids. The less she became involved, the better off she would be when she finally got out of there.

The night was balmy, the heavens awash with stars twinkling against an ink-black sky. Dusty stood beside the corral, his right foot resting on the bottom rail, his gaze turned upward.

What's going on with Hal, Lord? How do I reach him?

The boy was sticking by his story that he didn't know who the man in the restaurant was or what he'd been talking about. Dusty was certain that wasn't the truth. At least not the whole truth. Still, he knew there was no way any of the boys could be meeting secretly—or otherwise—with a girl, so he'd decided not to press too hard. He needed to gain Hal's trust, and he was a long way from accomplishing that.

"Pretty, isn't it?"

Startled from his thoughts, he turned to find Karen standing not far from him. He hadn't heard her approach.

"What?" he asked.

"The sky. You don't see stars like this in the city."

He leaned his back against the fence and looked up. "No, you don't. Guess I'd forgotten. Or maybe I didn't notice the difference when I was living in Chicago." He was silent a moment, then added, "I guess I take all this beauty for granted sometimes."

"It's easy to take things for granted when you're accustomed to them. I've done it all my life."

He purposefully didn't look at her. He hoped she would say more.

She moved a couple of steps closer. "Don't you get frustrated, trying to help somebody who doesn't want your help?"

"Who are we talking about?"

"Hal. He doesn't want your help. Doesn't it frustrate you?"

"Sometimes," he answered. "Sometimes I get plenty frustrated. But then I remember why God brought me to Idaho."

"You believe that, don't you? That God's got some grand design, and you're a part of it."

Over the years, he'd had similar questions posed to him. He'd asked them himself of Jock Carter.

"I don't understand you *or* my grandmother," Karen added in a whisper.

He turned his gaze in her direction again, but the darkness kept him from reading her expression. "Maybe you're trying too hard to understand us. And, yes, I really do believe it. That God has a grand design, and that I'm part of it. I even believe *you're* part of it."

She released a sigh as she came to stand beside him at the fence. She placed her arms on the top rail, then rested her chin on her forearms.

Dusty turned to face the same direction and waited. Over the years he'd learned patience was often the key. If he remained silent, eventually the other person began to talk.

Karen didn't disappoint him.

"Tell me about Billy," she said softly.

"Billy?" He smiled to himself, picturing the boy in his mind. "Comes from a warm, loving home. Lost his mother over a year ago in a shooting accident. His younger brother was playing with their father's handgun. Billy grabbed for it just as their mom entered the bedroom. It went off. She was killed instantly."

"Oh no."

"Billy felt responsible, and he hated himself. He told everyone that he should've died. Not his mom."

"How tragic. But I thought they, the boys, were all...you know, in trouble with the law. That sort of thing."

"No. Just at-risk. And that can mean many things."

"Billy's such a sweet kid."

"Yeah, he is." Dusty glanced at Karen. A shimmer of light from the just-rising moon played across her pale hair. "You wouldn't have known him only a few months ago. He didn't talk to anybody. Never smiled. His family was afraid he would try to take his own life. He was that despondent."

There was a lengthy silence before she asked, "And coming here made such a difference in him?"

"No. It happened before he came here."

"What *did* make the difference?"

"God worked a miracle."

"A miracle," she whispered. "Too bad I don't believe in them."

She looked so sad; Dusty's heart tightened in his chest. He had to resist the urge to take her in his arms and offer comfort. He sensed it would be a mistake if he did.

Saturday, November 14, 1936

Dear Diary,

Mikkel came to see Papa today. He asked to speak to him alone. They were closed in the parlor for such a long time. Mama seemed nervous. I have never seen her so jumpy before. Every time the wind made the house creak, she looked toward the parlor door.

When Mikkel left, he spoke hardly a word to me. In fact, he scarcely looked in my direction. And Papa looked grim. I could hear him and Mama talking in their bedroom long after they are usually asleep.

Is Papa in some sort of trouble with the church?

Esther

Sunday, November 22, 1936

Dear Diary,

Mama announced this morning, before we went to church, that she has invited Mikkel Christiansen to take Thanksgiving dinner with us, and he has accepted. Sophia acted as if Mama did it just for her. On the ride to church, she pinched me and said, "I will sit next to Pastor Christiansen when he comes to dinner on Thursday."

Nothing has been right between Sophia and me for months, but it has been worse since the night of the blizzard, when Mikkel brought me home from the Tallman farm. The way she has acted, you would think I had the ability to make it snow.

It is sad, losing my sister as my friend. I know, deep down, that she loves me, but she has set herself against me. She can tell what I want, just as I can tell with her. We are transparent to each other, now as always. And no matter which one of us catches Mikkel's eye, or even if neither of us does, I think this will remain a wall between us.

Believing that makes me want to cry.

Esther

Eight

Over the next ten days, Sophia observed her granddaughter as she was drawn, little by little, into the daily life of the ranch. Karen spent less time in her room. She even managed to look if not happy at least less miserable.

Sophia had Billy to thank for it. The boy had become almost a shadow to Karen. He found countless reasons to come to the house and linger in her company, and Karen responded to him as she had to no one else, talking with him, smiling, sharing an occasional confidence.

Hal, on the other hand, was a source of deep concern for Sophia. On the surface he was the same. He'd always been surly and somewhat arrogant, straining against the restrictions placed upon him at the ranch. He wasn't used to anyone caring where he was, what he did, who he was with. But something had changed inside the boy since that Sunday at the restaurant, and it wasn't a change for the better.

Sophia spent her mornings, as usual, in prayer, fervently seeking the will of the Father for everyone at the Golden T.

Karen wasn't certain how it had happened, but by the end of her second week in Idaho, she'd begun rising with the sun and not resenting it. She'd even started helping with some of the chores around the place. She would have been completely inept if it hadn't been for Billy. He never pointed out how stupid she was for not knowing something. He just calmly told her how to do this or where to find that, and then he continued with whatever story he'd been telling before the interruption.

It surprised her, this friendship with the boy. She hadn't spent much time around children. She'd believed kids were better cared for by nannies or shipped off to boarding schools, as she'd been.

But she *liked* being with Billy. His smile alone could brighten her entire day. She couldn't help wondering what the "miracle" had been that gave him back his ability to smile, not because it was expected of him but because he was truly happy.

Maybe someday she would ask him.

It was Friday evening, and Dusty, his assistant, Grant Ludwig, and the four boys had returned from the Yuli Basterra farm where they'd been baling hay the past week. They were a dirty, sweaty bunch, if Karen had ever seen one. And yet, she found herself smiling as she watched the good-natured pushing and shoving that went on while they stood on the porch and gave Sophia a quick rundown of their day.

"All right, fellas," Dusty said at last. "Time to wash up for supper. Unless my nose is totally out of whack from too much hay dust, I'd guess Miss Sophie's got a roast in the oven." He winked at the elderly woman.

"It's a roast, all right," Sophia replied, "but I didn't have anything to do with it. Karen made supper tonight."

Dusty's eyes widened as he looked at her. "*You* did?"

Indignation welled in her chest. He didn't have to sound and look so surprised. But before she could tell him to jump off a bridge or something, he grinned, and the sting was removed from his words.

"We'd better hurry, boys. I don't know about you, but I'm starved."

"So'm I!" Billy exclaimed before he took off running toward the bunkhouse. "I get the shower first."

The other boys followed him.

"Will you stay and eat with us, Grant?" Sophia asked.

"Thanks, Miss Sophie, but I've got a date tonight. I'd better get home and clean up or Wendy won't want anything to do with me." He bent his hat brim at Karen. "Evening, Karen." He turned. "See you on Sunday, Dusty." Then he strode toward his pickup.

"That's a man in love," Sophia said as they watched him walk away.

"Grant?" Dusty asked. "You think so?"

"Without a doubt. Wendy Aberdeen is a lucky girl. He'll make her a wonderful husband. He has the heart of a servant and will cherish her."

Her gaze still on Grant as he got into his truck and drove away, Karen felt a twinge of envy for the "lucky girl." What was it like to be cherished? To be loved and accepted? The entire concept was outside Karen's realm of experience. She didn't know if she believed in it.

"Are you all right, my dear?"

Karen blinked, then glanced at her grandmother. "I'm fine," she lied. "I'd better check the roast." Without looking at anyone else, she hurried inside.

❧

The supper was surprisingly good. Dusty wouldn't have believed it if he hadn't tasted it himself. He suspected Sophia had given plenty of advice to her granddaughter.

Finished with his dessert, Dusty shoved his plate away and let out a sigh of satisfaction. "That was great, Karen," he said, not for the first time.

"I'm glad you enjoyed it." Blushing, she rose from her chair and reached for his plate.

He stopped her with his fingers on the back of her wrist. "It's Hal and Billy's turn to clear the table." When she met his gaze, he said, "Sit down and relax. You deserve it."

Her blush intensified, but she did as he'd asked.

He tipped his chair back on two legs. "Hal's got some good news for you."

"Good news?" Karen glanced toward Hal. "About my car?"

"Yeah," the boy answered. "I've located that carburetor we needed. Good price, too. And I think I've found a guy who'll let me use his body shop to paint it when we're ready." Hal shifted his gaze to Dusty. "But we're gonna have to raise some up-front money or nothing's gonna get done."

It was a challenge of sorts, and Dusty recognized it. Hal was asking how much faith and trust they were going to put in him. From the look on Hal's face, he didn't expect them to have much.

Unlike the other three boys, Hal Junker hadn't been sent to the Golden T by his parents. He had none to send him. He'd come to Dusty by way of some concerned members of a local church who were aware of the boy's situation, people who'd seen that this young man was headed for serious trouble unless someone intervened. And the Junker family, if it could be called that, didn't particularly care if the camp made a difference for Hal or not.

Dusty didn't want him to be disappointed again. Somehow, he had to raise the necessary funds so Hal could fix that car. He wanted the boy to succeed at something. He wanted to prove he trusted him.

We're ripe for a miracle here, God. Show me what I need to do. Keep me on the right path.

"Dusty...," Sophia said.

He looked at her.

"The Lord will provide. He always does."

He nodded. Over the years he'd learned a lot from this woman. She'd been a good example of walking by faith and not by sight.

"Gosh, Miss Butler!" Billy exclaimed. "That looks awful. What happened?"

Dusty turned his head in time to see Karen pulling her arm from the boy's grasp. She quickly rolled down her shirt sleeve, then rose from her chair and hurried out of the house. The screen door swung closed behind her with a *bang!*

"I didn't mean to upset her," Billy said. "I thought she was hurt."

Sophia comforted him with a pat on the back. "It's okay,

Billy." She glanced at Dusty. "Would you mind talking to her?"

"No." He rose and went outside, just in time to see Karen disappearing into the barn. He followed her. The old building was filled with shadows. Dusty paused inside the doorway to give his eyes a moment to adjust.

"You didn't have to come after me."

He looked in the direction of her voice. "Sophia asked me to."

"I'm okay." She stepped forward, into the faint light coming through the doorway at his back.

"Are you?"

"Trying to rescue me, Mr. Stoddard?"

He smiled, answering softly, "Maybe." He moved across the barn. When he stood before her, he asked, "Care to tell me what happened?"

"You must have guessed by now."

Yes, he had guessed, but he didn't say so.

She held out her arms, wrists up, exposing the scars, clear even in the dim light. She held the position until he'd looked at what she defiantly showed him.

"Why?" he asked as he lifted his gaze to meet hers once again.

She released a humorless laugh. "Why not?"

"Many reasons."

"Not for me." She turned her back toward him.

He could have pressed her. He could have tried to force the story from her. He didn't. Instead, he waited.

"My mother never believed I would amount to anything. She was right. I couldn't even succeed at taking my own life." Again Karen laughed, a harsh sound in the cavernous barn. "I'm completely hopeless. Just like she said."

"No one is hopeless."

She whirled around. Her eyes spanked with contempt. "Are you going to give me the Jesus-loves-you spiel like they feed you at your church? If so, don't bother."

"It's true, whether you want to hear it or not. Truth isn't altered by unbelief. It's still truth."

"You don't know anything about me or my life," she snapped. "Do you?"

He could hear the deep hurt behind her words. "Not as much as I'd like to know."

"Why? Why would you like to know?"

He stared into her eyes, pondering her question, and was surprised when the answer came to him.

"Why?" she demanded again.

"Because I care about you, Karen."

....

Thanksgiving Day, 1936

Dear Diary,

   This has been the most delightful day, despite my misgivings about Sophia and me. Mikkel diplomatically (whether he knew it or not) placed himself between us, and he never seemed to prefer one over the other. He talked to us both, as well as to Mama and Papa.

   Mama outdid herself. In addition to the huge turkey, roasted a golden brown the way Papa likes it best, there was dressing and stuffed celery and mashed sweet potatoes and cranberry relish and butternut squash soup and peas with baby onions in that yummy cream sauce. And for dessert, we had a choice of mince or apple pie and spiced ginger cake.

   I heard Papa tell Mama it was almost sinful how much food we had on our table, and then Mama got all worried that her cooking was prideful rather than hospitable and maybe she had offended the pastor.

   I do not think Mikkel was offended. I think he was happy. I think he loved being with a family for Thanksgiving. I have never before thought about him being lonely, so far from the rest of his kin, but I should have. I would be lonely if I were taken a thousand or two thousand miles away from Mama and Papa and Sophia.

But today he was happy. He laughed a lot. He has the most wonderful laugh. When I hear it, I feel all warm in my stomach. It is a beautiful feeling. And terrifying, too.

After we were stuffed full of Mama's delicious dinner, we went outside and built snowmen. Mikkel made a competition of it, but we did not get far before a snowball fight broke out. I do not know who started it, but I know we were all sopping wet when we came in. Even Mikkel. We stood dripping on Mama's kitchen floor. Mikkel tried to look chagrined, but he was not successful. Even Mama was laughing, especially after he put on some of Papa's bib overalls while his clothes dried by the stove. They hit him mid-shin and had room for half another person in the backside. He looked so funny.

Sophia told me later that it was not proper for me to be laughing at a minister the way I laughed at Mikkel. But I think she is wrong. I think God made laughter. I think He meant for us to laugh and play and enjoy the beauty of the world. And I do not think so simply because Mikkel has said it from the pulpit. I believe it in my heart. As if God were whispering it to me there.

Does God talk to people that way? Sometimes I think that is what Mikkel has been teaching. But then I think, Why would God bother to talk to me? I am nobody important. I am not special. I do not have any unique talents. Not like Mikkel. He can change lives with his preaching. He is the sort of person God can use. When I listen to him on Sundays, I feel different.

But I am not like him. I am just ordinary. I am just Esther. It is not a bad thing to be, but it is not special either.

But then I think Mikkel wants me to think that it _is_ special. That _I_ am special.

It is confusing sometimes.

Jeg forstår ikke.

That is Danish for, "I do not understand."

Esther

Sunday, December 13, 1936

Dear Diary,

Jesus lives! Like scales falling from my eyes, I see it now. I understood today for the first time what I have been hearing preached since I was a little girl. I thought I understood, but I never did.

Jesus went to the cross to pay for my sins, and then He rose again. He is not just in heaven, far, far away. Like Grandma Jessie. He is here with me.

Oh, there are no words to explain it. But Mikkel understood, and he shares my joy.

I am reborn, and nothing shall ever be the same for me again.

Esther

With a groan of frustration, Karen opened her eyes and looked at the illuminated face of the clock radio. It was three o'clock, and she hadn't slept a wink. The top sheet and blanket were a tangled mess around her feet from all her tossing and turning. The underside of her eyelids seemed made of sandpaper. She had a nagging headache, and her stomach felt as if it were tied in a knot.

No one is hopeless, Karen.

"Go away," she whispered.

It's true, whether you want to hear it or not.

She put a pillow over her face. "Leave me alone, Dusty Stoddard."

I care about you, Karen.

How could he care about her? He didn't *know* her. Why had he said it?

She pushed aside the pillow and sat up, reaching for the bedside lamp at the same time. Muted light spilled from beneath the rose-colored lampshade.

"I don't want his pity."

She got out of bed and stepped to the window. A sliver of moon bathed Sophia's garden in a pale, white light. A warm breeze caused the branches of the old willow to sway, like a dancer to some unheard melody.

Karen opened the window as wide as it could go, then knelt on the floor and rested her arms on the sill. She drew in a deep breath and released it on a sigh.

"What am I doing in this place?"

I BROUGHT YOU HERE.

A quiver ran through her.

It wasn't bad enough she'd lost everything she'd held dear. It wasn't bad enough she'd wanted to die and had tried to take her own life. Now she was going insane, too. After all, only crazy people heard voices in their heads.

She turned from the window and sat on the floor with her back against the wall. Her gaze fell on the books on the nightstand. The journals her grandmother had wanted her to read.

Why not begin now? Those diaries would most likely put her to sleep in a hurry.

She reached for the top one and opened it. The first page was dated Saturday, February 14, 1931. *Dear Diary*, Esther had written in a girlish scrawl. *My name is Esther Ruth Thompson, and today is my twelfth birthday. Because I am always writing stories on whatever paper I can find, Mama and Papa gave me this journal to keep my thoughts in. So today I begin writing the story of my life…*

Karen scanned a few more entries. Esther described the family farm and introduced the members of her family, including her elder sister, Sophia. She even wrote about the dogs and the barnyard cats. The writing was childish and simple and not particularly entertaining. If there had been another book handy, Karen would have put the diary aside. But there wasn't anything else to read, and it was better to read this than to imagine she was hearing things. It was better than remembering the sound of Dusty's voice as he'd said he cared about her or dwelling on memories of her own past.

Dusty wasn't certain what caused it, but suddenly he was wide awake. He sat up and looked through the open doorway into the main room of the bunkhouse.

There it was again. A creaking floorboard. One of the boys was up. Probably using the bathroom.

And yet something in his spirit remained disturbed. Something wasn't right.

He glanced at his clock. It was after three o'clock. He rose and moved quietly toward the door. There was enough moonlight coming through the windows to make it easy to see Hal as he shucked off his clothes and got into his bed.

The boy had been outside, Dusty realized. It must have been the sound of the closing door that had awakened him.

"Where you been?" Billy whispered sleepily, echoing Dusty's thoughts.

"Nowhere, punk," Hal answered. "Go back to sleep."

Billy murmured something unintelligible, rolled over, and was silent once more.

Father, I feel as if Hal's slipping out of my reach. How can I help him? Soften his heart, Lord. Make him willing to listen. Don't let him make the same mistakes I made. Protect him. O God, protect him from himself.

Dusty returned to his bed, but sleep evaded him. Instead, his thoughts carried him back to his troubled youth—to the night of his sixteenth birthday.

The August night was hot and sticky, and the air conditioner was on the fritz. About as lousy a scenario as one could imagine for a guy's birthday.

Dusty's dad had been sick all day, feeling so rotten he hadn't gotten out of bed even once. The plan had been to celebrate with dinner out, his dad and him and his best friend, Pete Gold. But with the old man sick, that had been canceled.

It made Dusty mad. He felt like his dad got sick on purpose, just to spoil their plans. It wouldn't surprise him if it were true. Raine Stoddard was an old fogy, always down on whatever Dusty wanted to do. They fought all the time, over everything. Why would his dad want to spend a night on the town with the son he disapproved of in so many ways?

He was sitting on the front stoop, muttering obscenities and blaming his dad for every miserable thing in his life when Pete pulled to the curb in a souped-up Chevy, the powerful engine rumbling noisily.

"Hey, Dusty!" Pete yelled through the open window on the passenger side. "Get over here."

Dusty was down the walk in a flash. Leaning on the car door, he looked in at his friend. "Where'd you get the fancy wheels?"

"My aunt gave it to me. Get in."

He knew he shouldn't. His dad was sick. But hey, it was his birthday. He didn't want to stay home on his birthday.

Dusty opened the car door and slid in. "Let's go."

Tires squealing, the Chevy shot forward, leaving a patch of rubber on the pavement behind them.

They cruised around Chicago for the next few hours. They bought beer at a corner grocery store from a clerk who pretended

Pete wasn't underage. Outside a popular dance club, they picked up a couple of girls they knew from school.

Dusty was behind the wheel by that time. Pete was too wasted to drive. When Pete saw a row of flagpoles lining a sidewalk, he got the idea to grab one of the flags right off a pole as they drove past. Dusty told him he was crazy, but Pete insisted, and the two girls were yelling, "Go for it!"

Pete sat in the open window on the passenger side of the car. "Faster!" he shouted. He gripped the roof of the car and leaned out as far as he could go.

Dusty gunned it, pressing the gas pedal all the way to the floor. The Chevy responded with power. Pete reached for the first flag, whooping a cry of victory as his hand closed around the fabric.

And then suddenly he was gone, yanked clean out of the car.

Dusty slammed on the brakes, threw open his door, and hit the ground running.

But Pete was beyond help. He was already dead.

And that was only the beginning of the nightmare.

Dusty covered his face with his arm as he stifled a groan. He didn't want to relive the days and weeks immediately following that dreadful night. It didn't serve any purpose. What he wanted was to save the boys who came to the Golden T Youth

Camp from experiencing similar sorrows, from making similar mistakes. He wanted to rescue them, turn their lives around, help them find a better way.

It was easy to get into trouble in this world. He'd been a rebellious, mouthy, out-of-control kid, but that wasn't always the way of it. Sometimes it was the quiet ones who took a misstep and were plunged into misery.

But Hal…Hal was a lot like Dusty had been. Except Dusty hadn't been deserted and rejected by his parents. Dusty's father had loved him. Loved him more than he'd realized at the time.

It wasn't until it was too late that he'd seen the truth.

❦

The golden fingers of dawn were stretching above the eastern horizon by the time Karen closed Esther's first journal. Seeing that the sun was nearly up, she glanced with surprise at the bedside clock. She'd been reading for over two hours!

If that wasn't a sign of sheer boredom, she didn't know what would be. Reading a young girl's diary for all that time. And it wasn't as if Esther Thompson's life had been an exciting one. It was one of utter simplicity.

And yet, something had held Karen's attention. Something in Esther's story…

She gave her head a quick shake before pushing herself up from the floor.

"Ooh," she groaned, feeling how stiff she was from sitting in one spot for so long.

She stretched from side to side, leaned down to touch the palms of her hands to the floor, then reached up over her head. She was ready to crawl back into bed, in the hopes of getting at least a little shuteye, when she heard Sophia's voice raised in song.

Karen turned toward the window and looked out.

"Holy, holy, holy…," Sophia sang as she moved with slow steps along a path that wound through the garden.

She really believes it. She really believes God's up there, listening to her. It isn't just a Sunday thing with her.

Karen leaned her shoulder against the window frame, a small frown furrowing her brow.

Why? she wondered. *What makes my grandmother believe?*

In the back of her mind, she heard another voice singing. Dusty's voice. Though it was only a memory from the previous Sunday's church service, it seemed as if he were actually harmonizing with Sophia.

He believed too, she thought. Both of them believed in God in a way she'd never imagined believing. They had…*something.* Something she didn't have. Like a secret that gave them great joy.

It bothered Karen. It bothered her a lot.

···

Saturday, February 13, 1937

Dear Diary,

Today, Sophia turned nineteen, and tomorrow is my eighteenth birthday. Mama has made new dresses for us to wear to church, and Papa gave us both pretty new hats. Sophia said I should have had to wait for my actual birthday before Mama and Papa gave me my presents.

It breaks my heart that we have grown so far apart. It has been worse since I accepted Christ as my Savior and Lord. Sophia has distanced herself more than ever before, and I cannot reach her, no matter how much I try. And I _have_ tried. So very hard.

The Scriptures say in Luke that henceforth there shall be five in one house divided, three against two, and two against three. Surely that describes Sophia and me. But, oh, how I pray it will not continue to be true of us. I want to share this joy with my beloved sister. This above all else I want to share with her.

Last week Sophia accused me of getting religion only to impress Mikkel. She called me a hypocrite and worse. Her words seemed to crucify my Lord all over again, and they nearly broke my heart.

I pray for her. I will pray for her all the days of my life.

Father in heaven, help Sophia to see what it is I have found in You. Help her to see the abundance of life You have poured out upon me. Amen.

Esther

....

Sunday, February 14, 1937

Dear Diary,

Today, Mikkel asked me to marry him!

And I said Yes!!!

When he came to see Papa all those many weeks ago (that time I wondered if Papa could be in trouble of some sort), it was to ask for permission to court me and, when the time came, to propose marriage. He told me he was waiting for two things to happen. First, that I would come to know Jesus in my heart, and second, that I turn eighteen.

As of today, both conditions were met, and so after church services, Mikkel came to call on me. He declared his devotion in the sweetest of fashions, taking me by the hand and dropping to one knee, and then he asked for my hand in marriage. I was speechless at first. My heart raced so fast I was certain he must hear it. I could not speak and had to nod my answer. He smiled and kissed me.

He would like us to be married this summer, immediately after I graduate.

I have hoped this would happen almost from the moment I

first saw him. For months I have hoped. But I never believed he would choose me.

I love him more than I ever thought possible, and he loves me. What a miracle!

Mikkel warned me that life as a minister's wife will not be an easy one. I do not care. I am not afraid. If I am with him and can serve our Lord too, what have I to fear?

Esther

P.S. Sophia looked at me tonight as if I were a boil that needed to be pricked. She has stopped speaking to me altogether.

Ten

Standing in the corral in the shade of the barn, Karen gripped the horse's halter. "Easy, fella," she crooned.

Dusty braced the gelding's leg between his knees while cleaning dried blood from a gash that ran from knee to fetlock.

"Is it bad?" Billy asked.

"It'll mend okay," Dusty answered the boy without looking up. "But you won't be able to ride him for several weeks."

"I never shoulda left the trail. You told us not to, and I did it anyway." Billy glanced at Karen with tear-filled eyes. "This is my fault."

"You didn't mean for it to happen," she reassured him. "You couldn't—"

"Billy's right. He shouldn't have left the trail. He was told about the barbed wire up there." Dusty carefully set the horse's hoof on the ground, then straightened, his gaze instantly clashing with hers. "He has to take responsibility for his own actions."

Isn't that a little harsh? she wanted to ask.

His eyes clearly gave his answer. *No.*

You big bully.

Stay out of it, princess.

She wanted to hit him. The overbearing, sanctimonious, hick from the sticks. Never in her life had she detested a man the way she detested Dusty Stoddard.

I wish he'd kiss me. Her heart somersaulted at the surprising thought. *Oh no!*

She couldn't be falling for this backwoods cowboy. But she was. She was falling for him, and she was falling for him hard.

Dusty hunkered down and took Billy gently by the arms. "Son, it's going to be your responsibility to take care of Sundowner. You'll have to treat that leg with salve twice a day, morning and evening."

"I'll do it, Dusty. I promise." The boy continued his battle with tears.

"Maybe Miss Karen would be willing to help you." Dusty glanced at her a second time, his gaze no longer stern.

This cannot be happening to me, she thought as she stared at him.

"You know horses, Karen. Would you help Billy with Sundowner? Hold him like you're doing now while Billy dresses the wound?"

Was she still holding the horse's halter? She'd forgotten.

I can't get involved with these people. I can't fall for this man. I don't belong here. I belong in Los Angeles. I belong with my friends at the country club, and…

"Karen?"

She gave her head a slight shake, then nodded. "Yes. Of course I'll help Billy." *But only until I get some money together and get out of here. Only until then.*

The sound of an automobile coming up the drive was the perfect excuse for her to break eye contact before he could guess what she was thinking and feeling.

Dusty stepped away from the horse, his gaze on the car as they waited to see who their visitor was. A moment later, he muttered something under his breath, then strode toward the corral gate.

"That's the man from the restaurant," Billy said. "The one who was mad at Junkman."

This can't be good, Karen thought. Then she asked, "Where is he?"

"Him and the others are helping Miss Sophie weed her vegetable garden."

"Maybe you'd better join them." She gave Billy a little shove. "And don't say anything about that man being here."

"Are you—?"

"Go on. Do as I say." She unbuckled the lead from Sundowner's halter and followed Billy across the corral.

She approached the car as the visitor demanded, "Where is he? Where is that—" He called Hal a foul name.

Dusty's face darkened, but he managed to hold his temper. "Watch what you're saying, sir."

The man reached into the car and hauled a young girl out, forcing her to stand right next to him, his hand locked around her upper arm like a vice. Her face was as white as a sheet, and her eyes were swollen from crying.

"Daddy, please," she whimpered.

"He got her pregnant."

Dusty must have heard Karen's small gasp, for he turned his head to look in her direction. For an instant, she caught a glimpse of how much he cared, of how much he gave of himself to the boys who stayed at the ranch.

Instinctively, she moved to stand beside him.

"I'm going to have that kid put in jail. You hear me, Stoddard?"

Dusty seemed to come to himself. Calmly, he said, "May I have your name, sir?"

"Call. Olen Call." He gave the girl's arm a rough yank. "And this little tramp is Patty."

"Karen." Dusty's controlled tone of voice couldn't hide his anger from her. "Would you mind taking Patty into the house while I have a talk with Mr. Call?"

"Of course." She moved forward and gently drew the girl away from her father. "Come with me, Patty. I'll see if there isn't some lemonade in the refrigerator."

❦

Ofttimes, when Sophia closed her eyes, her mind carried her back through the years for brief visits with old friends and beloved family members. It was particularly easy to do when she sat in the shade of the willow tree on a warm June day.

Today she'd been remembering her first summer as Bradley's wife. She'd been happy, despite the arduous work of getting their little spread started. She'd loved riding horses and driving cattle with him and their cowhand, Lucky Sam Peterman. She'd been young, slender, pretty, and filled with dreams and plans for the future.

"I want a dozen children, Bradley, and I want all of them to look like you."

"No, they've gotta look like you, sweet pea."

She'd loved her husband very much. And yet, even so, there was a part of her heart she'd withheld from him throughout their marriage.

"Why can't you let go of Mikkel?" Bradley had asked once. *"I want your whole heart."*

"I don't know what you're talking about."

"Don't you? Then write to your sister before it's too late. The war's over. Write to her."

Of course, it had already been too late, though they hadn't known it at the time. It had already been too late to tell Esther how much she loved her, that it hadn't been Esther's fault Mikkel loved her and not Sophia, that she missed her sister and was sorry. So sorry.

She released a sigh. Those weren't the memories she'd been anticipating. The Lord knew she had a lifetime of regrets.

"Praise God for setting me free from regrets," she whispered, then she opened her eyes.

Billy came running around the corner of the house. He stopped abruptly, an anxious gaze locked on Hal.

"Billy, what is it?" she called to him.

The boy glanced her way, waging a valiant effort to hide his feelings. "Nothin'."

Sophia wasn't fooled. With a tiny groan, she pushed herself up from the bench and walked toward Billy. She saw him look at the three other boys who were busy weeding, then back at her. Whatever was wrong, it had something to do with Hal.

"Did Dusty send you for me?" she asked, watching him closely.

He shook his head.

"How is your horse?"

"He's gonna be okay." Another anxious glance toward Hal. "Dusty says I can't ride him for a while, and I'm gonna have to tend to his leg, but he's gonna be okay."

Sophia touched his shoulder. Speaking softly, she said, "What is it, Billy? Something's bothering you."

"Miss Karen told me not to say anything."

She raised an eyebrow.

Billy's resolve crumbled before her look. "It's that man. The one who came to the restaurant. The one who was so mad at Junkman."

"What about him?"

"He's here."

"Oh, dear." It was her turn to glance toward Hal and the others. Fortunately, they'd given scant notice to the elderly woman and young boy. "You'd better stay here." She pressed her index finger to her lips. "Miss Karen was right. Don't say anything until we know why he's come."

She followed the path toward the side of the house.

O Lord, my heart is full of fear. Protect Hal. Protect all these boys. Keep us in the center of Your will. Give Dusty wisdom. You are an awesome God, and we trust in Your goodness and mercy all the days of our lives. Whatever is about to happen, help us to keep our eyes on You. Amen.

Rounding the corner, she saw the automobile and the two

men. Though they weren't shouting, each man's body proclaimed his anger in the way he stood and faced the other.

Where was Karen?

Dusty glanced toward Sophia. He stared at her for a moment, then jerked his head toward the house before returning his attention to the other man.

Sophia climbed the few steps to the porch, then entered the house. She found Karen in the kitchen, seated at the table with a young girl who was weeping inconsolably into her hands while Karen patted her back.

You keep that sleazeball away from my daughter, or I'll have him thrown in jail.

With the memory of those words ringing in her ears, Sophia understood the situation without further explanation, and her heart sank.

"Grandmother."

It was the first time Karen had called Sophia that, but this wasn't the moment to take pleasure in it. "Yes." She moved forward again. "I'm here."

The girl choked back a sob as she lowered her hands.

She's so young, Lord. She can't be more than fifteen.

"Patty!" came a shout from outside.

The girl bolted from her seat.

"Patty, get out here! *Now!*"

"He's gonna make me have an abortion," she whispered, then she ran from the house.

O, Father God. No!

Sophia turned and followed after Patty as fast as her old legs would carry her. She reached the porch in time to see the girl's father grab her by the arm and force her into the car with a none-too-gentle shove. Before Sophia could step off the porch, the man got behind the wheel and started the engine. He said something to Dusty through the open window, then drove away, a spray of dirt and gravel flying up behind his rear tires.

Karen's fingers closed around Sophia's arm. "Dusty will take care of it."

"I hope so, dear," Sophia replied while patting Karen's hand. "Dear God, I hope so."

Sunday, May 9, 1937

Dear Diary,

Sophia has steadfastly refused to be my maid of honor.
Mikkel has tried talking to her, but she will not relent. I can see
the sadness in her eyes and the bitterness, too. I want so much to
help her, but she will have no part in it.

Mama is beside herself. I am getting married in less than a
month. She is making my wedding gown. And all the while, her
daughters are at war.

Papa has warned Sophia that she will one day regret her
decision, but Sophia insists she will not.

Father in heaven, is there no way for me to reach my sister?
Please soften her heart toward me. All my life she has been there
for me. We learned to play the piano together. She taught me to
swim when I was too afraid to get in the water. She helped me
with my algebra or I would have surely failed that subject. I
cannot help loving Mikkel, nor am I sorry I am to marry him.
But what about Sophia?

Esther

....

Wednesday, June 2, 1937

Dear Diary,

I am frightened.

My wedding gown is finished and hanging in the parlor.
Delphia has her bridesmaid gown. She says it is the loveliest
dress she has ever owned and that my mama is a wonder. Some
gifts have been delivered and are sitting on the table, prettily
wrapped. Mrs. Booher at the bakery says my cake will be large
enough to feed the entire church congregation, all of whom are
expected to be there for the wedding on Saturday morning.

I love Mikkel. I have come to love him more every single day.
But I am still frightened.

Today he told me that we will be leaving later this summer for
Denmark where he intends to assist his grandfather in his
church. I am more than frightened. I am terrified. I have never
gone farther from home than to Boise, less than a hundred miles
away. Mikkel says it will only be for a year. Two at the most.
But how shall I get along? I have learned only a little of the
Danish Mikkel has tried to teach me.

I long to talk to Sophia about my fears. She has been such a
rock for me. Always she has listened and advised. But it is

useless to try to talk to her now. She wants nothing to do with me. She will not listen or advise. She says she is not coming to the wedding.

I don't believe her. She will come. She must. She could not hate me that much.

Oh, Sophia, you were my closest and dearest companion. You were more than my sister. You were my friend. Why have you deserted me?

But God hasn't deserted me. Even in my fear and uncertainty, I feel Him near, offering comfort and courage. In my weakness, He is strong. His strength is perfect and His grace is sufficient.

Esther

Karen paced the tiny parlor of the ranch house. Every once in a while, she paused and looked toward the front door, wondering what was happening in the bunkhouse between Dusty and Hal. Then she started pacing again.

"Sit down, dear," her grandmother commanded gently. "Your worry will change nothing."

"How can you *not* worry?"

"The Bible says, 'And who of you by being worried can add a single hour to his life?' So that's what I try to practice. Not to worry."

"And you succeed?"

Sophia shook her head. "Not every time. But the older I get, the more often I've seen the hand of God miraculously change circumstances and bring good out of all kinds of disasters."

"Miracles." Karen's tone mocked the word. "You and Dusty talk like they happen every day."

"They do."

She whirled around, ready to tell her grandmother she was either senile or a fool. One or the other. But something in the elderly woman's expression stopped her.

Sophia's smile was tender, the look in her eyes slightly distant, as if she could see something Karen couldn't. "Thou wilt keep him in perfect peace, whose mind is stayed on thee," she said softly, more to herself than to her granddaughter.

"And you can be at peace over Junkman's pregnant girl-friend? And what about her father? Did you see the way he treated her? He called her a tramp. She's only fifteen, for crying out loud."

Sophia sighed. "Fifteen. That young. I'd hoped I was wrong." She sighed again, then added, "I'm not saying the days ahead of us will be easy. There are consequences for all of our actions, for the foolish choices we make when we insist upon our own way. But that doesn't mean God won't be there with us. It doesn't mean He won't forgive us and meet us at the point of our need. Jesus loves us."

"Oh, honestly," Karen muttered before striding out of the house.

Billy, Noah, and Ted were standing in the corral; their gazes were turned toward the bunkhouse. For an instant, she considered joining them. Maybe she could put their minds at ease. But she quickly discarded that notion.

How could she ease their minds when she couldn't ease her own?

She took off in the opposite direction, walking down the dirt drive toward the highway.

Miracles…

Perfect peace…

Right. Like such things existed in this world.

Jesus loves us, her grandmother had said, and there hadn't been a shred of doubt in her statement.

Karen halted in her tracks, looked upward, and cried, "If You love us, then prove it. Find a solution to Patty's problem, if You can."

She half expected a bolt from heaven to strike her dead.

It didn't.

Of course it didn't. God wasn't interested in their problems. They were going to have to muddle through this on their own.

They?

As in, us?

As in, me, too?

Karen groaned and resumed walking.

This was not her problem, she reminded herself. This was *their* problem—Dusty's and Sophia's and Hal's and Patty's—but not hers. She wasn't anybody's counselor. She wasn't anybody's friend or mom or sister or aunt. She had no words of wisdom to dispense to others. She wasn't responsible for anybody but herself.

And she had plenty of trouble trying to cope with that.

"I don't want to be here. I don't want to be involved in their lives or in their problems. I don't want to live on this falling-down ranch. I hate the sagebrush and the bugs and the snakes and the dirt and the wind. I hate it all."

So why didn't she swallow her tattered pride, pick up the phone, and throw herself on Mac's mercy? If she told him how miserable she was, he would pay for her transportation back to California. He was a kind and generous man, an old and good friend. He would let her stay in his home again, as he'd done before.

Sure, Mac would give her charity—if that was what she wanted.

Yes, she could go back to California. Back to L.A., where everyone was whispering behind their hands about her: *Poor Karen Butler. Her father was a crook... Poor Karen. Her father killed himself... Did you know she tried to commit suicide? Have you heard that she...*

It was too awful to contemplate, let alone endure.

Why don't you just kill yourself and get it over with? Do it right this time.

She stopped again. Her breath caught painfully in her throat even as her pulse began to race. Perspiration broke out on her forehead. She wondered if she would be sick.

She knew that dark, twisted voice, the one tempting her to take the easy way out. She'd listened to it before. Her father had listened to it too.

Go ahead. Do it. No one would miss you.

As soon as those words passed through her mind, another thought followed: *Grandmother would miss me. Billy would miss me. Maybe Dusty...*

She sank onto the ground and began to sob, overwhelmed by the horrible pain in her chest.

"All right," Hal said at last, his tone belligerent, his stance stiff. "So I slept with her. I didn't mean for her to get pregnant. It's her own fault. She should've been on the pill."

"Placing the blame on Patty isn't going to help matters." Dusty glanced out the window of his room and saw Karen walking down the drive. Briefly, he wondered where she was going.

"Are we finished yet?" Hal started for the door.

Dusty's attention returned to the boy. "Stay right where you are, Hal Junker. We're *not* finished."

"What d'you want from me? What's the big deal? Kids my age have sex. So what? It's a fact of life." He released a guttural sound, then faced Dusty again. "Patty probably got pregnant on purpose. You saw her old man. Who wouldn't want to get away from him? But I'm not gonna marry her, baby or no baby. And that's something you can't make me do."

"Hal—"

The boy swore at him. "Save it. I'm through listenin' to you." He slammed out of the room.

Dusty stared at the closed door, debating whether or not to go after him. Finally he decided it would be better to let the kid cool off a bit before they tried talking again.

Besides, he wasn't sure himself what needed to be done. Hal was sixteen. Patty was fifteen. Marriage wasn't the answer. The best thing was for the baby to be placed for adoption. But what Mr. Call wanted was Hal's hide nailed to the barn door. Period.

❧

It was the strangest thing. One moment Karen was sobbing inconsolably, and the next, she grew quiet. Her unhappiness and despair were gone. Her desire to run away was gone. Vanished. As if cut from her heart by a surgeon's knife. She looked at the scars on her wrists again, symbols of all that was wrong about her, and she realized she was no longer afraid.

The older I get—Sophia's voice repeated in her mind—*the*

more times I've seen the hand of God miraculously change cir-
cumstances and bring good out of all kinds of disasters.

Was it possible?

She looked up at the blue sky, dotted with cumulus clouds.

Was it possible?

She stood, still looking upward. A moment later, she heard the roar of an engine. She turned to see her Mustang barreling down the drive, coming directly toward her. Just as she took a step back, the car swerved, missing her by mere inches. And then it was past her.

Hal! That was Hal behind the wheel, driving like a maniac.

Heart hammering, she spun toward the house. "Dusty! Dusty, come quick!" She took off running. "Dusty!"

Even before her frantic cries, Dusty must have heard Hal driving away, for he appeared instantly through the kitchen doorway, Sophia right on his heels.

"It was Hal. He's taken my car."

Dusty leapt off the porch and raced toward his pickup truck. Karen headed in the same direction, yanking open the passenger-side door as he turned the key in the ignition.

"I'm going with you," she said needlessly.

He didn't offer any argument.

The truck raced down the drive. A haze of dust hovered at the junction with the highway, proclaiming Hal's recent exit. Dusty braked to a halt and stared west.

"Did you see which way he turned?"

"No," she answered, gazing down the highway to the east. If that was the direction Hal had taken, the swells of rolling desert obscured any sign of the battered Mustang.

With a few muttered words of frustration, Dusty laid his forehead on the back of his hands where they gripped the steering wheel.

"We'll find him," she said without much confidence.

He turned his head enough so he could look at her. "It never solves anything to run away. Ultimately, you're running from yourself." He sat up straight. "And there's no escape."

Karen wanted to touch his shoulder. She wanted to help him in some way. Worry darkened his eyes and creased his brow. He was suffering because he loved Hal. Despite everything that boy had done, Dusty loved him. She didn't understand, but she wanted to. She wished she could.

He pressed on the accelerator and turned left onto the highway, headed toward the small town of Murphy. "There wasn't much gas in the Mustang. He'll need a service station."

They made it about a mile down the road, driving about twenty miles per hour over the speed limit. Then the truck suddenly coughed, sputtered, and died. As it rolled to a stop, Dusty slapped his right hand against the steering wheel in frustration while staring at the gas gauge.

"He siphoned my tank!"

They sat in silence for a long while, both of them gazing straight ahead, staring at the point where the road disappeared over another swell in the land.

Finally, Karen looked at him. "You can't save them all, Dusty. No matter how hard you try. Even I know that."

Saturday, June 5, 1937

Dear Diary,

It is 4:00 in the morning. My wedding day. The house is quiet. Papa will not be up to milk the cows for another hour or so. The rooster has yet to crow. For now, the air is cold and I am wrapped in a blanket as I sit, writing in my journal, occasionally glancing out the window so that I might see the sun rise.

Today, I become Mrs. Mikkel Christiansen. Tonight I will lie down with my husband. Mama has explained to me what to expect on my wedding night. I am not certain I completely understand, but Mama was so embarrassed as she tried to explain the act of marriage that I could not ask her any questions.

Strangely, my fears have subsided. I am at peace. God has said a man is to leave his mother and father and cleave to his wife. He has said the marriage bed is undefiled. I know in my heart Mikkel loves me as Christ loves the church, enough to sacrifice himself for me. Because of that, I know I can trust him with my body, my mind, my heart, my soul.

I pray I will be a good wife to him and that our marriage will *be blessed with children. I pray I will be able to minister to God's people at my husband's side. I feel very certain the future that lies before us will be a simple and tranquil one. That is all I want or need.*

Father God, keep me ever mindful of You as I step into this new phase of my life. In Jesus' name, Amen.

Esther

Sunday, June 20, 1937

Dear Diary,

This morning, Mikkel and I bade farewell to our congregation. Tomorrow we leave on the train and begin our journey to Denmark.

It was a tearful parting at church. So many people who have touched my life through the years. So many friends whom I will miss. Not knowing when, if ever, we will return to Oregon made it all the more difficult. For even if Mikkel and I are only in Denmark a year or two, as he believes is true, the Lord may call him to minister anywhere else in the world.

I have promised many people that I will write to them, and they have all promised to write me in return.

Except for Sophia. She is as cold and unyielding as ever. She does not seem to care that I am going away and we may never see each other again. My heart is broken.

My beloved Mikkel tries to comfort me. He says I should not despair, that one day Sophia will find the truth. He says we must pray for her salvation, that we must forgive her hardness of heart and trust the Holy Spirit will hear our prayers.

O God, please make it so.

Esther

Twelve

You can't save them all, Dusty. No matter how hard you try. Even I know that.

Karen's softly spoken admonition dogged Dusty's thoughts in the anxious days that followed Hal's disappearance. Those words were in the back of his mind when he talked to the police. They were in the back of his mind when he drove to Kuna on the outside chance Hal had gone to see Patty; he hadn't. They were in the back of his mind when he prowled the streets of Caldwell and Nampa and Boise on warm summer evenings, searching for any sign of the boy or the old Mustang in the crowds of teens who congregated on street corners.

You can't save them all, Dusty. No matter how hard you try.

What could he have done differently? What could he have said differently?

There were so many things that could happen to Hal out there. So many things that could go wrong.

You can't save them all, Dusty.

When she heard the piano music, Karen set Esther's diary aside and left her bedroom. She paused at the parlor entrance, watching Sophia's arthritic fingers move over the keys, plucking out the melody of a vaguely familiar hymn. Karen waited until her grandmother stopped playing, then crossed the room to stand at the side of the old upright.

Sophia offered a sad smile. "I used to play well." She held up her hands, crooked fingers extended. "The spirit is willing, but the flesh is weak."

"It was lovely, all the same."

"I was remembering the way my sister and I used to play duets when we were girls. My, those were delightful evenings."

"I've been reading her journals," Karen said. "I didn't think I would find them interesting, but…well, they are a bit captivating, aren't they?"

Her grandmother's smile broadened.

Karen glanced toward the kitchen door. "It's quiet today. Where is everyone?"

"Grant took the boys into town to pick up supplies. And Dusty…" She let her voice drift into silence as she shook her head. Then, more softly, she said, "He's trying to repair the old bridge over Bonnet Creek."

Karen sat on the piano bench beside her grandmother. "He's taking this thing with Hal awfully hard."

"Yes."

"Why is that? Hal and Patty must have been seeing each other before Hal came to the Golden T. I mean, the boys have only been at the ranch since the start of summer. She was already pregnant by then. And Dusty couldn't have prevented Hal from taking off the way he did. So why is he acting like it's his fault?"

Sophia turned a thoughtful gaze on Karen. "I think you should ask him that yourself."

"He doesn't want to talk to me."

"Try anyway."

Karen couldn't deny she'd like to follow her grandmother's advice. She wanted to understand Dusty. She wanted to know about his past, about his thoughts and his beliefs, about so many things.

"Go on, dear. Just follow the creek up the draw. You'll find him easy enough."

Against her better judgment, led by her heart and not her head, Karen rose to her feet. She took a few steps toward the door, then stopped and glanced behind her. "If God is love, the way you say, why is this happening to all of you?"

"I don't always know God's purpose," Sophia answered after

a thoughtful pause. "But if I need to know, He'll reveal it to me."

Karen shook her head in bemusement and left the house.

❧

The July sun beat down on Dusty's back. His shirt was damp with his own perspiration, and his muscles ached from hours of exertion. But he didn't stop to sit in the shade, didn't try to take a rest. He wanted this bridge fixed. He wanted anyone who came up this trail to be able to use it. It had been in disrepair for too many years.

HEAR ME, MY SON, the beloved Voice spoke to his heart. ANYONE WHO SEPARATES HIMSELF FROM ME, SETS UP HIS IDOLS IN HIS HEART, PUTS RIGHT BEFORE HIS FACE THE STUMBLING BLOCK OF HIS INIQUITY.

Ezekiel, chapter 14, verse 7. He'd read that passage this morning, and he hadn't been able to escape the words since.

"I don't understand, Lord. I haven't any idols in my heart." Kneeling on the ground, he held a nail against a plank of wood and raised his hammer. "I haven't separated myself from You. I'm trying to serve You." He struck the head of the nail. "Everything I do is because I want to serve You. This ranch." He hit it again. "These boys." And again. "Everything is for You."

He straightened his back, resting his bottom against the heels of his boots, then wiped the sweat from his forehead with the back of his wrist.

FOR THE LORD, WHOSE NAME IS JEALOUS, IS A JEALOUS GOD.

He gazed upward. "I have no idols. I serve no other gods."

The silence in his heart was more eloquent—and more disturbing—than any audible voice could be.

Dusty rose from the ground and walked to the stack of lumber he'd earlier hauled up the trail using a team of horses and an old rickety wagon that wasn't in much better shape than the bridge he was attempting to repair. Selecting another plank, he started to slide it from the stack. He stopped when he heard a sound behind him.

Turning, he saw Karen riding the black-and-white paint toward him.

She stopped her horse, then slipped from the saddle. She patted the gelding's neck with one hand while holding the ends of the reins in the other. Shifting her weight from one foot to the other, she glanced toward the bridge, then back at Dusty.

"Could you use some help?"

"*You* want to help?"

He'd meant for her to be insulted by both his question and his tone. He'd meant for her to become angry and leave. She didn't do either.

"Yes, I want to help."

"All right." He turned his back toward her. "Grab the other end of this, and help me carry it to the bridge."

She did as he'd instructed.

After the board was set in place, she took a step backward onto firmer ground. "Now tell me how I can *really* help." There was a stubborn spark in her light blue eyes.

He saw the challenge in them, but he hadn't the strength to do battle with her today.

"You can't," he said as he knelt and reached for the hammer and nails.

"Sometimes it helps to talk. Remember?"

He set the hammer down again, then lowered his head toward his chest and pressed the palms of his hands against his thighs. "I'm tired," he said under his breath. "So doggone tired."

"Correct me if I'm wrong. After all, I'm new around here. But it seems to me you can't possibly take one summer and expect to turn around the lives of every boy who sets foot on this ranch. They can't all be success stories. So why are you beating yourself up over Hal?"

"I can't save them all," he said softly. Then, a little louder, he added, "I can't save *any* of them." Understanding swept through him. He raised his eyes and looked at her again. "Idols in my heart. My efforts to save Hal have become idols in my heart."

"Excuse me?"

"It's what He's been trying to tell me all morning. No. For much longer than that."

"Who's been trying to tell you?"

"God."

She frowned.

"You were right. *I've* been trying to save them. And I can't."

Confusion darkened her pretty face. "Isn't that why you run this camp? To give them some sort of chance?"

If he told her what God had revealed to him, that he'd been trying to do the work of the Holy Spirit, she wouldn't understand. Some things had to be spiritually discerned, and Karen wasn't ready yet.

But she wanted to understand. He could see that.

Karen watched the expression on his face, saw the way his brows drew together, could tell he was trying to think of a polite way to tell her to mind her own business.

"I made a mistake coming up here. I'll leave you alone." She turned to leave.

"Wait."

She stopped and looked over her shoulder. He was standing now.

"Please." He held out his arm toward her. "Let's talk."

She raised an eyebrow, expressing her skepticism.

"Please. I'm sorry I was rude. I took my frustration out on you, and that was wrong of me." He motioned toward the creek. "Come on. We'll sit in the shade. I could use a rest. I've got a jar of Sophia's lemonade sitting in the water to stay cool."

"I don't want to be in your way." She turned fully toward him.

"You won't be." His smile was both gentle and earnest. "You aren't. Honest."

Her better judgment told her she should return to the house. Her heart begged her to stay.

Her heart won.

With a nod, she said, "Lead the way, and I'll follow." She didn't take his hand.

He walked down a steep embankment, then followed the creek about twenty yards to a place where a couple of tall cottonwoods grew along the bank. There was a large boulder halfway in the water, and Dusty motioned toward it.

"Take your shoes off," he said. "Sit a spell."

"You sound like the intro to the *Beverly Hillbillies*."

He laughed, a genuine sound of pleasure. "Guess I do, at that."

Dusty leaned against the large rock and, with a grunt, pulled off one of his boots, then the other. When he was barefoot, his boots and socks safely placed away from the water's edge and his pant legs rolled up to midcalf, he waded into the stream, sucking in a quick breath when his feet first touched the water.

"Cold?" she asked.

"Not at all. It's perfect." He grimaced—or was he trying to grin around his chattering teeth? "Come on and join me."

Her pulse quickened. She wondered if he had any idea what he did to her. And if he did, was there even a small chance she affected him in the same way?

"Come on, K-Karen. Don't be a scaredy-cat."

"A *what?*"

"You heard me."

"Your lips are turning blue."

"Naw. It's just shadows from the trees." He pointed toward the spreading branches of the cottonwoods. "It's n-not c-cold, M-miss B-butler."

She knew he was exaggerating his stutter, and she couldn't help smiling at his efforts. It was good to see him in a teasing mood.

He grinned, a charming, carefree sort of smile.

Her heart flipped, like flapjacks on her grandmother's griddle.

His grin faded. "Take your boots off, Karen," he said softly. "It really does feel good."

She realized she would have done anything to please him at that precise moment. She sat on the boulder and removed her boots and socks. Then she yanked her narrow-leg jeans up her calves as high as they would go—which wasn't very far. They were certain to get wet.

"Here," Dusty said from behind her. "Just stay seated and turn around. I'll join you."

She did as she was told, a little disappointed not to be standing with him in the middle of the creek. Maybe if she'd gone to him when he first called to her, he would have taken her in his arms. Maybe he would have kissed her.

Instead, they sat side by side on the large rock, their feet dangling in the icy stream. They weren't quite touching, but they were close. The silence of the desert surrounded them, broken only by the gurgling music of the creek and the whisper of a hot summer's breeze rustling the leaves of the cottonwoods.

After a long silence, Dusty said, "Karen?"

She turned to look at him. He was watching her with eyes darkened by deep thoughts, his expression solemn.

"What is it?" she asked.

"There's something I'd like to tell you." He hesitated, as if having second thoughts. Then he continued, "I want to tell you about the night my best friend died."

....

Friday, August 20, 1937

Dear Diary,

I have been a poor chronicler of events. So much has happened since my last entry, I scarcely know where to begin.

Mikkel and I traveled by rail across the vast United States. How provincial I felt as we were carried from one state to another. America is so much more than the wide swath of Snake River and rolling farmlands of eastern Oregon. I never imagined anything like the majestic Rocky Mountains or the endless prairies east of them or the crowded cities beyond that.

We had a section in the sleeping car, which made our lengthy journey more comfortable than it would have been otherwise. The train was air-conditioned. Such a luxury in the middle of summer.

During the day, we spent many pleasant hours in the observation car. Mikkel knows no strangers, and he initiated many conversations with other passengers. I felt a special thrill whenever he introduced me by saying, "And this is my wife, Esther Christiansen."

I felt quite pampered by the porters who saw to our needs and answered my many questions. We took most of our meals on the train, but occasionally we ate in a rail station's modern café. The food in those cafés was good, and the staff behind the counters were faultlessly cheerful to their customers.

I must admit, despite the comfort of our train travel, I was thankful when we reached New York City. I was ready to put solid ground beneath my feet for a time.

But if I felt provincial before, I now felt positively dull-witted. So many people. Such tall buildings. I could not begin to describe it for I do not have the vocabulary. I was a foreigner in a strange land, and my fears I had thought laid to rest returned. If I felt so out of place in New York City, where everyone was American and spoke English, how was I going to feel once we reached Denmark?

But Mikkel eased my fears, encouraging me to read my Bible and promising that I would find answers therein. And so I did. Psalm 119:19 says, "I am a stranger in the earth: hide not thy commandments from me."

I am a stranger on earth, for my portion is in heaven with the Lord my God. Jesus said, "Lo, I am with you always, even unto the end of the world." Thus, while I may be a stranger, I am never alone. What a glorious promise!

But I digress.

Our ocean voyage is better not talked about. I was miserably sick most of the time. Poor Mikkel. He was forever waiting on me. Unfailingly patient and caring. If anything would make me want to remain in Europe, it would be the thought of the return voyage.

Be that as it may, I have fallen in love with Copenhagen and with Mikkel's "bedstefar" (that is Danish for grandfather). Fritz Christiansen is a man of seventy-three years. He is round and plump with a bushy snow-white beard and thinning white hair on his head. He is not nearly as tall as Mikkel, but their eyes are very much the same. Pale blue and penetrating. He has a wonderful laugh, one that rises from deep in his chest. He has welcomed me into his home like a long-lost granddaughter. Though he speaks hardly any English and my Danish is faltering, we have formed a strong bond.

One last thing, for it grows late.

I should like to tell you about where we are living. The house is narrow and three stories tall with an attic besides. Very different from the farmhouse where I grew up. It is in the western quarter of Copenhagen, set among other homes very similar to it.

The city of Copenhagen is many hundreds of years older than the tiny town of my birth. It is cooler and more damp than I am used to, but I think I shall become accustomed to the difference. There is a university not far from the house, a school with some five thousand students.

Now if only I could find someone whom I could talk to, I would be happy, for Mikkel is gone much of the day, already involved with the members of Grandfather Fritz's church.

Esther

"His name was Pete." Dusty stared into the gurgling stream. "Pete Gold. We met in the seventh grade and became fast friends." He shook his head. "My dad really disliked Pete. Maybe that's why we became inseparable. I wanted to spite my dad."

Karen thought of her relationship with her own father. She'd done just the opposite. She'd done anything and everything she could to try to please him, to earn his approval and affection.

"My mom died when I was five. My dad raised me alone. Dad was a tough, don't-argue-with-me kind of guy, and he wasn't afraid to apply the palm of his hand to my backside when he thought I needed it. And I needed it often. More than he knew. Especially after I fell in with Pete. We were a couple of inexperienced punks looking for trouble, and we found plenty of it too."

Karen wondered if he exaggerated. The Dusty she'd come to know during the past month was about as straight and narrow as any person she'd met.

"We ended up with a few minor marks on our juvenile records. Nothing too serious. We managed to avoid the cops on the big stuff. Dumb luck mostly." He glanced at the sky, frowning. "Dad and I fought a lot by the time I was in high school. I thought he was a real square. He thought I was a real delinquent."

No wonder he'd been so sensitive when she'd used that word to describe the boys at the Golden T.

Dusty shook his head as he returned his gaze to her. "Later, I could see that my dad loved me and how hard he tried to save me from myself. But I couldn't see it then."

"Hindsight," she whispered. "Everything's easier in hindsight."

"The night of my sixteenth birthday, Dad was sick. He wasn't the sort to take to his bed for no reason, but I was mad 'cause we'd made plans and he was breaking them. So when Pete showed up in a car, I took off with him."

In a low voice, he told her the story of a night spent drinking beer and cruising the streets of Chicago. It was a sadly too-common story that ended in tragedy.

"Turned out, Pete's aunt hadn't given him that car. He'd stolen it. The police arrested me, and my dad had to get up from his sickbed to bail me out of jail. He was just a working stiff. Never made much money, but he put everything he owned in hock to hire the best attorney he could find."

Dusty turned his head away, but the crack in his voice as he continued his story confirmed the depth of his emotions.

"The next weeks were awful. There was Pete's funeral, seeing his mom weeping next to his casket. There were the meetings with attorneys and the hearings and wondering if I was going to end up in jail. And Dad...he kept getting sicker and sicker. But I hardly noticed. I was too caught up in my own problems. Me, me, me."

He fell silent.

Karen wanted to touch him, wanted to take hold of his hand and squeeze, wanted to offer some sort of comfort.

He slid off the boulder. His feet hit the water with a splash. With his back to her, he lifted a hand to his face, and she suspected he was wiping away his tears. Then his shoulders rose and fell as he drew in a deep breath and released it. When he faced her again, he'd regained control.

"Dad lived long enough for me to get off on some legal technicality. I didn't have any other family, and there wasn't any money left after the hospitals and lawyers were done. So I threw a few things into a duffel bag and left Chicago. Hitchhiked my way across the country, doing odd jobs, stealing when I had to, surviving the best way I knew how."

She nodded. No wonder he'd been haunted by Hal taking off the way he had.

"Took me about a year to wind up in Owyhee County. Jock Carter found me trying to keep warm in a threadbare sleeping bag on a frigid October night. He took me back to his ranch, fed me, clothed me, took care of me."

Dusty searched for the right words. Everything else he'd told her had been history. Now what he said, if her heart was ready, could change her future.

"Jock was a true witness of Christ's love. He ran a place for boys, a lot like this one, only it operated year-round. Watching him, I came to understand the forgiveness Jesus was offering me if I'd give my life to Him."

Karen was concentrating on what he said—he could tell by the look in her eyes and the way she worried her lower lip between her teeth.

"I accepted Jesus as my Lord and Savior when I was eighteen. It radically changed my life." He glanced downstream, in the direction of the ranch. "Ultimately, it's God's unconditional love and forgiveness that I hope each of the boys will find."

After a moment of silence, Karen said, "Tell me something, Dusty."

He met her gaze. "Sure."

"If you believe God's forgiveness is unconditional, why are you trying so hard to earn it?"

Her question caught him unprepared. His mind went blank; he couldn't think of an answer.

She turned away from the stream, stood on dry ground, then reached for her socks and boots.

"Maybe I'm wrong," she said as she yanked on the first boot, "but it seems to me you're still feeling guilty about Pete and your dad and who knows what else." She pulled on the second boot, then straightened. "Awhile ago you said God was telling you that you've been trying to save these kids and you can't. Maybe that's true. Looks to me like you're trying to save yourself, too."

Unable to form a reply, Dusty watched her leave.

Was she right? Was that what he'd been doing?

She's not a believer. She didn't understand what I was telling her.

But did he think God couldn't use an unbeliever to speak to him? In fact, it seemed the Lord had used her twice today already. First up by the bridge. Now here.

Does that mean my work has all been in vain, Lord? I've believed You placed me here, that You wanted me to open this camp. I've believed it was Your will I continue Jock's work. Have I been wrong?

OPEN YOUR HANDS, MY SON.

He held his breath, and his pulse quickened as he waited.

OPEN YOUR HEART. OPEN AND LET GO.

Let go of what, Lord?

RELEASE WHATEVER FILLS YOUR HANDS AND YOUR HEART, AND RECEIVE THE ABUNDANCE I OFFER YOU. RECEIVE FROM ME.

Jesus?

YOU ARE ACCEPTED IN THE BELOVED, MY SON.

Dusty stepped out of the creek, overwhelmed by the outpouring of love that filled his heart. Not his love for God, but the Father's love for him.

He didn't want to set up idols. He didn't want to negate the work of Christ by trying to achieve his own salvation through good works. He wanted to be squarely in the midst of God's perfect will.

"Lord," he whispered, his face and hands—open hands—raised toward heaven, "I thank You."

And in that moment, he truly and finally let go of the past.

It was one of those soft summer evenings when the air was freshened by the green scent of irrigated alfalfa fields and the more pungent aroma of sage. The evening star twinkled in a sky not yet gone dark. Basalt outcrops, rising unexpectedly from the forbidding Owyhee Range, resembled ruins of ancient citadels with their highest ramparts kissed gold by the last rays of a sinking sun.

Sophia watched the dying of the day from her bench in the garden.

It was a familiar summertime ritual, one she had observed for more than fifty years. In the beginning, of course, Bradley had been beside her.

I still miss him. Even after all these years.

It was easy to imagine her husband sitting there, his arm draped over her shoulders in that relaxed, devoted manner of his. She could see them both clearly in her mind's eye, so young, so full of hopes and dreams.

It's true. Youth is wasted on the young. It's too bad we have to get old before we understand it.

"Grandmother? Are you out here?"

"Yes, I'm here. On the bench."

Karen appeared on the path as it spilled through the abundance of flowers and shrubs that made this garden Sophia's special oasis. "I wondered where you'd disappeared to."

"The evening was too lovely to ignore."

"It is nice tonight, isn't it?"

"Sit beside me, dear." She patted the bench.

Karen did so, then turned her gaze beyond the boundaries of the ranch. "There's a kind of haunting beauty about this place. When I first came, I thought the only word to describe it was *desolate,* but I was wrong. It...oh, I don't know. It sort of grows on you."

Sophia laughed softly in agreement.

"I'm still afraid I'll find a rattlesnake at every turn," her granddaughter added with a shudder.

"Not an unreasonable concern."

"Oh, *that* reassures me."

"Snakes aren't all bad. They eat the slugs and insects that could ruin this garden."

"Everything's got a purpose. Is that what you're telling me?"

"Yes, I guess it is." Sophia took hold of Karen's hand and squeezed it. "You've found some degree of contentment here with us, haven't you, my dear?"

"Yes. I have." There was a look of real affection in her eyes.

Should I tell her, Lord? Is now the time to tell her about Esther and Mikkel and her mother?

"I talked to Dusty this afternoon," Karen said. "Like you told me to."

"And?"

"I think I understand him a little better." A frown narrowed her eyes. "But in some ways I'm more confused than ever."

"About Dusty?"

"Him...and other things, too."

"Keep seeking, dear. You'll find your answers as long as you seek them with an open heart."

The cloak of darkness fell over the garden and its inhabitants. The yawning stretch of desert surrounding them amplified the night sounds—the hoot of an owl, a coyote's mournful cry, a bullfrog's *ribbet, ribbet,* even the whine of a diesel engine as a truck, somewhere in the distance, sped along the ribbon of highway.

After a long while, Karen said softly, "Do you truly believe God is up there, listening to us, caring about us?"

Sophia's old heart fluttered, quickened by the question. "Yes, I do. I don't just believe it. I *know* it."

"How can you know?"

Father, give me the right words. She's looking for You, whether she knows it or not.

"How can I know?" she answered at last. "Well, I believe the Bible is the final authority on everything. It's infallible, written by men as God directed them. It tells a story of God's great love for us. So great a love that He sent His own son to die for us. To die for my sins so I could be reconciled with Him."

"I've heard the story. Christmas. Easter. All that stuff. But I've never known anyone who lived it the way you do." Karen gave Sophia's hand a squeeze, then rose from the bench. "I don't think I ever could."

"I thought the same way at one time."

"*You* did?"

"Mmm. I did."

A pregnant pause followed Sophia's response, a pause that caused her to hope Karen would ask another question, give her a chance to say more. But it didn't happen.

Her granddaughter turned away. "Goodnight, Grandmother."

"Goodnight, Karen. Sleep well."

Tuesday, August 24, 1937

Dear Diary,

My heart is filled with joy. I am with child. It explains why I was so miserably ill during the ocean crossing.

Thank You, Father. Thank You for this most precious of gifts. My cup runneth over.

Esther

Thursday, September 9, 1937

Dear Diary,

Mama writes to tell me that Sophia has moved from home and is now living in Idaho where she has found employment doing clerical work. Mama says she has forwarded my letters to Sophia, but still I have received no replies. I fear she has thrown them away, unread.

I will continue to write and hope and pray. I wish very much that I could share my wonderful news with her. I wish she could be with me when the baby is born in March.

If my child is a girl, I will name her Sophia.

Esther

Dusty felt a lightness in his heart such as he hadn't felt before. He'd been a Christian for many years and had loved and served God to the best of his ability. But yesterday something wonderful had happened.

Yesterday, he'd discovered he didn't have to serve to the best of *his* ability; his own ability would never be enough. Now he understood he could serve to the best of *God's* ability. And God's ability—His power, His grace, His strength—was more than sufficient.

Dusty spent his morning prayer time in praise and worship. He couldn't think of a single thing to ask for, anything more that he needed.

His joy must have been both evident and contagious, for all the boys were in good moods that morning. When they had breakfast in the main house, there was plenty of laughter and good-natured teasing.

Dusty felt the curious glances of both Sophia and Karen. Later, he would find a moment to tell Sophia what had happened to him. Karen... He didn't know what he would say to Karen.

The phone rang, and Billy hopped up to answer it. "Hello?" After a moment's pause, he turned toward the table. "It's some guy asking for you, Miss Karen."

Her eyes widened. "For me?" She rose. "I wonder who it could be?"

Dusty wondered the same thing as he watched her cross the room and take the handset from Billy.

"Hello?" She listened, then grinned. "Mac!"

Mac? Mac who?

"Oh, I'm fine... I know I should have. I'm sorry... No, it isn't anything like I expected..."

Obviously it was someone from California. Someone special. Someone she cared about, judging by her smile and the tone of her voice.

"I wish I could, Mac. I appreciate it... I miss you, too."

Dusty felt like grinding his teeth. Why was that? His eyes widened in surprise when the answer came: He was *jealous!*

"Nobody could have done more." She turned her back toward the table and lowered her voice. "You needn't feel that way."

Just what did he have to be jealous about? It wasn't as if he had romantic feelings for Karen. For Pete's sake! He hadn't even *liked* her at first.

"That's sweet of you," she said softly.

"Come on, guys." Dusty stood. "We're expected at the Echeverria place in a half-hour."

"What're we doin' there?" Noah asked.

"Repairing the roof of his barn." His answer was followed by a trio of groans.

"All right," he overheard Karen say. "I promise, Mac. Thanks for calling... You, too. Bye."

He looked over his shoulder as she placed the handset in its cradle.

When their gazes met, she smiled and said, "That was my friend, Mac Gleason."

Friend? Was that all? Or was it something more? Why had Mac called her? What had he wanted?

"Where are you all going?" she asked, interrupting Dusty's mental interrogation.

"We're fixing a barn at the Echeverria farm," Billy answered. "Why don't you come with us? You'd like to see the lambs they've got."

She looked at Dusty. "Would you mind?"

"It wouldn't be much fun for you. The day promises to be a scorcher, and there wouldn't be much for you to do. You'd get bored."

"I can help carry lumber. Remember? I did it yesterday without breaking a single fingernail." Her smile was mischievous, the twinkle in her eyes teasing. "Didn't I?" Her smile vanished as quickly as it had come. "Unless you don't want me there."

What he feared was that he wanted her there *too* much. Seeing Karen as a woman and not only as Sophia's granddaughter was a complication he hadn't expected and didn't want.

At least, he didn't *think* he wanted it.

"Dusty?"

He gave his head a small shake to clear his thoughts, then turned toward the door. "You can come if you want. Be ready in twenty minutes." He strode out of the kitchen.

"Well, I'll be," Sophia said as Dusty disappeared through the doorway.

Karen looked at Sophia.

Her grandmother chuckled. "It seems you've done something no other woman has managed to do."

"What?"

"Become a bur under Dusty's saddle."

Karen couldn't think of a reply.

Sophia glanced at the three boys, each in turn. "I'll do the dishes today, fellas. Get going. Miss Karen can help me fill the cooler for your lunch."

Chairs scraped the kitchen floor as Ted, Noah, and Billy rose from the table.

As they left the house, Billy was heard asking the other two boys, "Did she mean Dusty wants to kiss Miss Karen?"

Noah and Ted replied with laughter.

Karen sank onto one of the vacated chairs, her gaze on her grandmother. "*Is* that what you meant?"

"In a roundabout way, yes."

"Oh." Elbows on the table, she covered her face with her hands. "Oh, dear."

"And what about you, Karen?"

She lowered her hands. "We have absolutely nothing in common. Look at us. He's lived this Spartan existence since he was sixteen or seventeen, and he *likes* it. I'm used to a totally different lifestyle. He's a cowboy. I'm a city girl. He thinks a vacation is an afternoon at the swimming hole. I think it's a month skiing in Saint-Moritz or a summer at a resort on the Côte d'Azur." She raised her hands in a gesture of futility. "We're just too different."

"Are you trying to convince me or yourself?"

She chose not to answer.

Sophia's expression was both gentle and patient. "The real difference, Karen, is one of faith—what Dusty believes about

God and what you believe. If anything will separate the two of you, it's that one. The other things, while they may seem important now, are actually quite trivial."

"Are they? All I wanted when I came here was a place to stay until I could get some money and return home. Or maybe a place to hide would be more truthful."

Her grandmother nodded.

"I never expected to start caring for him."

"One rarely does plan these things," Sophia answered.

"Maybe I shouldn't go with them. If he and I aren't meant for each other, it would be a mistake to—"

"Don't hide from life, Karen. You'll regret it if you do."

She lowered her gaze. So many things had happened in the past week. Too much to make sense of it all.

"Go with them," Sophia said as she rose from her chair. "Caring for someone else is worth the risk. Always."

⁓❧

"I asked Wendy to marry me," Grant announced just as Dusty reached the top of the ladder leaning against the Echeverria barn.

"You did?" Despite himself, Dusty's gaze dropped to the barnyard where Karen and Billy were unloading bundles of shingles from the back of an ancient two-ton truck.

"Yeah. The time was right. So I popped the question, and she said yes."

Dusty hadn't given much thought to marriage over the years. He'd had girlfriends, of course, but friends were all they'd turned out to be. Eventually, each one had drifted into other relationships. Most were married by now.

Married and happy, with kids of their own.

He watched as Karen set the bundle of shingles near the others she'd helped unload. She placed her fingers against the small of her spine and arched backward. After she straightened again, she wiped the perspiration from her brow with her forearm.

Marriage?

A wife?

Kids?

For him?

No. Maybe the time was right for Grant, but it wasn't for Dusty. The Golden T Youth Camp was barely getting by as it was. And even if he *was* looking for a wife—which he wasn't— Karen would definitely be the wrong woman to fill the bill.

He glanced at Grant. "When's the wedding date?"

"We decided on Thanksgiving Day. She's got quite a few relatives coming in for the holiday, and we thought we should take advantage of it."

"A wedding *and* turkey with dressing." He grinned. "Good planning."

Grant laughed as he offered Dusty a hand up onto the roof. "I was hoping you'd agree to be my best man."

"You know I'll do it." Once again, his gaze drifted downward.

"Hey, are you thinking what I think you are?"

Am I? He shrugged, frowned, then shook his head. "No."

"Okay. I can take a hint. I won't ask anything more."

They set to work, but Dusty found himself pausing after a short while to look in Karen's direction.

She was pretty. He'd always been aware of that. And despite a lot of negative first impressions, he'd found plenty to like about her during the past month. The way she treated Sophia for one. The way she responded to Billy for another.

But she wasn't a fellow believer, and the "be not unequally yoked" advice hadn't been included in God's Word without a reason. In his years as a Christian, he'd seen the problems caused when people went against that basic principle.

But if she was seeking the truth, wasn't that…?

No, he'd been right the first time. This wasn't the time for him to be thinking about things like love and marriage. After all, it was only yesterday God had set him free so he could serve Him even better than before.

Wednesday, November 24, 1937

Dear Diary,

Tomorrow is Thanksgiving Day. It is not a Danish holiday, but Mikkel, Grandfather Fritz, and I shall celebrate it in our home. Our dinner will be nothing like the one Mikkel shared with my family a year ago, for many of those food items are not readily available in Denmark. But that doesn't matter. We have much to be thankful for, and that is why we will gather together.

We have invited our neighbors to join us. Mr. and Mrs. Abrams are a young Jewish couple with two small children. Mikkel has formed a friendship with Isaac Abrams, and I hope to do the same with his wife, Hannah.

I do miss having a good friend. Another woman with whom I can share my hopes and dreams, my uncertainties and disappointments. Mikkel has tried valiantly to fill the void left by Sophia, but there are some things even he cannot do.

Esther

Monday, December 13, 1937

Dear Diary,

Mikkel had a dream last night, and he remains deeply
troubled by it. He fears war is on the horizon. Grandfather Fritz
says the dream was caused by nothing more than indigestion
from the large piece of pie Mikkel ate before going to bed.

Mikkel closed himself in his study for the better part of the
day, and I know he was in prayer much of that time.

I prefer to believe Grandfather Fritz is right.

I am beginning to be very round with child. I feel the baby
moving and am warmed by the knowledge of what God has
created.

Esther

Dusty's heart nearly stopped beating the day the sheriff's car came up the drive, trailed by a cloud of dust.

"Wait here," he said to the three boys who were helping him stack firewood against the south side of the house. If the sheriff's deputy was bringing bad news about Hal, Dusty wanted to hear it alone first, then break it to the others in the right way.

The deputy, Colin Reilly, unfolded his gangly, six-foot-seven-inch frame and stood beside the black-and-white car. He squinted against the bright midday sun as Dusty strode toward him. "Afternoon."

Dusty nodded his return greeting.

Colin wasn't the type to beat around the bush. "They found Miss Butler's car in Portland, what's left of it. It's been stripped."

"And Hal?"

"No sign of him. They think he abandoned the car because it quit running, although they can't be sure there wasn't foul play." Colin tipped his hat slightly back on his head. "Has he got friends over that way?"

"Not that I know of. He grew up in this area, shuffled between different family members about every four to six months. I doubt any of them would know either."

"Yeah, we haven't had much help from any of the Junkers."

"Has Hal tried to contact the girl? Patty Call?"

"No, and we'd know if he did. Mr. Call would make sure of that." Colin shook his head. "He's a hard, unforgiving man."

Dusty glanced toward the house, then back again. "Want to come inside out of this heat?"

"No. Can't stay. Just wanted to give you the news in person." He tugged on his hat brim. "Miss Butler will need to decide what she wants done with what's left of the vehicle."

"I'll tell her."

The deputy got into the sheriff's car, started the engine, and with a wave out the window drove away.

Dusty watched until Colin reached the highway, then turned toward the house. By that time, Karen was approaching.

"Is it Hal?" she asked. "Have they found him?"

"No, but they found your car."

"Where?"

"In Portland."

"He made it that far?" She stopped before him. "I didn't think the Mustang had that many miles left in it."

"The kid's good with engines."

"Dusty?" Her voice lowered. "Is Hal going to be all right?"

"I don't know. I pray he will."

"I wish I believed your prayers would make a difference." Worry was etched in her pretty features, an earnest concern for someone other than herself.

Dusty wondered if she was aware how much she'd changed in the weeks she'd been at the ranch.

Or how much she'd changed him.

Impulsively, he reached out, taking hold of her hand and squeezing with his fingers. "Prayer makes a difference, Karen. Just not always in the way we expect."

Her glance fell to their joined hands.

He was tempted to step closer, to brush the loose tendril of hair from her temple, maybe to kiss her neck below her ear.

She looked up.

The air was hot, still, and unbroken by sound.

"Do you know why I came here, Dusty?" She withdrew her hand and took a step backward. "I thought a ranch meant money, and I figured, since my grandmother was so old, that I could hang around until she died and then inherit it, sell it, and go back to L.A. That was all I wanted."

"And what do you want now?"

There was a glimmer of tears in her eyes. "I don't know. I honestly don't know." She spun on her heel and strode away.

As he watched her go, Dusty recalled a verse from that morning's Bible reading: *"'For I know the plans that I have for you,' declares the Lord, 'plans for welfare and not for calamity to give you a future and a hope.'"*

He felt comforted by the words. He had plenty of reasons to hope in the future because God already had plans for him. Good plans. Plans for his welfare and not for calamity.

He didn't know for certain what would happen with this ranch, with Hal, with Karen. He didn't have a vision of the future. He didn't have a detailed blueprint of what tomorrow would bring. He didn't need one.

He had God's promises instead.

I never should have told him why I came here, Karen silently berated herself. *Why did I tell Dusty the truth about myself?*

She skirted the house, going instead into Sophia's garden. She followed the dirt-and-stone path that wound through the flowers and shrubs and trees, a garden that was watered and tended with loving care by an old woman. The vegetable patch was planted to provide food for the table, but the rest was there for pleasure, a feast for the eyes and the soul.

Karen felt in need of that feast now.

I don't know who I am anymore. I don't know what I want.

California seemed far away. Not in miles, although it certainly was that. No, it was something much more than physical distance she felt.

What's happened to me?

Nothing made any sense. The despair that had once driven her to attempt to take her own life was gone, yet she remained confused and longing for answers. Was her confusion only because of this attraction she felt for Dusty Stoddard?

Of course. That had to be it. Falling for Dusty would confuse any normal, cosmopolitan woman of her generation.

If they'd been in Los Angeles, instead of stuck in the middle of nowhere, she wouldn't have noticed him at all, let alone felt any attraction for him. He wasn't her type. The plain truth was, in a county of nearly five million acres and less than ten thousand people, he was the only available man she'd seen above the age of twenty. That was the single reason for her attraction to him.

Well, that and his rugged good looks. Those didn't hurt either.

She stopped in the middle of the path, the hot July sun beating down on her head and back.

No, that wasn't the truth. There was much more about Dusty that appealed to her. There was his depth of character, a strength of purpose, that set him apart from any of the men of her previous acquaintance.

But that's merely admiration. Nothing more.

If that were true, how did she explain the things she'd felt that day at Bonnet Creek? If that were true, how did she explain accompanying Dusty and the others the day they'd worked on the Echeverria barn?

I wanted to help. That's all.

Who was she kidding?

I wanted to be with him. I wanted to be with Dusty.

As she continued along the path, she recalled the feel of Dusty's hand holding hers. She recalled the heated look in his dark eyes. She wasn't mistaken. He'd wanted to kiss her. And she would have let him if he'd tried.

"No wonder Mother thought me a lost cause," she muttered. "Even when I know something isn't good for me, I want it."

She arrived at the bench beneath the willow and sat down with a sigh.

"O God," she whispered. She hadn't meant it as a prayer, and yet somehow it became one.

She looked upward.

"What am I to do?"

WAIT.

Her breath caught, and a fluttering sensation swept through

her. The word was there and then it was gone, but it had been oh so real.

"Wait for what?" she asked softly.

She heard no reply, only the rustle of leaves as they danced to the tune of the never-ceasing wind blowing across the Owyhee desert.

Tuesday, February 1, 1938

Dear Diary,

I love being married!

It struck me this morning how very blessed I am. It was God who brought Mikkel into my life. Without Him, what were the chances of Mikkel leaving Wisconsin and coming to our small town in Oregon just so that he and I could meet?

None, indeed, without the divine hand of God guiding him there.

Mikkel and I begin every day with Bible reading and prayer. I learn so much in those quiet times together, just the two of us with our Lord, praying in agreement, talking about God's holy word. But there is more I yearn to know and understand. Mikkel tells me I must be patient. That life is a continuous lesson to be learned one step at a time.

Oh, but I am an impatient woman. I hope our baby is like Mikkel and not me.

Father in heaven, may this child I carry in my womb be a child of God from an early age. May he be trained up in the way he should go so that when he is old, he will not depart from it. Amen.

Esther

August arrived at the Golden T Ranch, a month of hot winds, blowing sands, relentless sun, and scant chance of rain.

Hal had been gone more than five weeks, but there was still no word of his whereabouts. Daily Sophia and Dusty prayed, asking God to protect him. Beyond that, all they could do was trust and hope.

As for the other boys, Dusty was pleased with the progress they'd made. Each had come to the Golden T with unique needs and ways of acting out those needs. And each had responded positively to the love and discipline that were the hallmarks of this youth camp. Noah had made a commitment to Christ in late July. Billy, who had experienced the changing power of God's grace earlier in the year, had become the older boy's mentor. And Ted, who had been the most resistant to church and the message of the gospel, seemed more open now, giving Dusty hope that he, too, would find peace with God.

But tonight he wasn't thinking about the well-being of his boys. He was thinking about Karen, a particularly easy thing to do, sitting as they were across a campfire from each other. They weren't alone, of course. Ted, Noah, and Billy were with them, as was Sophia. The youth group from church had joined them too, along with Grant, Wendy, the youth pastor, and his wife.

The barbecue was an annual event at the Golden T, and everyone looked forward to it. Plenty of food. Plenty of good company, games, and laughter. And after nightfall, a marshmallow roast and songfest around a large campfire.

Karen and Billy sat side by side in lawn chairs, each of them holding straightened wire hangers toward the fire. Karen smiled brightly, something she hadn't done much lately. At least not when Dusty was around. He didn't have to be an Einstein to understand she was doing her best to keep him at arm's length. She was probably right, too, but it didn't change the way he felt about her.

He'd never seen Karen look lovelier than she did tonight. Flickering firelight turned her pale hair from the color of wheat to a coppery orange. He wished he could run his fingers through it, feel its silkiness.

Could she be the one for me, Lord? Or am I getting my eyes off of You?

"You lost another one?" Billy cried as Karen's marshmallow

dropped into the fire, his tone clearly indicating what he thought of her roasting skills. "You'd better let me do it for you."

"Maybe I'd better." She shook her head, still smiling. "I told you I've never done this before."

"How'd you get to be so old without learning how to roast marshmallows?"

Again she laughed. "So old?" She looked up, and her gaze met Dusty's. For a change, her smile didn't fade away.

Encouraged, he asked, "Yes, how *did* you get to be so old, Miss Butler, without knowing something that important?"

"I honestly don't know, sir."

"All of what? Twenty-eight?"

"Twenty-seven, thank you very much. And *you're* old enough to know you should never ask a lady her age."

His grin broadened. "Oops. Sorry."

"How come?" Billy interjected with his usual curiosity.

"Basic rules of life, my young friend," Dusty answered. "Just basic rules of life."

"Sounds dumb. People ask me how old I am, and I don't mind."

Karen laughed again. "You have a point."

"Get your guitar, Dusty," Grant interrupted from somewhere beyond the ring of firelight. "We're ready to sing."

Karen looked away, and the moment of easy camaraderie was broken.

As Dusty strummed his guitar, Karen stood and stepped into the shadow of night. At the same time, others moved closer until she was the only one not included in the group.

By her own choice.

I'm in love with him.

She couldn't think of anything worse that could happen to her than to fall in love with Dusty Stoddard. It was all wrong. For both of them. It would only lead to heartache. She wasn't about to stay in Idaho any longer than she had to, and she couldn't imagine Dusty living in Los Angeles.

Voices joined the music of the guitar. "Amazing grace…"

Dusty played with his eyes closed, his face tilted upward. His expression was… How could she describe it? More than peaceful. More than joyful. Simply *more*.

His thoughts had been centered on her earlier, when their gazes met across the campfire, before the singing had begun. She'd seen it in his eyes. But he wasn't thinking about her now. He was totally focused on the God he sang about.

Just once I'd like to come first in somebody's life.

She could almost hear Dusty saying, "God loved you first, Karen."

But that's not what I mean.

A new melody arose, the voices harmonizing as perfectly as any trained choir. "Great is Thy faithfulness…"

I can't believe in God the way they do. I just can't. It isn't in me. I'm not like that.

⁂

Later that night, after the young people from church had left with the other adults and Dusty and the boys had retired to the bunkhouse, Sophia rapped on Karen's bedroom door.

"Yes?"

Sophia turned the knob and pushed the door open.

Wearing a silky yellow nightgown, Karen sat on the stool in front of the dressing table, her back toward the door. Her hair fell loose about her shoulders, and she held a brush in her right hand. When she saw Sophia's reflection in the mirror, she twisted on the stool.

"Are you too tired to talk?" Sophia asked.

"No." Karen shook her head. "Come in."

"I have a favor to ask." She stepped into the bedroom.

"Sure. What is it?"

"I'd like you to drive me to Boise tomorrow. I need to attend to a few errands, and I hate to bother Dusty with them. Do you mind?"

"Of course not. I'd be glad to."

Sophia sat on the edge of the bed. "Did you have a good time tonight?"

"Yes," Karen answered as she turned toward the mirror and resumed brushing her hair.

Sophia recognized the action for what it was. In her younger days she, too, had distanced herself from those who loved her. Self-protection had become self-destruction.

What can I say to help Karen find her way?

As that thought lifted toward heaven, her gaze alighted on an old rag doll atop the bureau. "Oh, my," she whispered. She pushed herself up from the bed and crossed the room. A tight band seemed to wrap itself around her chest as she reached out to finger the threadbare dress on the doll. "Esther's doll."

"No," Karen said. "It was my mother's."

"Maggie kept it." She could barely speak around the lump in her throat. Tears stung her eyes.

"I found it in a trunk after Mother died."

Sophia turned toward Karen. "Are you still reading Esther's journals?"

"Now and then. Why?"

"I taught Esther how to make dolls like this one when we were girls." She smiled sadly at the memory. "We were very close, my sister and I. We had wonderful times together when we were growing up." She brushed a tear from her cheek. "She writes about our doll making in one of her journals. She made this particular doll when she was living in Denmark during the war."

"She did?" Karen rose from the bench. "What was she doing there?"

"Mikkel, her husband, was a minister in Copenhagen. They went there to help Mikkel's grandfather who was also a minister. That was in the thirties, before the war. Esther never returned to America." She blinked back more tears. "That doll belonged to her daughter."

"Her daughter? We have family in Europe?"

"No," Sophia answered softly. "Not any longer."

Karen frowned, then lifted the doll from the bureau. "I never figured out why Mother kept it. She liked fancy, expensive things. She had a collection of antique porcelain dolls that was worth a small fortune. But Mother wasn't the sentimental type. That's why this doll seemed such a strange thing for her to keep, even in a trunk." Her voice drifted into silence as she turned the doll over and over in her hands.

Should I tell her? Is now the time?

No, her heart replied. The answer for Karen lay in Esther's journals. Sophia would have to be patient and trust the Lord's timing.

She patted her granddaughter's shoulder, then leaned forward and kissed her cheek. "Maybe your mother was more sentimental than either of us realized." She walked toward the door. "We should leave about 8:30 in the morning, if that's all right with you."

"Sure. I'm up early these days. I'll be ready to go when you are."

Karen continued to stare at the object in her hands long after the door closed behind her grandmother. She'd felt an odd affection for the rag doll from the first moment she'd found it in her mother's trunk alongside the beaded handbags, sequined evening gowns, and fur coats that were no longer in vogue. The doll had seemed out of place with those costly things. Lonely, like Karen herself. She'd kept the doll with her ever since.

"Why was Grandmother near tears because of you?" she whispered as she set the rag doll on the bureau again.

Still puzzling, she turned off the overhead light and climbed into bed. She lay in the darkness for a short while, trying to sleep, then gave up, switched on the bedside lamp, picked up another of Esther's journals, and began to read.

....

Sunday, February 13, 1938

Dear Diary,

Today is Sophia's twentieth birthday, and tomorrow I shall turn nineteen.

I wrote to her again today, with hopes that this time she will read the letter. I am convinced if she was reading them she would have answered. Still, I tried. I told her, as I have said before in my letters, that if this baby is a girl, I shall name her Sophia.

How very much I miss my sister!

I love Mikkel and Grandfather Fritz, but they are men and often do not understand me. I am very fond of Hannah Abrams, and we are becoming good friends, despite the way we struggle to communicate. My Danish is wretched and her English is not much better. More than that, we are from such different backgrounds that we can never be as close as Sophia and I once were.

Romans 8:28 says all things work together for good to them that love God, to them who are the called according to his purpose. I know I was called, and I do want to walk according to his purpose. But sometimes I cannot help wondering why things must be the way they are.

I suppose that is very unfaithlike of me and I should repent of it.

Things will be better once the baby comes. Only another month.

Esther

Tuesday, April 12, 1938

Our little Sophie died today. She was one month old.

Seventeen

Sophia gazed out the van window as the vehicle sped along I-84 toward the capital city. The foothills along the Boise Front were brown in the waning weeks of summer. Only the mile-high peaks of the mountains were green, blanketed as they were by pine trees.

"I remember when I first came to Boise," she said softly. "My goodness. That was more than sixty years ago."

"I'll bet it's changed a lot since then," Karen commented.

"Yes. It certainly has." She chuckled. "How fast are you driving, dear?"

"Sixty-five. Why? Does it feel like I'm speeding? I can slow down if you like."

"No. You're fine. I was simply remembering how we thought thirty miles an hour was going dangerously fast. Most of the roads were dirt and gravel, and there was certainly nothing resembling an Interstate." She looked at her granddaughter. "Dutch Tallman, a childhood friend of ours, drove me to Boise in his Model T. It took us the better part of a day to get there from our farm in Oregon."

"How old were you?"

"Nineteen."

"Why'd you leave Oregon?"

Again, she gazed out the window toward the mountains. "Oh, there were many reasons. Mostly because I was running away." She paused, then added, "From myself. I was an angry and bitter girl."

"You?"

Sophie smiled sadly at the surprise in her granddaughter's voice. "Yes. And I wasted far too many years wrapped up in those emotions. Too many years." She closed her eyes. "But God was merciful. He loved and blessed me despite my many shortcomings. And Bradley loved me despite them too. We had a good marriage, he and I. A good life together."

"I wish I could have known my grandfather."

Sophia envisioned both Mikkel and Bradley. "Me too."

They continued in silence, Sophia's thoughts drifting from one memory to another, moving through the years and events that formed the tapestry of her life until she returned to the present. Her gaze focused once again on the foothills against which the city of Boise was nestled. Before she knew it the weather would turn cold and the leaves would change and the snows would come.

"Our boys will be going home in another three weeks," she said to herself. Then she sighed. "The place is much too quiet after they leave."

"What do you and Dusty do to fill your time during the winter? I mean, it isn't as if the Golden T is a working ranch with lots of cattle and so forth. So what do you do with yourselves all winter long?"

"Afraid you'll be bored, my dear?"

"Frankly, yes."

Sophia smiled. "Well, I do a great deal of reading. Thank the Lord my sight remains good. And Dusty…he'll continue his studies at the university."

"He'll *what?*"

"He's working toward his master's degree. He's only able to take one or two classes each semester because of the cost, but he's very close now. You're surprised, aren't you?"

"Yes."

"You shouldn't be. Dusty's intelligent. More than that, he's dedicated. Years ago, he could have had a scholarship, but he believed he was supposed to keep working with Jock, helping with the boys. So he turned it down and settled for taking what courses he could each school year. After Jock died, Dusty felt called to continue the work." She glanced at the road ahead of them. "I'm sure he could have had a thriving counseling practice long before now if that's what he'd wanted. But Dusty is motivated by other things than worldly success. His whole heart wants him to be smack-dab in the middle of God's will."

There was a lengthy silence before Karen asked, "How does a person know what God's will is, Grandmother?"

"You start by making Jesus your Savior," she answered without hesitation. "Once you've done that, He'll reveal His will in countless ways."

"And what would I have to give up?"

Sophia pondered the question for several seconds before she quietly and honestly answered, "Everything, Karen."

Everything, Karen.

Those two words haunted Karen throughout the day as she escorted her grandmother from one location to another.

Everything, Karen.

What if she didn't want to give up everything? What about the free gift of salvation and forgiveness and all that other stuff she'd heard preached?

Everything, Karen.

That was too much to ask of anybody. Besides, Karen had already lost everything, thanks to her father. So what else did she have to give?

What do You want from me anyway?

EVERYTHING, KAREN.

※

"Gee, Miss Sophie's gonna be surprised," Billy said, grinning from ear to ear.

"She certainly is," Dusty answered as he started up the ladder.

He'd been waiting several weeks for Sophia to take one of her rare trips into the city. He'd dropped a number of hints, and finally, she'd taken the bait. So while she and Karen were gone for the day, Dusty and the boys were painting the house with bright yellow paint purchased by a member of their church.

His grin, he thought as he applied the brush to the faded siding, must look a lot like Billy's.

Many times he'd heard the story of the day Bradley Taylor had painted the small ranch house, a surprise for his wife who, so the story went, had often complained about the drabness of their surroundings in those early years before the trees had grown tall and the garden had flourished. And so Bradley had made it less drab. Sophia had returned from a day of helping a sick neighbor to find her house sporting a coat of the brightest shade of yellow she had ever seen.

More than once, Dusty had offered to paint the place for her, but she repeatedly said there were other things the youth camp needed more than to be gussied up. True, perhaps, but he was glad they could do it anyway.

"You think we'll get it done before they get back?" Noah asked from his perch atop another ladder.

"I hope so. I gave Miss Karen a list of things to do, besides whatever errands Miss Sophie has."

Ted slapped paint on the porch railing. "Bet Miss Karen would've liked to help us."

Dusty considered the comment a moment, then decided Ted was right. Karen would have liked to help. He grinned. Weeks ago, the last of her manicured nails had been clipped short.

I think I love her, Lord. Now what?

He'd like to tell her how he felt, but he knew he couldn't. Not yet. Not until she made a decision for Christ.

And if she never does?

His chest tightened.

What if she never does?

After all these years of working with and counseling troubled teens, he knew not everyone who was presented with the gospel accepted it. Many rejected it. He supposed the majority rejected it. Karen could reject it too. No matter how much he wanted it to be otherwise.

If she had the wherewithal to return to California, would she? Or was there a chance she would want to stay? Was it possible she might care for him too? And if she did care, would it be so terrible to ask her to marry him? Would God really object?

He frowned, not liking the confusion and uncertainty of his thoughts and feelings.

Show me what to do, Jesus. And if You don't mean for me to feel this way about Karen, please take it from my heart.

Their last stop for the day was at the mall.

"Why don't you treat yourself to a milk shake or a sundae," Sophia suggested while pointing at a nearby bench. "Then you can wait for me there. I'm going into the Christian bookstore. I won't be but a moment."

Karen didn't want anything to eat, but she was more than willing to sit down. She was exhausted. Her grandmother, on the other hand, seemed brimming with energy.

With a sigh, she settled onto the bench and allowed her eyes to drift closed. The sounds of the busy mall slowly faded into the background.

Dusty Stoddard, studying for his master's degree. Imagine that.

I'm a snob.

It wasn't a flattering discovery about herself. She'd judged him as an uneducated cowboy, even after all these weeks, even once she'd come to know him. Even after she'd fallen in love with him. She'd assumed it was good intentions alone that guided him in his work. That he had no ambitions or dreams of his own. She'd thought him merely guided by his religious principles and nothing more.

And maybe that would be enough for someone like him.

Karen had a college degree, and look at her. She was virtually useless. Dusty, on the other hand, had done something useful with his life from an early age. Who was she to judge anyone else? She knew nothing of any value. Nothing.

For the Lord gives wisdom; from His mouth come knowledge and understanding.

Who'd told her that? she wondered. Her grandmother? Dusty? Or maybe she'd heard it at their church. Well, it didn't matter who'd said it. She didn't believe it anyway.

"I'm back."

Karen opened her eyes to see Sophia coming toward her, a small sack clutched against her chest, held there with both arms.

"No ice cream?" Sophia asked.

"No. I wasn't hungry. Would you like me to get you something?"

Her grandmother sat on the bench next to her. "No, thank you, dear." She opened the sack. "I bought something for you." She placed a box on Karen's lap. "I wanted you to have a Bible of your own, for when we go to church."

"I'm not sure I want to go to church again," she said as she stared at the gift. "It only confuses me."

"I know," Sophia whispered. "I know."

Karen intentionally didn't look at her grandmother. She knew she would see compassion in the elderly woman's eyes, and she didn't want to see it. She was tired of seeing it.

Sophia's hand covered hers. "It's all right, my dear child. Understanding doesn't happen overnight."

Karen nodded, unwilling to admit she didn't think understanding would ever come, no matter how much time passed. She simply couldn't believe the things Sophia believed, the things Dusty believed. She couldn't.

EVERYTHING, KAREN.

Or maybe she could...and was afraid.

Thanksgiving Day, 1938

Dear Diary,

This was our second Thanksgiving in Denmark. Hannah and Isaac and their children, Ben and Ruth, joined us for dinner. Before we said grace, Isaac announced Hannah is expecting again.

I tried not to show my grief when he told us the news. I mourn my baby so, despite all the time that has passed. Often, I wish I could leave this place and return home to Mama and Papa and the old farm, yet I could never tell Mikkel how I feel. He loves the people here. He loves his work. He knows he is walking in God's will.

What is God's will for me? I do not know. Whatever it is, I feel far from it.

Esther

....

Tuesday, February 14, 1939

Dear Diary,

Today was my twentieth birthday. Hannah and Isaac joined Grandfather Fritz, Mikkel, and me for a little party. Hannah baked a cake, and Isaac gave me a beautiful Star of David, the Mogen David, that he carved himself. He said it is a symbol of hope and strength to all Jews.

Mikkel gave me a copy of Hannah Whitall Smith's book, The Christian's Secret of a Happy Life and also John Bunyan's The Pilgrim's Progress. I look forward to reading them both.

Of course, this day is more than just my birthday. Two years ago, Mikkel proposed to me while down on one knee. This morning, he knelt beside the bed, took hold of my hand, and told me that it was the wisest thing he ever did, asking me to be his wife.

What wonderful words to hear! They made me cry.

I love him so much, and my heart breaks because I have been unable to conceive again. I know Mikkel wants children as much as I do. Many children.

The doctor says I should not worry. That there is no reason I should not have another child. But in my darkest moments, I wonder.

Maybe these thoughts are worsened because of Hannah. She is so happily pregnant. Plump and gay. And beautiful, too, with her shiny dark hair and large brown eyes. She is my dearest friend in Copenhagen, and she has taught me a great deal about God's chosen people.

I was dreadfully ignorant of so much before coming to Denmark.

One thing I do tease Hannah about—she is horribly superstitious. She will not discuss names for the baby before its birth. To do so, she says, would be to invite spirits to affect the child in some way. She says that to know a person's name is to know his being, and, therefore, to speak the child's name before it is born could control its destiny.

And another thing that is not considered is naming a child after someone living, even to do them honor, just as I named my beloved Sophie after my sister. Hannah says to do so might cause the soul of the one so honored to be transported to the baby. Not only could this affect the character of the infant but it could cost the life of the elder person.

They seem so strange to me, these Jewish beliefs and customs, but I suppose no more strange than many of my American beliefs and customs seem to her. Different, we may be, but we are also very much the same.

And God loves all of us. No matter our color. No matter our nationalities.

Why can't the world understand this? There is so much hate and fear in Europe now. I scarcely gave notice when Nazi forces marched into Austria last March because it was on the same day Sophie was born, and I think Mikkel has tried to shield me from the worst. Sometimes he and Grandfather talk in Danish about the events transpiring. I can only understand part of what they are saying, but it is enough to make me wonder how long we will be safe here.

And so I cling ever harder to God's word in Isaiah that says, "Hast thou not known? hast thou not heard, that the everlasting God, the LORD, the Creator of the ends of the earth, fainteth not, neither is weary? there is no searching of his understanding. He giveth power to the faint; and to them that have no might he increaseth strength. Even the youths shall faint and be weary, and the young men shall utterly fall: But they that wait upon the LORD shall renew their strength; they shall mount up with wings as eagles; they shall run, and not be weary; and they shall walk, and not faint."

Esther

Eighteen

As far as Dusty was concerned, Sophia's reaction to the newly painted house was everything he and the boys had hoped for and then some. Despite her long day in the city, she walked around the house, not once but twice, admiring and commenting upon the job they'd done. She didn't seem to notice any of the imperfections, although they were obvious to all.

"What d'you think, Miss Karen?" Billy asked as he took hold of her hand.

"I think it's wonderful," she answered. "I wish I could have helped."

"I told Dusty that's how you'd feel."

"You did?" She glanced over her shoulder.

Their gazes met, and Dusty's sudden need to draw her into his arms and kiss her almost overwhelmed him. And the wanting was more than physical desire. It was something deeper, unlike anything he'd felt before in his life.

There was no more trying to deny it. He'd fallen in love with Karen Butler.

"I sure did," Billy said in answer to her question. "But Dusty was countin' on you to keep Miss Sophie away all day so we could get it done."

She returned her gaze to the boy at her side. "Dusty knows best, doesn't he?"

Not always, Karen.

Dusty stopped, letting the others move on without him.

Father, is this something You want for me? I've never given much thought to loving a woman or getting married. It seemed like You had other plans for my life. But has that changed, Lord?

His prayer had barely taken wing when he heard a voice behind him say, "Mr. Stoddard?"

He turned, and there stood Patty Call. Her face was flushed from the heat; sweat trickled near her temples. A backpack was slung over her left shoulder, and with her right hand, she clutched a duffel bag.

"Mr. Stoddard, I'm looking for Junkman. Has he come back? Do you know where he is?"

"No. We haven't heard from him."

She started to cry. Silent tears, streaking her cheeks.

"Let's go inside, Patty. You look tired."

"My dad kicked me out. He told me never to come back."

Dusty clenched his jaw, but he tried to keep his voice neutral. "Come on. It's hot out here." He put his hand on her shoulder and gently propelled her forward.

"I…I didn't know where else to go." Her words ended on a sob.

He drew her a little closer as they walked. "I'm glad you came. We'll figure this out. Don't worry."

Just before they reached the corner of the front porch, Sophia, Karen, and the three boys rounded the opposite corner. For a moment, Dusty's gaze met Karen's. Surprise was the first thing he read in her eyes, followed immediately by empathy and compassion. She left the others and strode forward.

"Patty," she said softly. She didn't ask how the girl was or what was wrong. She simply opened her arms and let Patty rush into them. While stroking the girl's hair with one hand, she looked at Dusty.

He gave his head a slow shake, then tipped it toward the house.

Karen nodded in understanding, and wordlessly, she guided the weeping girl up the porch steps and into the house.

"Boys," Sophia said, "go wash up for supper. We'll call you when it's time to eat."

Nobody argued.

Even though Dusty's gaze remained on the front door, he was aware of Sophia's slow approach, could sense the heaviness of her heart. It matched his own.

"What happened?"

"She said her dad kicked her out of the house and told her not to come back."

"Oh, Dusty. No."

He let out a deep sigh. "I'll have to let him know she's here. Maybe he's over being angry." He met Sophia's watery blue gaze. "We'd better get inside. Karen isn't used to dealing with stuff like this."

"It looked like she was handling it just fine. What more does that little girl need than someone reaching out in love?"

Dusty knew she was right.

"Karen's not the same spoiled rich girl who arrived here two months ago," Sophia said. "She's changed."

"You know what I feel for her, don't you?"

"Yes, I know."

"She isn't a Christian."

Sophia touched his arm with her fingertips. "Then we'll have to trust the Lord about that, too. We trust Him for everything else."

❦

Fury burned in Karen's chest as she listened to Patty between sobs.

"He...he told me if I...refused again, then he...he'd wash

his hands of…of me. But I didn't…I didn't want an abortion. I…I don't think it's right, and I was…scared."

Karen wished she could cut out Olen Call's heart. Only she doubted he had one.

Patty looked up. "I know what I did was wr-wrong. But I…I couldn't let a doctor kill the baby. It isn't her fault—this baby's—what I did."

Karen heard the floorboards squeak and was relieved to see Dusty and Sophia enter the parlor. Dusty looked at her briefly. Then he crossed the short distance separating them and sat on the sofa next to Patty.

Karen gave the girl a comforting squeeze. "Tell Mr. Stoddard what you told me while I get you a glass of water and a cloth to wash your face."

"Don't go!" Patty cried as she grabbed hold of Karen's hand.

"It's all right. I'm just going into—"

"I'll get the water and washcloth," Sophia interrupted. "You sit still."

Karen had no other choice. Patty had a death grip on her by this time.

"You tell him," the girl said in a hoarse whisper. "Please." Then she hid her face against Karen's chest and began to weep anew.

Speaking in a low voice, Karen repeated what Patty had told her. When she was finished, they sat in silence until Sophia returned to the parlor. The three adults exchanged glances while Patty wiped her face with the moistened washcloth and sipped water from the glass.

Finally, Dusty spoke. "Patty, I'm going to call your father. He'll have to know where you are."

"He won't care."

Karen was glad Dusty didn't try to tell the girl she was wrong. There was no sense in pretending.

"I'll have to call him anyway. But I don't want you to be afraid. We're going to do everything in our power to see that you're well taken care of. Will you trust me about that?"

Patty nodded.

"And Patty…" He hooked her hair behind her ear, then cupped her chin with his hand. "It took a lot of courage, making the decision not to abort your baby."

Sophia held out her hand. "I think you should come and lie down for a while, dear child."

Patty hesitated only a moment, then took the elderly woman's hand and followed her out of the parlor.

"She's a baby having a baby," Karen said softly. "Maybe it would have been better if she'd just gone through—"

"No," he interrupted. "It wouldn't."

She looked at him. "How can you be so sure?"

"God puts great value on every human life. He knew that baby before it was formed. It isn't the baby's fault how it was conceived or that its parents are too young. When we take a human life, young or old, we're playing God."

"You're twisting this all around. In case you're not aware of it, women earned the right to control their own bodies a couple of decades ago. You religious fanatics are all the same, trying to make other people live the way you think they should."

She'd said it to get a rise out of him. She failed.

"I can't force anyone to do anything, Karen. I can only try to walk as Jesus walked. He never took a single life during His time on earth. He healed the sick. He gave sight to the blind. He raised the dead. But He never took a life."

"Even if that's true, it was two thousand years ago." She rose from the sofa. "What good does it do Patty?"

"More than you know."

Karen didn't hear what was said when Dusty telephoned Olen Call to inform him his daughter was at the Golden T. Whatever was said, it upset him. He scarcely spoke during supper, and he excused himself without eating half the food on his plate. A short while later, those in the kitchen could hear the sounds of wood being split.

He was still at it at nine-thirty that evening when Karen stepped onto the porch.

The sky had clouded over, obscuring the sun as it sank in the west. A cooling breeze swept across the rolling countryside, bringing with it the scent of sage and rain.

Karen crossed her arms over her chest and watched as he worked off his frustration. She was actually glad to see his anger—it made him seem more approachable.

What makes him so different from other men I've known?

Dusty leaned his ax against a nearby bench, then picked up the garden hose, turned the faucet, and drank his fill. When he was finished, he bent forward at the waist and held the hose above his head, letting the water drench him.

She couldn't help smiling as she observed him. There were models and actors in Los Angeles who would sell their souls to look as ruggedly handsome as Dusty looked right then.

Drawn as irresistibly as a moth to a flame, Karen left the porch and strode across the yard. When Dusty straightened and their eyes met, he dropped the hose and turned off the faucet, then used both hands to push his damp hair back from his face.

I'm in love with you, Dusty. Do you find me desirable at all? Do you like me just the least little bit?

Those thoughts tumbled through her mind, but she didn't say any of them aloud. Instead, she asked, "Care to talk about it?"

"I'm not sure I'm ready yet." He reached for his T-shirt and slipped it over his head. "I'm too blasted mad."

"You can't chop wood all night long."

"I might need to." He looked up at the clouds. "But I guess you're right. Looks like it's going to dump rain on me pretty soon."

"Patty went to bed. I think she's asleep now."

"Poor kid. I'll never understand how a father can reject his daughter like that. No matter what she's done. No matter how often I see it, I can't understand it."

Karen stuffed her fingers into the back pockets of her Levi's, determined not to think of her own father. "Dusty, I'm sorry for what I said earlier. About religious fanatics."

"I wasn't insulted." He surprised her with a brief smile. "It's the truth. I'd like to change the world to my way of thinking. If that makes me a fanatic, I guess I'll accept the moniker."

"I've never known anyone like you," she muttered, echoing her earlier thought.

"Karen?" He stepped closer. "You were wonderful this afternoon."

She wasn't sure what he was talking about. She was too aware of how near he was standing and the way the shadow of a beard darkened his jaw. Would his skin feel rough if she ran her fingertips over his cheek?

"Let's find out," he said huskily. "Shall we?"

"Find out what?"

"This." He lowered his head toward hers.

Slowly…

Oh, so slowly.

When their lips met, Karen felt a quiver run the length of her. It stole the breath from her lungs and the strength from her knees.

She was no stranger to sexual attraction, but she was a complete neophyte when it came to true matters of the heart. Love changed everything, she realized now. And it frightened her.

Perhaps Dusty sensed her uncertainty, for he broke the kiss and drew back. Not far enough. She could still feel the heat of his body, still see the pulse in his throat.

"I guess that answered that," he said.

She meant to reply, but it appeared he'd stolen her ability to speak, too.

"It complicates things, Karen."

"What does?"

"Falling in love."

He couldn't possibly be saying he loved her. And she wasn't ready for him to know she loved him.

Not yet. Perhaps not ever.

Before she could make a huge mistake, she spun on her heel and walked away from him as quickly as her legs would carry her.

Wednesday, May 10, 1939

Dear Diary,

I received a letter from Mama today. Delphia is engaged to Dutch. They are planning a wedding for the Fourth of July. Sam Draker bought a big new tractor, and almost every farmer in the county showed up at the Draker farm the day it was delivered. The church elders have finally hired a new pastor, and he will arrive soon, much to Mama's relief since she says Elder Trenton's sermons are dry as toast.

Papa has been talking about selling the farm and moving to Boise in order to be closer to Sophia. Mama said he seems to be tired much of the time, and she fears for his health.

How would I imagine them as living anywhere else than our big old house on the farm? It would be so strange, as if I had lost something. When I am sad and homesick, I can close my eyes and see Mama in the kitchen, preparing one of her wonderful dinners. Or Papa sitting in the corner, smoking his pipe, his reading glasses perched on the end of his nose as he scours the newspaper.

Often I wish we could go home to America, but Mikkel is certain this is where God has planted us.

Why that is, I couldn't say, but here we will remain for now.

Esther

Thursday, June 8, 1939

Dear Diary,

Today Hannah was delivered of a beautiful baby girl, and I was with her when it happened. I had never helped at a birthing before and, while I have given birth myself, had never witnessed the miracle. Oh, praise God in the highest! If ever I had doubted the existence of our Creator, that doubt would have ended in the early hours of this morning.

What promise it holds, to see new life begin.

But the world is troubled, and Mikkel believes darker days are ahead of us. Germany has annexed Czechoslovakia, and Italy has annexed Albania. The threat to neighboring countries is clear, even to someone like me. Anti-Semitism is spreading at an alarming rate as Hitler's Nazi forces grow and strengthen. There are even some signs of it here in Denmark, although it is an unusual thing for these loving, caring people.

Yet despite all that is happening in the outside world, for this day we have seen the hand of God at work. A child has been born, healthy and squalling. A daughter for Hannah and Isaac. A sister for Ben and Ruth. A beautiful child with a future already foreseen by God.

Dear Father in heaven, You have promised that You will give

the desires of our hearts to those of us who seek Your face. I have tried to do so. I have tried to know Your calling and to walk as Jesus walked when He was here on this earth. Now I come to You, asking You to bless me with another child, a baby to hold in my arms and to love as I was loved by my own mother, as Hannah loves her children. Amen.

Esther

Nineteen

By morning, Karen had made up her mind. She had to leave this ranch on the edge of nowhere. She must look for employment and another place to live. If she had to, she would flip burgers at the local fast-food joint, but she was going to get out of here before it was too late.

It complicates things, Karen...

Maybe it was already too late.

"I'm *not* going to love him," she whispered, lying in her bed, staring at the ceiling as dawn's light crept across it. "Because he's right. It *does* complicate things, and I don't need complications. I'm not going to love him or these kids or even my grandmother."

Could anyone she knew—in the wildest stretch of their imaginations—picture her remaining at this joke of a ranch one moment longer than was absolutely necessary? Of course not. She was an outsider. She didn't think the way Sophia and

Dusty did. She missed the parties and glitter and beautiful people.

What did those beautiful people ever do for me?

She winced.

And what did I ever do for any of them?

She rolled over, covered her head with her pillow, and tried to blank out her thoughts. She was tired of this soul-searching. Life was simpler when she went through each day unawares, seeking nothing beyond the pleasure of the moment.

And what would I have to give up?

EVERYTHING, KAREN.

"No," she whispered. "No, no, no."

Dusty didn't hear much of the sermon that Sunday morning. His thoughts were back at the Golden T…with Karen. For the first time since her arrival, she hadn't come with them to church. She'd claimed she had a headache.

He suspected *he* was the cause of her headache, whether real or imagined.

Lord, I love her. I want her to work with me with these kids. Look how good she's been with Patty and with Billy. She's got a lot to give. I know she does. All she needs is You. So what should I do next?

He'd learned early in his Christian walk the importance of prayer. He'd learned to pray for things great and small, and he'd learned to watch with expectation to see how God answered. But suddenly he felt adrift at sea, as if he'd broken loose from his anchor.

Jesus...what's the answer?

Sophia's hand alighted on the back of his. He glanced at her and was comforted by the serenity he saw in her eyes. Blessed assurance. That was what he saw there. He wanted to know that same peace.

But I won't as long as I want my own way more than I want God's will.

He shifted his gaze forward again, toward the large cross hanging high above the pulpit, the focal point of the sanctuary. He knew he'd discovered the root of his disquiet. He didn't truly want God's answer unless it meant getting his own way.

SOLD OUT TO ME.

Ah, Lord, I am. I have been.

DO YOU TRUST ME, BELOVED?

You know I do, Lord.

DO YOU BELIEVE I LOVE YOU WITH AN EVERLASTING LOVE?

Yes.

DO YOU BELIEVE I LOVE KAREN WITH THE SAME LOVE?

Yes.

THEN GIVE HER TO ME.

Dusty's old pickup truck ran rough, and Karen wasn't an expert with a stick shift. But somehow she managed to drive without killing herself.

She'd found two hundred dollars in the lower drawer of her grandmother's dresser. It was now tucked safely in her purse. Her suitcase was in the truck bed, and Esther's diaries and the Bible Sophia had given her were lying on the seat beside her. She'd left a note, promising to repay the money as soon as she could. She'd also promised to return the truck, though why anyone in their right mind would want this piece of junk, she couldn't say.

At least she knew they wouldn't call the cops and have her arrested for car theft. That wasn't her grandmother's or Dusty's style. They would probably sit at the kitchen table and pray for her.

"I don't want their prayers. I'm sick to death of prayers."

Two hundred dollars wasn't going to last long. She would have to find an inexpensive room for the night, then start job hunting in the morning.

Doing what? Flipping those proverbial burgers?

She groaned. She'd learned to cook a few things since arriving at the Golden T, but she couldn't say she enjoyed it enough to do it eight hours a day, five days a week.

I can ask Mac for help.

She pressed her lips together, fighting the sudden urge to cry.

"Why? Why did this have to happen to me?"

She wasn't certain what she meant by *this*. Did she mean her father's suicide and her sudden loss of all her material possessions? Did she mean never knowing the love of her parents, no matter how hard she'd tried to earn it? Did she mean leaving behind California and everything familiar to her? Did she mean Grandmother Sophia? Or the boys, especially Billy? Or poor, distraught Patty?

Or did she mean Dusty?

"Oh, Dusty."

Tears swam before her eyes, blinding her. She quickly flicked them away. All she needed was to wreck his truck. Besides, if she was going to die, she didn't want it to be in a hunk of junk like this.

Seeing an exit up ahead, she made a quick decision, flipped on her turn signal, and drove off the freeway. She hadn't a clue where she was, but she didn't think it mattered much. Wherever it was, she was still lost.

So very lost.

❧

Dusty wasn't surprised when Sophia brought him a slip of paper with Karen's meticulous handwriting on it. He didn't have to read it to know what it said.

He read it anyway.

Karen had left them. She'd taken his truck and Sophia's meager savings, and she'd left them all.

"Don't lose hope," Sophia said softly after he'd finished.

"No," he answered, although he didn't feel hopeful.

"She took the Bible I bought her. And Esther's journals."

He nodded.

"Remember, you and I ran away too. But God was there to meet us in His own way, in His own timing. He'll do no less for Karen."

Dusty closed his hands into fists at his sides. "She doesn't even know she's running. Or what she's running from."

"Give her time. Give the Lord time to work in her."

"Sold out to Him," he whispered. "Complete trust."

"What?"

He met her gaze. "Just something the Lord told me this morning."

Sophia didn't press him to explain.

Dusty glanced toward the bunkhouse. "I'll have to tell the boys."

"And Patty."

All of a sudden, he felt like cursing. "How could she do this to them? She ought to know how much these kids love her. Especially Billy. And Patty. That girl went to her yesterday like a magnet. You saw how it was."

"Yes, I saw."

"Maybe getting Karen out of here was God's way of keeping me from making a mistake." He regretted the words the instant they were out of his mouth. "I'm sorry. I shouldn't have said that to you."

She squeezed his upper arm with frail fingers, smiling sadly. "I understand, Dusty." Then she turned and walked toward the house, leaving him standing in the yard.

He closed his eyes as the memory of Karen's voice played in his head. *You can't save them all.* His fingers crinkled the note in his hand into a small ball.

I turned loose of all that, Jesus, he silently protested. *Remember?*

NO ONE CAN COME TO ME UNLESS THE FATHER WHO SENT ME DRAWS HIM. JUST AS YOU WERE DRAWN.

He sighed as the argument drained out of him. He knew what God was speaking to his heart. This was about trusting Him. This was about faith. Believing the unseen even when everything inside him said there was no hope.

"For who has known the mind of the LORD," he quoted softly, "or who became His counselor? Or who has first given to Him that it might be paid back to him again? For from Him and through Him and to Him are all things."

With those words, he finally and completely relinquished the woman he loved, the woman he hoped to marry, to God.

The tiny motel room had stained, olive green shag carpet, curtains that sagged over one small window, an air conditioner that sounded as if it was about to explode, and a lumpy mattress. But it was the best Karen could afford if the two hundred dollars she'd stolen from her grandmother—correct that; the money she'd *borrowed*—was going to last until she got a job.

The busy street outside the motel whirred with traffic even this late on a Sunday night, and lights from the passing cars flashed through a tear in the curtains.

Unable to sleep, Karen switched on the lamp, sat up in bed, and turned on the television. The reception was poor; there was little more than fuzz on the screen. She would find no diversion there.

She glanced at the books on the table beside the bed. She'd been reading Esther's diaries for several weeks. It had surprised her, the way those simplistic entries had drawn her into the life of a woman she'd never known. She hadn't been able to leave the ranch without bringing the journals along. For some strange reason, she wanted to know what had happened to Esther.

But it was Sophia's other gift that drew her gaze tonight.

How many times this summer had she seen Sophia and Dusty reading their well-used Bibles, seen them turn those curling pages, pages filled with underlined and highlighted passages and personal notations in the margins? What, she wondered, caused them to do it, to read those same chapters and verses time and time again? She couldn't recall reading any book more than once. Not even the ones she'd raved about to others.

She reached out, touched the Bible, traced the lettering on the cover with the tip of her index finger. *Study Bible,* it read.

Her grandmother couldn't afford to buy this for her. It had been a sacrifice. One she'd gladly made because she loved Karen.

She lifted the book onto her lap. Ancient writings for an ancient religion—she'd heard a friend describe the Bible that way. And Christianity, he'd said, was a religion that had little to do with today's world. These were modern times, a time of science and knowledge, a period of history when the human race no longer needed to believe in something bigger, in someone omniscient.

But that isn't what Dusty and Grandmother believe. Why is that? What is it they find inside this book?

She drew the Bible against her chest as she closed her eyes. She imagined Dusty as he worked with those boys. His patience. His smile. His love for them even when they were unlovable. She pictured Sophia, old and frail, a woman who had few creature comforts in her latter years and yet who had an aura of joy for the life she led.

"I've been happy too," Karen whispered.

She remembered the day she'd been released from the desire to take her own life. It wasn't that things had become suddenly easier. It wasn't that her fortunes had been restored. No, there had simply been a lifting of oppression.

She recalled the way Billy's hand felt whenever it had slipped into hers. Dear, darling Billy. He loved Dusty and Sophia's God too. But he was young and moldable. He hadn't suffered life's many disappointments yet. As soon as that thought passed through her mind, she knew it was a lie. Billy had suffered, but he'd also overcome.

"Miracles. They all believe in miracles. But *I* don't. I *can't*."

She opened her eyes, glancing toward the diaries on the table. The story within them painted a picture of Sophia as an angry, bitter young woman, bitter because Mikkel had loved Esther and not her. Karen's mother had described Sophia in much the same way. Yet, that wasn't the woman Karen knew.

Maybe it *was* a miracle.

She looked up at the water-stained ceiling. "So tell me," she said softly. "Just where does a person have to go to get a miracle?"

Monday, September 4, 1939

Dear Diary,

England and France have declared war on Germany after the invasion of Poland. Mikkel says he should have sent me back to America months ago. But Grandfather Fritz insists Denmark will be all right. This nation remained neutral during the Great War, and he says the king will keep them so again. He says Mikkel worries needlessly. The Germans will leave us alone.

I pray Grandfather is right.

Esther

Saturday, October 28, 1939

Why God? Why? Why must I suffer? Why am I unable to give Mikkel a son or a daughter? Why did I miscarry before I could even share my secret hope with Mikkel, that I was at last pregnant again?

Christmas Day, 1939

Dear Diary,

Grandfather is ill. We had just returned from our Christmas morning service when he collapsed. Mikkel carried him to his room while I called for the doctor, and we waited long and agonizing minutes until he arrived.

The doctor says it is old age and we should not expect Grandfather to live more than another four to six months, although it is possible he will linger beyond that.

The vibrant old man I have known since coming to Denmark—the man who revealed to me his beloved Copenhagen, who took me for long walks down old streets and showed me the Citadel and the Royal Theatre and the university and the Botanical and Tivoli Gardens, and who loved me as if I were his own granddaughter—is dying.

It is too much, God. Too much. Must You take away everyone I love from me? My sister. My daughter. My unborn child. And now Grandfather Fritz. What lesson is this I must learn? Why? Why? Why? Am I like Job? Must I be stripped of everything?

Esther

Twenty

A week passed.

"Do you suppose Miss Karen's all right?" Billy asked at supper one night.

"She's in God's hands," Sophia answered.

The boy nodded. "Then she's all right."

Listening, Dusty thought it was no wonder Christ said they were to have faith like a little child's. He would do well to follow Billy's example.

Another week went by.

Dusty called in a few favors from his contacts at both the county and state level and obtained permission for Patty to remain at the Golden T during her pregnancy. Perhaps longer if circumstances didn't change with her father.

"You and I can do our homework together," Dusty told Patty after they'd decided to homeschool her. "Agreed?"

"Agreed," she answered, showing more animation than she had since her arrival at the ranch.

The final week of the youth camp's season was upon them, and everyone began to feel the regret of approaching separation. It was like this every year for Dusty. He poured all his efforts into helping his boys cope with whatever they had to face in their families, their homes, their communities, and then he hated to send them back to those same situations.

Some would write to him now and then. A few would even come for a visit. Most would simply disappear from his life, remembered in his prayers but never seen nor heard from again.

Much like Karen.

He'd foolishly thought the pain of her absence would lessen with time. It hadn't happened. At least not yet.

It was tradition for everyone at the Golden T to spend a full day at the Western Idaho State Fair before the boys left the ranch. This year was no different.

"Can I push your wheelchair first?" Billy asked Sophia as Dusty parked the van in the packed lot.

"If you'd like." She glanced at Dusty. "Renting that contraption is a foolish waste of money. You could have left me on a bench in the shade. I enjoy watching people. I would've been fine."

"Don't be silly. We *want* you with us. Don't we?"

A chorus of yeses resounded from the back of the van.

It didn't take long for everyone to disembark. Soon Sophia was seated in the wheelchair and being pushed by Billy toward the main gates. Patty stayed close to the elderly woman's side. The girl had bonded with Sophia, but Dusty suspected she missed Karen almost as much as he did.

One day. It'd be nice to go through one day without thinking of her.

He purchased their admission tickets. Then he gave them his standard speech about watching the time, and they decided on a meeting place. Monies were doled out. There was less than originally hoped for, thanks to Karen.

But he didn't want to think of that either. God had provided. What more could he want?

He checked his wristwatch. "Okay, it's one o'clock now. Everybody plan to meet by the fountain"—he pointed toward it—"at three-thirty. And don't be late."

The three boys took off. Patty didn't budge.

"Aren't you going, dear?" Sophia asked.

The girl shook her head. "I'd rather stay with you, if that's okay."

"Of course it is."

Patty looked toward the carnival grounds. "I can't go on the rides anyway since I'm pregnant."

Dusty had known his share of adults who didn't face their responsibilities as well as this girl faced hers.

"Come on." He put his arm around her shoulders at the same time she gripped the handles of the wheelchair. "Let's find something to eat. I've got money burning a hole in my pocket and hunger burning a hole in my stomach."

⁂

The fair had been in full swing for six days, and Karen had spent every one of them in her employer's booth on food row. Now, she knew more about dipping ice cream than she'd imagined there was to know.

On this Thursday afternoon, the August sun beat relentlessly down on the roadway outside the booth; mirages wavered above the blacktopped surface. To make matters worse, crying children, shouting mothers, and loud rock music blaring from speakers in the carnival combined into an ear-shattering cacophony.

And Karen put up with it all for minimum wage.

She leaned over the freezer compartment, grateful for the blast of cold air that hit her face as she scooped chocolate-chip ice cream into a cone. It momentarily eased the pounding in her head.

"Here you go. That'll be a dollar seventy-five." She handed

the cone to a small boy as his mother placed seven quarters on the stainless steel counter.

"Karen?"

She glanced over her shoulder at Toby, the owner's teenaged son. "Hmm?"

"I'm going for some chocolate syrup. Need me to bring anything else?"

"No. I don't think so."

"Okay. Back in ten."

She watched Toby leave through the rear of the booth. The kid reminded her a little of Hal Junker.

I wonder where Junkman is now?

The thought caused a twinge of pain, and she quickly blanked it out. If she thought about Junkman, then she would think about the other boys. If she thought about the other boys, then she would think about Sophia. And then she would think about Dusty. She couldn't handle that.

She turned toward the counter again—

And there he stood, as if in answer to her thoughts.

She saw her own surprise mirrored in Dusty's eyes.

"Karen."

Her mouth went dry.

"How are you?" he asked softly.

She swallowed, then moistened her lips with the tip of her tongue. "I...I'm fine."

"I thought you'd gone back to California."

"No." She shook her head. "No, I'm still here." She wiped her damp palms on her apron.

"Have you seen the boys?"

"They're here?"

"Yes." His dark, expressive eyes searched hers. There was no condemnation in them. Only tenderness. "Sophia's here too. She's with Patty."

"With Patty."

"Patty's staying with us through the winter." He paused a moment, then said, "She misses you. Everyone does."

It took all her resolve not to say she missed them, too, to keep from bursting into tears and rushing into his arms.

"Come home, Karen."

Home… Was the Golden T her home? Did she want it to be? She didn't know. She wasn't sure. She was confused.

She shook her head. "I can't."

"Sure you can."

She stared into the freezer compartment, unable to look at him any longer. "No." Oh, why did Toby have to be gone from the booth? If only she could turn and walk away. This was too hard. It was much too hard.

Dusty reached across the counter and took hold of her arm. She stared at his hand. The summer sun had bronzed his skin. There were tiny scars on several knuckles. It was a large, strong hand, and yet, like everything else about Dusty, it was gentle.

"Come home, Karen."

Blinded by tears, she took a step backward, out of his reach, then turned her back toward him. "I don't know where home is," she confessed in a strangled voice.

"Sure you do. You know. In your heart, you know. Home is with the people you love, with the people who love you."

"I don't belong with—" She stopped abruptly. She'd almost said she didn't belong with him. But she couldn't say it. Those words would reveal too much. Finally, she said, "I don't belong at the Golden T."

"You're running away. Just like I did. Just like your grandmother did. Just like Hal did. But you can't outrun God, Karen. I'm living proof of that. You'll find Him waiting for you wherever you go. So you might as well stop running."

"I can't come back. Don't ask me to." She swallowed the lump in her throat. "Please don't ask me to."

He sighed. "All right. I won't ask." There was a lengthy pause, then he added, "But I'll be praying for you. I won't stop doing that."

No, don't stop praying for me, Dusty. Please don't stop.

She blinked away hot tears, set her jaw, clenched her hands

into fists. She wasn't going to cry in front of him. No matter what else happened, she wasn't going to let him see her tears.

It took awhile, but once she'd regained a measure of control, she turned around.

Too late. Dusty was gone.

. . . .

Sunday, December 31, 1939

Dear Diary,

It is not "Why is this happening to me?" that I should be
asking of God. It is "How can I draw closer to You, Lord? How
can I take this experience, my own suffering and loss, and use it
to minister to others?"

I felt God stirring my heart this morning while Mikkel was
preaching. It wasn't anything he said specifically. It was purely
of the Holy Spirit, speaking quietly to me, reassuring me,
comforting me. Suddenly, I felt a peace I have not felt for a
long, long time. I let go of the hurt I was clinging to. I do not
know how else to describe it. I simply let go and told the Lord
that whatever happened, I was His. I will worship Him. I will
serve Him. No matter what, I will praise Him for all of my
days. I will go where He wants me to go. I will do what He
wants me to do.

And in that moment, I knew I would find God's will for my
life, that I would not live in vain, and that my descendants
would be able to say, "Esther Christiansen was a woman of God,
a woman who loved Jesus and who taught others to love the Lord
as well."

My descendants. I do not know if they will be few or if they will be as many as Abraham's. All I know is, the Lord told me there will be descendants.

Thank You, Jesus.

Esther

Twenty-One

You're running away...

For the eyes of the LORD move to and fro throughout the earth that He may strongly support those whose heart is completely His.

Just like I did...

The eyes of the LORD are toward the righteous, and His ears are open to their cry.

Just like your grandmother did...

My eyes shall be upon the faithful of the land, that they may dwell with me; He who walks in a blameless way is the one who will minister to me.

Just like Hal did...

The eyes of the LORD are in every place, watching the evil and the good.

But you can't outrun God, Karen...

You can't outrun God, Karen...
You can't outrun God...

❧

The tangerine light of dawn spread across the ceiling of Dusty's bedroom. It surprised him to find it there. He was usually awake long before sunup.

But, of course, the boys had left on Saturday, and today there was no need to rise early.

Sitting up, he raked his fingers through his hair and yawned. What he needed was a cup of coffee to clear the cobwebs. Then maybe he'd put his feet up and read a good book, just for the fun of it. A suspense novel. One of those books about the end times that had been getting such great reviews. Anything other than a textbook. He'd be getting his fill of those as soon as he was back at the university.

His eyes widened. The *university!* He'd be driving back and forth to school in Boise. But he couldn't leave Sophia and Patty alone all day with no transportation. Sophia was old and Patty was pregnant, and the Golden T was miles from anywhere. And, thanks to Karen, they were now short one vehicle.

Why didn't I think of this before?

He got out of bed, pulled on his jeans, dropped a T-shirt over his head, then slipped his feet into a pair of thongs. He needed that coffee before he'd be able to work through this latest problem.

Lord, we're gonna need plenty of help on this one.

He opened the bunkhouse door.

And there was his pickup, Karen seated inside, her forehead resting on the steering wheel.

He whispered her name as quickened strides carried him toward the truck. Sunlight glinted off the windshield, the reflection momentarily blinding him.

"Karen?" Hurrying around to the driver's side, he grabbed the handle and yanked the door open. "Karen, what's wrong?"

She lifted her head, and her gaze met his. "I came home. I'm tired of—"

Before she could finish whatever she was about to say, Dusty drew her out of the truck and into his arms. He held her tightly as he brushed his lips across the top of her head, all the while silently praying, *Thank You, Jesus. Thank You for bringing her home. Thank You. Thank You.*

He had no idea how much time passed before she pulled back from him, lifting her eyes toward his.

"I don't want to run away anymore, Dusty. I need to find answers."

He heard the heartache in her voice, and he longed to soothe it away. He longed to tell her he loved her. He longed to tell her he wanted to spend the rest of his life with her. But he kept silent, knowing he had to be patient. If ever there was a time to seek God's guidance, this was it.

Karen looked toward the house. "I don't have much of Grandmother's money left."

"It won't matter. She'll just be glad you're back."

"I...I'm sorry about taking your truck."

He gave her a tender smile. "You brought it back. The rest doesn't matter." He put his arm around her shoulders. "Let's get you inside."

She let him steer her toward the house, up the porch steps, and through the front door. They stopped, and Karen's gaze swept over the kitchen. The scent of freshly perked coffee filled the room.

"Sophia must be up," he said needlessly.

"She'll be in her garden." Karen stepped away from him. "Praying."

He watched her walk across the kitchen, putting more distance between them.

"She'll be out there praying for me," she added.

"Yes."

She turned toward him. "I don't know if I can ever believe the things you do. About God and Jesus and faith and...and love."

This is real love, he quoted silently, willing her to understand. *It is not that we loved God, but that He loved us and sent His Son as a sacrifice to take away our sins.*

"I've been reading the Bible she gave me."

He smiled.

"No need to look so pleased," she said with a note of irritation. "It doesn't mean I agree with it."

"Sorry," he answered, but his smile remained.

Whether Karen knew it or not, the Holy Spirit was at work in her heart, and he couldn't keep himself from silently rejoicing.

Seated beneath the willow, Sophia rejoiced as well. Before coming to the garden, she'd seen Karen in Dusty's truck, and she'd known the young woman had returned.

"And she who seeks the Truth shall find Him," she whispered.

Her gaze strayed to her vegetable patch. Ripening tomatoes hung on the vines. Three rows of cornstalks formed the southern border of the rectangle garden; their tassels bobbed and danced in a crisp morning breeze. Long, green tentacles from the zucchini plants spread in several directions.

It was easy now, as summer ended, to tell what each plant was. It was more difficult early in the season, especially for the untrained eye.

She remembered the day Billy had pulled up several young plants, thinking they were weeds. "It's hard to tell what they are when nothing's growin' on 'em," he'd said to her.

It's the same thing with people, isn't it, Lord? But You know what they are. You know who they are. You know who Karen is and what You have in store for her. And one day, we'll be able to see it too.

As if in response to her thoughts, she saw her granddaughter coming down the path toward her. Karen had lost weight in the past three weeks. Judging by the circles beneath her eyes, she hadn't been getting much sleep either.

"Hello, Grandmother."

"Come." Sophia patted the bench with her hand. "Sit beside me, dear. I've missed you."

"I've missed you, too." She sat as directed.

Sophia enfolded Karen's left hand in her right one and squeezed.

"I'm sorry I took your money."

"It's all right."

"No, it isn't. I know how little you have. And what you do have, you give to others. Me, I've just thought about myself." Karen closed her eyes. "I want my life to *mean* something. I want to be a better person than I am."

"Oh, my dear." Sophia released her granddaughter's hand, then put her arm around Karen's back and drew her close, stroking her hair with her hand. "I love you so much."

"No one ever loved me until you," she said in a hoarse whisper.

"You're wrong, Karen. You're so very wrong. You've been loved by God all your life."

"I want to believe that."

Sophia sent up a quick prayer. *Help me, Lord!*

Karen choked back a sob.

"Dear girl," Sophia murmured as she glanced up at the blue morning sky. "My dear, dear girl." She didn't know what else to say. Perhaps there wasn't anything else.

Dusty leaned his shoulder against the window frame in Sophia's bedroom, watching as Sophia comforted her grand-daughter. He saw the tremble of Karen's shoulders and knew she was crying.

His eyes suddenly misted, blurring his vision. He blinked rapidly, at the same time clearing his throat. He'd never been comfortable with his own tears, not even when there was no one else around to see them.

I SEE THEM.

I love her, but what if she never accepts You?

FAITH IS THE ASSURANCE OF THINGS HOPED FOR, THE CONVICTION OF THINGS NOT SEEN.

He closed his eyes and pressed his forehead against the windowpane. A deep sigh escaped him. Operating the Golden T

Youth Camp was a study in the faith walk. So why couldn't he seem to trust God to do what was best for him when it came to women?

No, not women.

Just one woman.

Just Karen.

....

Thursday, February 8, 1940

Dear Diary,

Mikkel has talked himself blue in the face, trying to convince
Isaac to take his family and leave Denmark now. But Isaac is
like Grandfather Fritz. He cannot believe the Germans would
march into a neutral country. Hannah is just as stubborn and
will do nothing to change Isaac's mind.

I feel my husband's concern. It is not lack of faith, for I know
Mikkel finds comfort in God. But he senses there is great peril.
He rarely sleeps and is gone for many hours every day.

This morning, he decided to make changes to the upper floors
of the house. He said we will need a place to hide our valuables
should the Nazis bring their war to Copenhagen. I know I looked
at him in utter surprise and confusion. "What valuables?" I
asked, but he only shook his head and said I must tell no one.
Not even Hannah. I will honor his request, of course, yet I
cannot understand it.

He has hidden our radio. He even lied to Grandfather about
it, saying it was broken. I have never known Mikkel to tell a lie,
but I can see it in his eyes. He thinks it is better for

Grandfather and for me not to know some things. And so he tries to protect us, as much as he is able.

I long to hear from Mama and Papa, but the war in the Atlantic has disrupted mail service. I write to them often and hope my letters get through.

I write to Sophia as well. How my heart aches to hear from her again. It has been nearly three years since we last spoke. Such a very long time to have silence between sisters.

Esther

Tuesday, April 9, 1940

Germany has invaded Denmark. They took control of the Citadel by 5:00 this morning. The citizens of Copenhagen awakened to find Nazi troops crowding the streets and squadrons of aircraft circling over our heads. After some resistance, King Christian X ordered his troops to lay down their arms.

Despite everything Mikkel said in the past, I was as surprised as almost everyone else. I wanted to believe we would be spared.

Now the war is here.

Esther

Twenty-Two

Karen's return to the Golden T was celebrated much like the return of the prodigal son.

In the afternoon, Dusty and Karen went for a horseback ride. They followed a trail down to the Snake River where they watched birds of prey circling above the high bluffs. Dusty didn't force her to talk, for which she was grateful. She wasn't ready.

After their ride, Dusty fired up the grill to barbecue steaks, a rare extravagance. Patty had baked a cake, and Sophia had squeezed lemons for her famous lemonade. They ate their supper while sitting around a campfire and visited into the evening, watching as dusk gave over to night and stars blanketed the heavens.

Karen hadn't expected to find her spirits lifting, like a heavy load from her shoulders, but they did. And she gave herself permission to feel happy and deeply loved. She knew there was much left unsettled, so many things within her heart she still had to work through. Tomorrow, she would have to face herself again. But not tonight. She wanted to enjoy this one night.

Tomorrow came sooner than she'd anticipated.

She hadn't been asleep long when she heard her name, coming from a great distance. Like climbing out of a well, she forced herself awake, but not until she felt her shoulder being shaken.

"Karen, wake up. Wake up. Please."

Blinking against the light, she finally realized who was speaking. "Patty, what is it?"

"It's Miss Sophie. She's sick. She's not breathing right."

Karen was out of bed in an instant. "Get Dusty," she ordered as she rushed from her room and into her grandmother's.

The bedside lamp was on, spilling a golden light onto the elderly woman where she lay, her back propped by several pillows. Her eyes were closed, her mouth parted slightly. A definite, though soft, wheezing sound could be heard with each rise and fall of her chest.

"Grandmother?" Karen fought hard to keep fear from seeping into her voice. "Patty says you're not feeling well." She leaned over the bed and took hold of Sophia's hand.

"Hard…to breathe."

O God. Please don't take her now. Not now.

She heard the screen door slam, and she looked over her shoulder as Dusty came into view. Their gazes met, holding for a heartbeat. Then he strode to the opposite side of the bed and assumed a similar position to hers. A few moments later, after studying the woman's shallow breathing and her pale countenance, he released her hand and left the room, a deep frown drawing his brows close together.

"Patty," Karen whispered. "Stay with her."

She hurried after Dusty. She found him in the kitchen, the telephone in hand.

"Who are you calling?" she asked, although she knew.

"An ambulance."

She clutched the back of a kitchen chair. "You don't think—?"

Her question was cut short when Dusty's phone call was answered. He quickly gave a brief description of Sophia's problem, followed by meticulous directions to the Golden T.

After he hung up the phone, she asked, "How long will it take them to get here?"

"They've got a lot of miles to cover."

It was an unsatisfactory answer, but it was the best she was going to get. Dusty was already walking back to the bedroom. She followed, pausing in the open doorway to watch as he took Sophia's hand for a second time, dropped to his knees beside the bed, and began to pray.

It was a long night.

The sun was well up before Dusty drove the van toward the ranch. Karen sat, cloaked in silence, in the front passenger seat. An exhausted Patty slept in the seat behind him.

A mild heart attack, a doctor at the hospital had finally told them, but the prognosis was good, taking into consideration Sophia's age.

It wasn't as if Dusty didn't know she was old and could go at any time. But knowing in his head and accepting in his heart were two different things. He loved Sophia Taylor. While not related by blood, she was the only family he had left in the world.

I'm not ready for this, Lord. Purely selfish on my part. I know she'll be going to a better place when the time comes, and I shouldn't want to keep her here. But I do.

He glanced toward Karen.

She's not ready either. She needs Sophia, and she's just beginning to understand her need for You. Without her grandmother here to—

He stopped the thought before he could finish it.

Let us keep Sophia awhile longer, Father. Let her share her wisdom and love with us.

Arriving home, Dusty brought the van to a stop near the porch. The front door stood open, a reminder of how quickly they'd left. How many hours ago had that been? It seemed an eternity.

"Are we home?" Karen asked softly.

"Yes." He cut the engine. "We're home." He opened his door and got out, then went around and slid open the side door, reaching in to give Patty a gentle shake. "Wake up, Patty."

The girl barely stirred.

Recognizing the inevitable, he stepped into the van, lifted Patty into his arms, and carried her to the house. She mumbled something unintelligible when he laid her on her cot in Sophia's room, then she rolled onto her side, undisturbed.

Wishing he could sleep that soundly, Dusty removed Patty's shoes and socks, pulled the sheet and blanket over her, then left the bedroom.

Karen was in the kitchen, putting on a pot of coffee.

"Shouldn't you try to get some sleep?" he asked.

"I don't think I could." She looked over her shoulder. "Is Patty okay?"

"I doubt she'll wake up until evening. You know how it is with teenagers."

Karen nodded. "Yes." She retrieved a coffee mug from the dish drain and held it up, questioning him with her eyes.

"Sure. Why not? I probably wouldn't sleep either."

She set the mug, along with one for herself, on the table. Then she opened the refrigerator and took the creamer from the door.

"I could scramble some eggs," she said as she placed the carton in the center of the table.

"No, thanks. Not hungry."

He sat on a chair while she returned to the counter and stood before the coffeepot, watching it brew. The seconds dragged by in silence, both of them lost in thought.

"Dusty?" Karen turned to look at him. "Would you answer a question for me?"

"Of course. If I can. What is it?"

"I was wondering…" She paused, worrying her lower lip. "I was wondering, if God's supposed to love us so much, why does He let good people like my grandmother suffer?"

Dusty released a humorless chuckle. "You don't ask easy ones, do you? I'm not sure I'm thinking clearly enough to answer that."

"You mean you don't know the answer." She sounded suddenly angry.

"No," he answered firmly. "That's not what I mean. I mean it's not something I can answer in fifteen seconds after a long, sleepless night."

She glared at him, and behind her veneer of anger, he recognized her confusion and emotional pain.

He sighed. "Get the coffee, and we'll talk."

A few moments later, she set steaming mugs on the table, then sat on a chair opposite him.

Help me out here, Lord.

"Years ago," he began after a short while, "when I was a brand-new believer, I asked the same sort of question of Jock. I guess this sorta serves me right." He shrugged, making light of it while waiting for a bolt of inspired knowledge to strike him.

It didn't. He was going to have to wade through these waters as best he could, trusting the Lord would stop him if he spoke in error.

"First of all, I believe the answers for everything are in the Bible. So when you ask a question like that, all I know how to do is answer with Scripture."

She nodded but said nothing as she sipped her coffee.

"Second, I don't have a corner on truth. But I know Who *has* the answers. I haven't learned all He has to teach me. And I never will. There'll be something new to learn, right up to the day I die."

Again she acknowledged his words with a nod.

"Okay." He folded his hands on the table before him and leaned forward. "I believe we live in a natural, fallen world. Suffering was introduced because mankind chose to sin rather than to walk with God. And because of that, bad things happen to everybody, the just and the unjust. Pain is a part of life, and so's death. Some pain's even good for us. If you touch a hot burner on the stove, it's pain that causes you to pull back. If you didn't feel anything, you could lose your hand."

He wondered what she was thinking behind those pale blue eyes.

"But for believers, God causes all things to work together for good, even those things the devil means for ill. God the Father is sovereign. He knows what's best for us. He allows us to go through times of testing and trial for our own good and for the greater good of His kingdom."

"How could my grandmother's suffering help His kingdom? She's just an old woman who wants to serve Him."

Dusty raked the fingers of both hands through his hair. "I don't know. I'm not saying it will in this case. It may simply be Sophia's time because her body's worn out. But you asked about the suffering of people in general, not specifically your grandmother."

"You're right. Go on."

"Sometimes suffering's because we've got to be disciplined, like one of our boys. When those kids are here, they live by strict rules, and when they disobey, they get punished. The discipline that's rendered is another expression of my love for them. It's for their good, not because I take pleasure in punishing them."

"I suppose I can accept that," she answered softly.

"Sometimes the suffering we endure is a direct result of our own rebellion, and we're reaping the natural result of our actions. Sometimes God lets us go through stuff so we can use the experience to help others at a later time. And sometimes it happens to strengthen our faith."

"That doesn't sound very loving to me."

"God's nature is love. That never changes."

It was her turn to sigh. She looked away from him, staring out the window.

Dusty stood and walked into the parlor where he took a tattered Bible off the bookshelf. Then he returned to the kitchen, sat down, and opened it.

"Let me read what it says here. 'Dear brothers and sisters, whenever trouble comes your way, let it be an opportunity for joy. For when your faith is tested, your endurance has a chance to grow. So let it grow, for when your endurance is fully developed, you will be strong in character and ready for anything.'"

He paused, waiting, hoping she would look at him again. She didn't.

He closed the Bible. "That's the best answer I have for you. I could have spent my life asking God why my mom died when I was little, why He took my dad away when I needed him most, why I was such a rotten kid who never showed my dad I loved him, why He allowed my best friend to die because of my reckless behavior, why I had to tramp across the country and go hungry and be cold and do without. But maybe all those things happened so I could do exactly what I'm doing now. Maybe it was so I could make a difference in life instead of just going through it. Maybe it's because God loved me enough to want me to know Him. To know Jock and Sophia and kids like Billy and Noah and Ted and Hal and Patty." He reached across the table and covered the back of her hand with his. "Maybe it's because He loves me so much He wanted me to know you."

Her gaze darted back to him, and her eyes widened.

Maybe it's because He wants me to love you.

Karen stood. "Thanks for explaining what you believe. I…I'll think on it." She stepped toward the kitchen doorway. "I think I'll lie down after all." She hurried from the room.

Dusty wondered if he'd made a mistake, saying what he had about God wanting the two of them to meet.

Or had his mistake been not telling her he loved her?

Wednesday, April 10, 1940

Hear me when I call, O God of my righteousness: thou hast enlarged me when I was in distress; have mercy upon me, and hear my prayer. O ye sons of men, how long will ye turn my glory into shame? how long will ye love vanity, and seek after leasing? But know that the LORD hath set apart him that is godly for himself: the LORD will hear when I call unto him. Stand in awe, and sin not: commune with your own heart upon your bed, and be still. Offer the sacrifices of righteousness, and put your trust in the LORD. There be many that say, Who will shew us any good? LORD, lift thou up the light of thy countenance upon us. Thou hast put gladness in my heart, more than in the time that their corn and their wine increased. I will both lay me down in peace, and sleep: for thou, LORD, only makest me dwell in safety. (Psalm 4)

Amen

Sunday, June 23, 1940

Dear Diary,

There is a false normalcy in Copenhagen. We go about our daily lives, but we are surrounded by German soldiers. They seek to be friendly, to pretend they are not invaders in this democratic nation. Even I, young and unsophisticated as I am, know better. They are not our friends.

Hannah and Isaac continue to worship at the synagogue, so far undisturbed. But I see the fear in their eyes. The threat is there. We hear rumors of the deportation of Jews. The thought of my friends being imprisoned for the duration of the war is unbearable to me. They have done nothing wrong. Isaac is a tailor, Hannah a mother who tends to her children and her home.

I asked Mikkel why God allowed evil, such as war and the killing of the innocent, to remain on this earth. He said evil is the result of mankind's corruption of free will. God cannot give us free will to do good, but take away our free will when we choose to do evil. God has spent eternity calling us to Himself, but it is up to us to choose to follow His way, the way of goodness and righteousness.

Mikkel reminded me again of Romans 8:28. But how, I asked him, could any of this work together for good? And he answered me, "I do not know the mind of God, but I do know those who trust in Jesus Christ were predestined to be conformed to His image. Perhaps that is why we are here."

Father God, I am not a brilliant woman. I was only an average student in school. I know so little of the world. Even after nearly three years in Denmark, I struggle with the language and often feel like an outsider. I read my Bible daily, and I try hard to understand what You are telling me. But some things are beyond me. I am just a simple Oregon farm girl. For what purpose did you place me here?

Esther

Karen kept her promise to Dusty. She thought about what he'd told her. She considered his words often, pondering them, trying to understand.

She also thought about what he *hadn't* said. If things were different, she might have asked him if he wished to say more.

But things weren't different.

Sophia spent a week in the hospital. Dusty, Karen, and Patty visited her every day. The daily trip to and from town was tiring for them all, but no one complained.

Dusty made the difficult but necessary decision to forego his studies that semester. As he explained to Karen, Sophia would need lots of care when she was released from the hospital, more than one person could handle. And there were bound to be expenses not covered by insurance, which meant they would need every penny they could scrape together. There wouldn't be any left over for textbooks or gasoline for transportation. After all, it was a long drive from the ranch to the university.

On the day Sophia was to be discharged, Karen dropped Dusty at the hospital in the morning, then drove Patty to her monthly prenatal exam. They were lucky to find empty chairs in the obstetrician's waiting room. It was obvious Dr. Waters was a popular physician. Either that or there was a major baby boom in progress.

The moment she met Dr. Clark Waters, she knew it was the former reason. He could have been the role model for TV's *Marcus Welby, M.D.* The doctor had a round face, creased by time and frequent smiles. He appeared to be about sixty years old, although his build was that of a much younger man. He had a full head of salt-and-pepper hair. His hazel eyes revealed a gentle concern for his patients. Even his voice was perfect, soft and reassuring.

How could one worry with Dr. Waters in charge?

If I were having a baby, I'd want him taking care of me.

On the heels of that thought came another.

If I were having Dusty's baby, I'd want Dr. Waters taking care of us.

Something strange and warm curled inside her belly as she imagined herself sitting in the rocking chair on the front porch at the ranch while holding a baby on her lap.

Never in her life had Karen felt the slightest twinge of maternal instincts. When other women had spoken of their ticking biological clocks, she'd felt confused. It had seemed a great nonsense to her. But in that moment, she knew precisely what all the fuss was about.

"May I have a word in private with you, Miss Butler?"

Heat rose in her cheeks. She hoped the doctor hadn't read her mind. "Of course." She reached for her purse on the floor next to her chair.

Dr. Waters led the way out of the examination room, and Karen followed.

"Is there a problem?" she asked as the door closed behind her.

"Beyond Patty's youthfulness, no." He stopped and turned toward her, speaking in that comforting, perfectly modulated voice of his. "I anticipate no physical problems with this pregnancy. But given her family situation and her age, I'd like her to receive some specialized counseling."

"Mr. Stoddard *is* a counselor. And a good one."

The doctor shook his head. "I know Dusty from church, and I agree. He does fine work. But this is a little different. I don't mean to sound sexist, but I believe she needs a woman counselor, one trained in counseling girls in Patty's situation. Patty has a lot to face in the coming months."

Karen nodded, conceding the point. "We want to do whatever's necessary for her well-being." *But will we have the money to pay for it?*

"I took the liberty of discussing Patty with Victoria Dickson." Dr. Waters drew a card from the pocket of his white coat. "Dusty knows Victoria. She used to attend our church before moving to Boise to open a counseling center there."

"Boise," she whispered beneath her breath, thinking of money again, this time in relation to the cost of gas.

Couldn't You give us a break? Did it have to be so far away?

"You look good," Dusty said with a grin, then leaned over to kiss Sophia's forehead.

"Ha!" The elderly woman swatted his arm. "Are you going to start lying to me just because I've been under the weather? I look dreadful, like anyone my age after a week in the hospital. Thank God I'm going home."

"Thank God, indeed."

"What a bother this has been for you."

"You're never a bother, Sophia."

She reached up to touch his cheek. He covered her hand with his and held it there, holding it close, by his gesture telling her how much she was loved.

"So when do they let me out?" she asked with false brightness, at the same time using a tissue to wipe away a few tears.

"There's some paperwork to take care of first. They're doing that now. Should be done by the time Karen and Patty are back from the obstetrician's."

Sophia's brows drew together in a frown. "How is Karen? Really."

"Seeking and resisting at the same time." He sat on the foot of the bed.

"That's how it was for me." She sighed. "I wonder why acceptance comes easily to some, but others of us fight the whole way to the foot of the cross?"

"I don't know."

"Dusty?"

He lifted an eyebrow. "Hmm."

"When we get home, there are some things we must discuss. About my will and the provisions I've made."

"Hey, you're not dying anytime soon. There's no hurry to—"

"I'm nearly eighty-two. Whether I live another week or another decade, my time on earth is short. We must have this discussion, you and Karen and I."

He nodded his acquiescence, knowing there was no point in arguing with her. When Sophia made up her mind, she could be a most intractable woman.

While Dusty and Karen helped Sophia settle into her room, Patty told her all that had happened during the past week, ending with, "Dr. Waters let Karen listen to the baby's heartbeat this morning."

Dusty stopped what he was doing and looked at Karen. "You got to listen?"

"Yes." She remembered the awesome sound coming through the stethoscope.

"Dr. Waters says," Patty continued, "that if the baby comes at the end of December when it's due, I could be back at my own school by mid-January." She hesitated, then added, "Unless my dad won't let me go home again."

Karen sent Patty an empathetic glance. She knew how it felt to be unwanted. She also knew it was much too easy, even for a girl as young as Patty, to hide her true feelings. Karen had done it for years. To be honest, she was still doing it.

She remembered the card in her coat pocket and knew she must give it to Dusty as soon as they had a moment alone. She didn't want Patty becoming an expert at running away from herself, at hiding what was in her heart so deep no one could reach her.

"Everybody out," Dusty said, breaking into Karen's thoughts. "Sophia needs rest."

"All I do is rest," the older woman groused, but it was half-hearted at best. She'd been worn out by the trip home, and it showed.

Karen leaned over the bed and kissed her grandmother on the forehead. "You take a nap. When you wake up, I'll fix you something to eat."

"Thank you, dear."

Karen led the way out of the bedroom, followed by Patty. Dusty left the door ajar, in case Sophia needed to call for something.

"Do you care if I listen to some CDs over in the bunkhouse?" Patty asked Dusty when they reached the kitchen.

"No. Go ahead."

A few minutes later, the girl was out the door, her CD player in one hand, a case of CDs in the other.

"She should have a room of her own," Karen said as soon as Patty was out of hearing. "I'll sleep on the cot in Grandmother's room, and Patty can have mine. She needs her own space more than I do."

She looked toward Dusty and found him staring at her, his expression inscrutable.

After a breathless moment, she was compelled to ask, "What are you looking at?"

"At someone special," he answered. "At someone very, very special."

Thursday, July 4, 1940

Dear Diary,

In America today, they are celebrating a people's right to rule.
How far away and strange that seems with our streets occupied
by the Germans.

The youth associations in Denmark have combined to form
Dansk Ungdomssamvirke, which means Danish Youth
Cooperation. Mikkel has participated somewhat in their
formation. He hopes they will serve to strengthen national
morale. But there is more he is not telling me. I can see it in his
eyes—they give away the truth.

I have always thought Mikkel's eyes a window into his soul,
and after three years of marriage, I have learned to read him
well. He has seen more than he tells me when he goes about his
church work. Death perhaps. Suffering most definitely. But I
try not to ask, for it is clear he does not wish me to know.

I fear Mikkel does too much, takes too many risks. I have
cautioned him. He is an American. He should try to be
inconspicuous. But he does not listen. Mikkel would never ignore
anyone who is in need.

Still, he must agree with me to a small degree, for he has forbidden me to speak English outside of the house. Even here he wishes I would speak Danish. But it is hard for me. The words remain foreign on my tongue, and I must stop and translate things in my head first.

I wish I were smarter. Not just with languages but with many other things besides.

Esther

Tuesday, September 17, 1940

Dear Diary,

Today, Grandfather Fritz went home to be with the Lord. Mikkel and I were with him at the end.

Before he breathed his last, he looked at Mikkel and said, "I am proud of you. Be strong. Listen to God. He will lead you. Always do what is right."

And Mikkel promised he would.

Then Grandfather looked at me. His hand, quivering and frail, skin like parchment, tightened around mine. "Remember this," he said. "Esther never faltered. Esther fulfilled her destiny, serving where she was planted. Remember it always, Esther. Remember."

I wanted to ask what he meant, but he closed his eyes and was gone. He went so peacefully. And willingly.

But I do not know what he meant. I do not feel I have fulfilled my destiny. I do not feel I have served anyone. What special thing did Grandfather think I have done that caused him to say this?

Or maybe he did not know what he was saying. Perhaps it was only the talk of an old and wandering mind.

Esther

Twenty-Four

Dusty enjoyed watching Karen come into her own. It was difficult to remember the spoiled, emotionally withdrawn poor-little-rich-girl who'd arrived at the beginning of summer. That woman had little in common with the Karen he saw before him now.

He suspected she was unaware of her own transformation. Tenderly caring for Sophia and willingly giving up her bedroom to Patty were only two of the more obvious ways in which she'd changed. There were countless little things that added up to the whole.

I love her more every day, Lord, he thought as he saddled his horse one morning, five days after Sophia's return home. *When do I get to tell her? Or will I never get to?*

He feared the latter might be God's answer. Especially if she didn't come to Christ.

He hadn't much to offer Karen. He owned his horse and tack and an old truck. He had a few changes of clothes and three Bibles and numerous other books he'd collected over the years. Little else belonged to him. He wasn't complaining. He'd lost his desire to acquire *things* long ago. Still, he could understand that a woman might want something more secure when she chose a husband.

And yet he continued to think about her, to envision a future with her, to hope…

A familiar Bible verse came to him: *Hope that is seen is not hope; for who hopes for what he already sees? But if we hope for what we do not see, with perseverance we wait eagerly for it.*

"Are You trying to tell me something, Lord? That it's okay to hope for this?"

His horse nickered.

Dusty leaned his forehead against the animal's neck. "O God, I do hope for it. I can't stop hoping. But more than anything, I want what You want for me, and I don't know what that is. Not in this case."

"Dusty?"

At Karen's voice, his breath caught in his chest. He turned toward the barn doorway. "You're up early." He hoped he sounded normal.

"I wondered if I could join you. I could help you round up those cows for Mr. Basterra. Patty says she'll take care of

Grandmother while we're gone." She hesitated a moment before adding, "Unless you'd rather be alone?"

"No." He grinned, feeling his pulse quicken. "I'd like it if you'd come with me."

"Great." She returned his smile. "I'll saddle the paint."

Sunlight played across the steep walls of the canyon and glittered on the surface of the water. The golden glow gave a false promise of warmth.

Karen shrugged deeper into her coat and tried not to shiver.

"Want to head back?" Dusty asked, breaking the silence that had accompanied them on the ride down to the river.

She glanced his way. "No. I'm okay."

His gaze didn't waver from hers.

For some reason, she thought of Esther and Mikkel. Sophia's sister had left everything she'd known and followed her husband across an ocean, to a country where she didn't even speak the language, all because she'd loved him.

Would I have that kind of courage? Or that kind of faith in anything or anyone?

"A penny for your thoughts."

She gave her head a small shake. "I was thinking of Great-Aunt Esther. Do you know about her?"

"Some."

"Grandmother gave me her diaries. I didn't think I'd be interested, but I've been reading them over the summer. A little here. A little there. Many of the entries are simple recountings of daily activities, but some…" She allowed her words to drift into silence, not knowing how to express what she was feeling. Finally, she said, "She was married to a minister."

"Yes. I knew that."

Karen frowned. "Her first baby died. A little girl she'd name for Grandmother. She was only a month old. And later Esther miscarried another baby. Grandmother, her own sister, wouldn't answer her letters. She was a foreigner in the middle of an occupied country in World War II." She looked away from him, staring toward the rim of the canyon walls. "And yet she never lost faith in the goodness of God."

"God *is* good," he replied softly before nudging his horse into the lead as the trail narrowed, forcing them to ride single file.

Would I have enough courage to follow him anywhere? she wondered as she stared at his back. *If he asked me to, would I go to another country, give up everything comfortable and familiar because I loved him?*

Her parents had done little together, beyond what was expected of them in their social circles. What they had done as a couple had been for display, not out of devotion. Karen knew with certainty that her mother would never have considered doing what Esther Christiansen had done. Not for an instant.

Did Mother and Dad love each other in the beginning? At least a little?

She would never know.

Did either of them ever love me?

That question hurt more, and it couldn't be answered either.

She looked up at the canopy of blue beyond the canyon walls. *Will I ever understand? Will I ever believe?*

Of all the seasons, Sophia enjoyed autumn the most. There was something about the crispness in the air, about the changing of colors that had a calming affect. Perhaps it was an instinctive settling-in as nature prepared for the coming winter.

Dusty had forbidden her to walk out to the garden in the mornings as had been her habit for many years. Instead, she sat in a rocking chair on the front porch, bundled in some old, familiar quilts. Her Bible lay open on her lap, but she wasn't reading it now. Her eyes were closed, and she slept, dreaming…

Esther looked stunning in her wedding gown. It was a simple white dress, without costly pearls and beads, as befit the bride of a poor but honorable country preacher. Yet, there was a radiance about the bride that made the gown seem far more than it was.

"Please come," she said, turning from the mirror.

"I can't," Sophia answered. "You know why."

"I love you. You're my only sister."

"I've hated you. I've resented you. Because of Mikkel. I coveted Mikkel. I wanted him for myself."

"Yes."

"How could you forgive me?"

"It was easy, Sophia."

In the blink of an eye, the wedding dress was gone. Esther looked older, more tired, and yet the radiance remained.

"Sophia, all will be well."

"How can you be so sure?"

"Because I've seen it."

"I failed Maggie. I failed you and Mikkel. You sent her to me, and I failed you both. I loved her, you know. Like she was my own blood."

"I know. And deep down, Margaret Rose knew it too. But don't look back, dearest sister. Look up!"

"I've missed you all these years, Esther. All these years."

Esther's smile was sad as she stepped backward, fading from view. "Don't let Karen go," she called softly. "Promise you won't let her go."

"I won't. I won't let her go. I promise."

The cool morning gave way to warmth as the sun approached its zenith. Dusty and Karen located the dozen stray cattle and drove them to the Basterra farm without mishap or problems.

As soon as they herded the cows into a pen near the barn, Dusty asked Yuli Basterra if he could use the telephone.

"Sure. You know where it is."

"Be right back," Dusty told Karen before walking to the house.

The kitchen was filled with delicious cooking aromas, and his stomach growled in response. He ignored it as he lifted the receiver and dialed the number of the ranch. It was answered on the third ring.

"Hi, Patty. I thought I'd better check in. How's Miss Sophie doing?"

"She's okay. She's resting out on the front porch."

"I told her to stay in bed."

With the mouthpiece covered, muffling her voice, Dusty could hear Patty repeating what he'd said to Sophia. Then she paused, giggled, and said, "Miss Sophie wants me to say you told her she couldn't go out to the garden, and she didn't." Another pause, then, "She says to quit clucking over her like an old wet hen and enjoy the beautiful day with your beautiful companion."

"Not bad advice." He grinned. "Tell her I'm going to follow it."

He hung up the phone, then walked outside. Karen was waiting for him beside the holding pen, talking with Yuli and Celia Basterra.

"Would you like to stay for lunch?" Celia asked when she saw Dusty.

"Thanks for the invitation, but we'd better get back to the Golden T."

"Cold fried chicken and apple-walnut salad," she said. "And freshly baked oatmeal-raisin cookies for dessert."

"So that's what smelled so good in there." Dusty glanced toward Karen. If she was as hungry as he was…

"Thirty minutes is all it will take to eat." Yuli slapped Dusty on the back. "Not worth riding home hungry to save thirty minutes. Celia's fried chicken is the best, and her cookies have won awards at the fair."

Smiling her reply, Karen nodded.

"Okay." Dusty laughed. "Okay. Don't torture us anymore. We'll stay."

A dust cloud rose above the road from the highway, alerting Sophia that she was about to have company. A number of people from church had come calling this past week, most of them bringing food. She wondered what delectable dish they would be sampling for supper tonight.

But it was a stranger who disembarked from the long, black luxury car after it came to a halt in front of the house.

Don't let Karen go, a small voice repeated in her heart.

A shiver ran through Sophia as the man walked toward the porch.

Thursday, May 8, 1941

Dear Diary,

It is true. Mikkel is working with the resistance. He does not know I have discovered the truth, and I am torn about what to do. I fear for him.

If the Germans were to discover it, what might they do to him?

Esther

Wednesday, June 18, 1941

Dear Diary,

I am pregnant. I can no longer doubt it. Tomorrow I will tell Mikkel. I am happy, and yet, I am afraid. Life here is tenuous. Is it right to bring a child into a world overrun with evil? Nutritious food is hard to come by. Everything is rationed due to the war.

And Mikkel takes so many risks. I know, even though he never tells me what he does. But I can see the truth in his eyes. He seldom sleeps.

When we were married four years ago this month, I thought we would live a quiet life, serving the people of this church in Copenhagen for a while, and then serving another in some small American town. I imagined us with a couple of children and a serene home life. I never suspected we would still be in Denmark four years later or that the world would be at war.

We do not know the future, do we, God? Only You know. But You are here with me. It is not Your desire for me to fear, for Your word says You have not given me a spirit of fear. Help me lean upon Your strength, no matter what the future holds. In Jesus' name. Amen.

Esther

P.S. I sometimes wonder if there is not more I could do to help. Surely it is God's will to stop the killing of innocent people.

Sunday, November 9, 1941

Dear Diary,

   Winter is hard upon us, and I am cold much of the time. I try not to complain, but it is hard not to sometimes.

   We are hiding two telegraphists from the British Secret Intelligence Service in the church. They parachuted into Denmark and made their way to Copenhagen. Their equipment was smashed upon landing, and they needed the aid of a Danish radio engineer who is working with the local resistance.

   Mikkel wants me to stop helping in the resistance efforts, especially now that I am so big with child. In truth, there is a part of me that wants to stop too. But as long as my husband is involved, as long as God is directing him to help end this war, how can I stay hidden in the house?

   And there is something inside of me, a place in my heart, that keeps driving me to do what I can. Even when I am afraid, there is a stronger sense of peace. So I continue because God sustains me.

   The LORD is my light and my salvation; whom shall I fear? the LORD is the strength of my life; of whom shall I be afraid? When the wicked, even mine enemies and my foes, came upon me to eat up my flesh, they stumbled and fell. Though an host should encamp against me, my heart shall not fear: though war should rise against me, in this will I be confident. One thing have I desired of the LORD, that will I seek after; that I may dwell in the house of the LORD all the days of my life, to behold the beauty of the LORD, and to enquire in his temple. For in the time of trouble he shall hide me in his pavilion: in the secret of his tabernacle shall he hide me; he shall set me up upon a rock. And now shall mine head be lifted up above mine enemies round about me: therefore will I offer in his tabernacle sacrifices of joy; I will sing, yea, I will sing praises unto the LORD. (Psalm 27:1-6)

Esther

Celia Basterra's cooking was everything Yuli had promised and then some. Karen hadn't realized how hungry she was until she started to dish up a second helping of crisp apple salad with marshmallows, walnuts, and some sort of sweet, creamy dressing.

"You'll have to give me the recipe for this salad," she told Celia.

"Oh, it's easy. I won't even have to write it down."

Karen released a self-deprecating laugh. "Trust me. You'll need to write it down. And include *all* the details. I'm a dreadful cook."

"Don't believe her," Dusty said to their hostess. "Karen may be a novice in the kitchen, but she's *not* dreadful. In fact, I think I've gained a few pounds since she came to the ranch."

The praise fell over Karen like a warm down comforter on a cold winter's night.

"I'd be happy to write it down," Celia said. "Just give me a minute or two." She rose from her chair and walked to an antique buffet on the far side of the large kitchen. Once there, she opened the lower right cabinet door and withdrew a recipe card from a box.

The phone rang.

"I'll get it, hon." Yuli crossed to the wall phone. "Hello?" After a moment's pause, he said, "Just a minute." He held out the phone. "Dusty, it's Miss Sophie."

Karen exchanged a quick glance with him before he went to take the phone from Yuli.

"Sophia? What is it?" He listened. Then his gaze darted back to Karen. "We're on our way."

She stood. The instant he said good-bye and hung up, she asked, "Is something wrong with Grandmother?"

"No." He shrugged. "We've got an unexpected guest at the ranch. That's all. But she wants us to hurry back."

His effort to look and sound nonchalant didn't fool her. She knew it was something more than what he was telling her. But she decided not to press for information. She would have her answers soon enough.

They thanked the Basterras for the delicious meal, then left the house. Minutes later, they were mounted on their horses and riding away from the farm. They followed the same trail as that morning, but they kept a faster pace on the return trip.

Dusty's haste wasn't lost on Karen. Admit it or not, he wasn't happy about the unnamed guest who was waiting at the Golden T.

❦

Sophia prayed silently and fervently as she watched Mac Gleason stroll around the barnyard. He looked at the outbuildings, corrals, and livestock as if he were actually interested in them. She knew better. This was a man in a hurry, eager to finish his business and be on his way.

Lord, I don't know what he wants here, but I pray your protection over all of us. Especially Karen, Father. She's so close to finding Your truth. So close. Prepare her heart. Open her eyes and her ears.

She remembered her dream of that morning.

Esther told me not to let Karen go. Lord, I don't know if that dream was merely a product of my own imagination or if it was Your way of speaking to me in advance. Whatever it was, I ask You to keep Karen here if that's what's best for her. Only You know what's best, but for myself, I want to keep her here. I love her. She is so dear to me, a treasure in my old age.

She remembered watching Dusty and Karen riding out this morning. They hadn't known she was up and about, of course, but she'd seen them, and she'd been glad.

Jesus, those two young people love each other. I can't help believing You brought them together for more than just one summer. Protect them, Lord. Protect them both. Help them to hear You.

"Miss Sophie?"

She opened her eyes. "Yes, Patty?"

"Is that man here to take Karen away?"

"I don't know." She took the girl's hand between both of hers. "He didn't tell me why he'd come. Only that he needs to see Karen."

"I don't like him."

Sophia shook her head. "Don't be quick to make judgments, my dear." Sound advice, even though she didn't want to follow it herself. Everything inside her wanted to dislike the stranger too. She feared his presence at the Golden T would spell trouble and heartache for them all.

Take this fear from me, Father. I know it isn't of You.

Dusty's mood grew darker the closer they got to the ranch. He tried to pray, but he couldn't. Maybe that was because he didn't want to ask for the Lord's will to be done. He wanted Karen to stay. He wanted Karen to marry him.

He'd never asked for much, but this he wanted. Wanted it with all his heart.

He didn't have to meet Mac Gleason to know that her friend, as she'd described him in the past, had come to take her back to California. What Dusty didn't know was, would she go?

❧

Karen squinted her eyes against the bright September sunlight as the horses trotted the last quarter mile. She could see the ranch house, and she could see the black automobile parked near the porch. It looked like a new-model Town Car. Not many of those driving around Owyhee County.

She glanced toward Dusty. They'd spoken nary a word for miles, and his forbidding expression didn't encourage her to try again.

She looked forward, this time noticing a man in a suit stepping off the porch. There was something familiar about—

"Mac?" she whispered. Then she grinned. "Mac!" She nudged the paint into a canter.

The minute she reached the barnyard, she drew her horse to a halt and slipped from the saddle. A few quick strides carried her to him and straight into his bear-hugging embrace.

"Oh, Mac, it's good to see you."

"I'd say the same, except I haven't got much of a look at you yet."

She stepped back and waited while he gave her a thorough perusal.

After a long while, he said, "You look more than good, Karen. You look happy."

"I *am* happy."

"Good." Mac looked behind her.

She turned to see Dusty dismounting. She walked over to him, took hold of his hand, then drew him back to where Mac was waiting. "Dusty, I want you to meet Mac Gleason, a dear and trusted friend. He was my father's attorney."

The two men shook hands.

"What brings you to Idaho?" Dusty asked, his voice a bit gruff. No. It was almost unfriendly.

That wasn't like him, Karen thought as she watched the two men.

They were each sizing up the other with wary gazes. She half expected them to start circling and growling like a couple of dogs fighting over a bone.

And I'm the bone! She nearly laughed aloud at the surprising insight.

She slipped her arm through Mac's and drew him toward the house. "Come onto the porch and sit down. I'm going to freshen up. We've been herding cattle, and I'm covered with dust from the trail."

"Herding cattle?" Mac chuckled.

She elbowed him. "Don't say it." She returned his grin. "Don't you dare say it."

Karen thought Dusty might follow her into the house, but he didn't. She paused in the doorway, glancing over her shoulder. He was sitting on the porch rail, watching their guest with obvious displeasure.

She decided she'd better hurry.

❧

Mac Gleason was old enough to be Karen's father. Pushing sixty, judging by the gray in his hair and his time-weathered face. Handsome. Distinguished looking in a suit that probably cost enough to support the youth camp for a full summer session. Or longer.

A dear and trusted friend, Karen had called him. Her father's attorney.

What was the honorable Mr. Gleason doing at the Golden T? Dusty had felt twinges of jealousy over this man before. He remembered when Mac had called Karen a couple of months ago. He'd feared then that they were or had been involved. He didn't think so anymore. Not after seeing them together. Yet he wasn't comforted. Mac Gleason had come to Idaho for a reason, and Dusty suspected the reason wasn't going to make him happy.

"Much better," Karen called as she came through the doorway.

Her gaze met Dusty's.

I should've told her I love her. I should've done it before now.

She glanced toward Mac. "I still can't believe you're here," she said to him. "Did you look around the place while you were waiting?"

"Yes."

"Too bad you didn't come this summer while the boys were here." She sat on the chair next to Mac. "Dusty runs a youth camp in the summer months. The boys live in the bunkhouse and learn to ride and rope and all sorts of things."

Mac looked at Dusty. "Really? Sounds interesting. You'll have to tell me more about it."

"Another time maybe," Dusty replied. "For now, why don't you tell us why you're here? It must be important for you to come all this way."

"Yes. It is important." Mac returned his gaze to Karen. "I've brought good news."

"Good news?" she echoed, sounding curious. Nothing more.

"Something's come to light, and I didn't want to tell you over the phone. Too good for that. It seems your father didn't leave you totally impoverished."

"What are you talking about, Mac?"

"There's money in an account we only recently discovered.

Money the IRS can't attach. It's complicated to explain, but the bottom line is, it's yours, Karen."

"What's mine?"

"Over three hundred thousand dollars."

"Three hundred..." Her eyes widened in disbelief. She looked at Dusty. "Three hundred thousand dollars?"

"Yes," Mac answered. "But I need you in California. This could take months to untangle."

Dusty pushed off the porch railing. "This sounds like something the two of you should talk over alone." He turned toward the steps. "I'll take care of the horses."

Then he strode away before anyone could see that his heart had just broken in two.

Thursday, December 11, 1941

Dear Diary,

It was reported on the BBC's Danish news bulletin that, in support of their Japanese ally, Germany and Italy have declared war upon America. Mikkel says it is all the more important our foreign identity be concealed. We have carried forged papers almost since the war began, but I wonder how long it will be before the German Gestapo finds us out.

My God reigns, and the joy of the Lord is my strength. God cannot fail, nor is He discouraged. He will keep me in perfect peace because I trust in Him.

Esther

Friday, January 2, 1942

Dear Diary,

I spent the day in the nursery. Mikkel was away again. He does not tell me where he goes or what he does. He says it is better I not know. My darling Mikkel seeks to protect me.

I grow eager for the birth of this baby. When my fear of the future threatens to overwhelm me, I remember the promise God gave me about my descendants. Faith is believing things not seen, not in believing those things that can be seen. And so by faith, I trust God will do all He has said He will do.

I made a rag doll for the baby. I remember many years ago when Sophia taught me how to make my first rag doll. I was six or seven at the time. We sat at the kitchen table. It was winter, as it is now, and there was snow on the ground. The wind blew around the corners of the house and whistled beneath the eaves, rattling the windowpanes. But Mama had a fire burning bright in the stove, and the kitchen was toasty warm.

Sophia was so very patient as she taught me what she knew. It was a wonderful day. I wish I had brought that doll with me from America instead of leaving it packed in a trunk in Papa's attic.

Does Sophia still have her doll? Does she ever look at it and remember me kindly?

I wish my sister could be with me when I give birth. I miss her in countless ways. I long to know if she has found contentment, if she has forgiven me, both for the wrongs she thinks I did her and for the wrongs I am guilty of.

Perhaps she is married. Perhaps she has a child or children of her own. It has been nearly three years since I have had a letter from home. It is terrible not to know how they fare in these troubled times.

O God in heaven, let Sophia know how much I love her, have always loved her.

Esther

Sophia awakened before dawn. She didn't rise to turn up the heat, even though the air in her bedroom was cold. To do so would risk waking Karen, who slept on the cot in the parlor. Instead, she remained in bed, her comforter tucked around her for warmth.

Father, I don't want Karen to leave us. Dusty doesn't want her to leave us. How do we stop her? Or should we try to stop her? Maybe she's meant to leave us. Was my dream of Esther from You? Was it a warning or merely my imagination? I don't know. I don't know what to do or what to say. Help me, Lord.

She opened her Bible, but the words seemed to float before her eyes, a jumble of letters that made no sense.

"Thou wilt keep him in perfect peace," she quoted from memory, the words as familiar to her as her own name, "whose mind is stayed on thee: because he trusteth in thee."

Poor Karen. It was clear she was torn, that she didn't know which direction to turn. And Sophia felt ill equipped to advise her. After all, three hundred thousand dollars was a fortune.

She closed her eyes and whispered, "Trust in the LORD with all thine heart; and lean not unto thine own understanding."

She knew she could play upon Karen's affection for her. If she protested that, because of her heart condition and poor health, she needed Karen to stay, then she would stay. But Sophia also knew she couldn't ask Karen *not* to go with her attorney. It wouldn't be fair. It wouldn't be reasonable.

Poor Dusty. She knew he was equally torn. Because he loved Karen, he wanted to do what was right. He didn't want to impose his wants and desires upon her. Poor boy. The poor dear boy. He thought he was hiding his true feelings, but Sophia could see through to his aching heart.

Jesus, apart from You, I'm helpless. I'm an old woman. I have little in the way of worldly possessions. I don't have any answers, but I know You have all the answers. You're the Author and Perfecter of my faith. We need to see You moving in a divine and miraculous way.

Karen wasn't asleep. She didn't think she'd slept more than half an hour all night long. She'd tossed and turned for hours.

What am I supposed to do? What's the right thing to do?

A year or two ago, she wouldn't have thought three hundred thousand dollars was all that much. She could have easily spent it in one summer in Europe. But those days were gone. Three hundred thousand dollars meant a lot. It could change everything.

Is this *what I have to give up, God? Then I'm not sure I can do it. Why* should *I do it?*

She'd seen the way Mac looked at the ranch. He'd been nothing short of appalled by the lack of amenities. It hadn't surprised her when he'd declined Dusty's offer of a bed in the bunkhouse, opting instead to drive to Nampa and stay in a motel. He'd promised to return this morning.

What am I going to tell him?

She wished her grandmother or Dusty had told her what to do, but they hadn't. Nor would they. She knew she would have to decide for herself.

"I wish I believed in You the way they do," she whispered.

She waited a moment. Hoping...

But God didn't speak.

With a sigh, she turned on the lamp next to her cot and reached for the twelfth of the thirteen journals.

"Maybe I shouldn't feel so sorry for myself. It could be worse. I could be in Esther's shoes, couldn't I?"

She opened the book and looked at the familiar script

without reading it. It was strange, how close she felt to this young woman. Through these entries, she'd watched Esther grow from an innocent child on an Oregon farm to a minister's wife living in a war-torn country, a woman living out each day with courage and faith.

She smoothed her fingers over the open book. "I wish I had her faith."

It seemed to Karen that Esther had never wavered. Not once in all those years. Not when her own sister had turned away in anger and bitterness. Not when she'd felt so alone and out of place in Denmark. Not even when her little daughter had died or when she'd miscarried her second child.

"What would Esther have done if she were me?" she asked aloud.

Of course, there was no answer to that question either.

She began to read, hoping it would take her mind off the decision she had yet to make.

Bundled in a down-filled coat, his breath forming tiny clouds in front of his face, Dusty set about his morning chores while the earth and sky blended together in shades of gray. According to the calendar, autumn was officially a week away, but Dusty knew it wouldn't be long before flurries of snow fell.

Would Karen be at the Golden T to see that first snowfall of the season? Or would she be enjoying the California sunshine with some of her old friends?

He wished he knew. He wished he could read her mind.

He'd almost gone up to the house to see her last night after Mac Gleason left. He'd almost told her he loved her and wanted her to stay, to marry him, to forget the money her attorney had found.

But he hadn't done it. He couldn't.

Not then. Not now.

This was a decision she had to make on her own. And whatever that decision was, Dusty was going to have to live with it too.

DELIGHT IN ME, MY SON, AND I WILL GIVE YOU THE DESIRES OF YOUR HEART. THAT IS MY PROMISE TO ALL WHO BELIEVE IN MY NAME.

The moment the Voice touched his heart, Dusty stopped in his tracks, struck by the truth. He'd been expecting the worst. He'd been preparing himself for heartache and disappointment.

But if he truly believed God wanted the best for him, then his expectations should be just the opposite. He should expect that, no matter what happened, joy would be the result. Joy rather than sorrow.

Forgive me, Father.

Once before he'd relinquished Karen into God's tender care, but somewhere along the line, he'd taken her back.

Lord, You have only good in mind for us. I give you Karen, and I trust You to do what is best in her life and in mine. You know I love her, but You love her even more. Whatever comes, whatever tomorrow may bring, I'll delight in You all the days of my life, for You are the foremost desire of my heart.

A sense of peace washed over him, pervaded him, the first peace he'd felt since learning of Mac Gleason's arrival at the Golden T.

"This is the day that the Lord has made," he said aloud as he looked up at the brightening sky. "I will rejoice and be glad in it."

Friday, January 9, 1942

Father God, we thank You for our daughter, Margaret Rose Christiansen, born at 2:00 this morning, healthy and beautiful. I give her to You, Jesus, and ask You to keep her safe. Draw her to You. Let her know You early in her earthly walk.

In Your blessed name I ask it. Amen.

Twenty-Seven

Karen stared at the words in the journal, awash in disbelief.

Margaret Rose Christiansen.

January 9, 1942.

It couldn't be. It couldn't mean...

But it could and it did.

Even as she tried to deny it, she knew it was true. Her mother was the daughter of Esther Christiansen, not of Sophia Taylor.

Which meant Karen wasn't Sophia's granddaughter.

Tears stung her eyes as a sharp sense of grief and loss pierced her heart. It was as if someone she loved had died.

Why didn't Grandmother tell me? She closed her eyes. *But she isn't really my grandmother, is she?*

Following on the heels of her hurt came anger.

Why does everyone lie to me?

But Sophia hadn't lied to her really. She'd given Karen these journals. She'd known if Karen read them she would realize what this entry meant.

But why? *Why?*

"If You're trying to tell me something, God," she muttered beneath her breath, "why don't You just come right out and say it, clear and plain?"

Her words were almost a dare to the Almighty.

"It was easier when I didn't care." She tossed aside the blankets, sat up, and reached for her robe. "It was easier when I didn't have any questions or want any answers." She rose from her cot and headed for the bathroom, pausing long enough in the hall to bump up the thermostat.

Three hundred thousand dollars would mean nice clothes, a nice home, a nice car. And a warm house without drafts! That kind of money would mean she could travel and go to parties. She could forget looking for answers. She could *live!*

She turned the faucet in the shower. While waiting for hot water to reach the bathroom, she shucked off her robe and pajamas. A couple of minutes later, she stood beneath the spray, her head dropped back as tiny needles of water massaged her scalp, steam forming a thick cloud around her.

For a short while, her mind was blank, aware only of the pleasurable feel of the hot water upon her skin. Then, unexpectedly, she thought of Alan Ivie, her erstwhile fiancé.

Wouldn't *he* be surprised if she returned to their former haunts, showing up at the same parties and charity events he attended?

When she'd first arrived in Idaho, that had been her greatest desire. To acquire enough money so she could return to Los Angeles, so she could go back to her old way of life, so she could make Alan and her other so-called friends regret how they'd treated her. It was all she'd thought about, all she'd dreamed about.

But now?

She pressed her back against the tiled wall. "What do I want now?"

Another image came to her mind. Another man, but this one as different from Alan as day was from night.

"Oh, Dusty." She closed her eyes. "What does any of this mean for us?"

WAIT.

Wait for what?

WAIT.

I'm tired of waiting.

She bumped her head against the shower wall.

I'm tired of wanting.

She bumped it again.

I'm tired of wondering.

And yet again.

"I'm tired...I'm tired...I'm *tired!*"

She didn't realize she was crying until she heard a soft rap on the door.

"Karen, are you okay?" Patty called from the hallway.

She turned off the shower. "Yes." She wiped away the tears. "I'm all right. I'll be out in a few minutes."

❧

The atmosphere at breakfast that Sunday morning was strained. Gazes met briefly, and then both parties looked away, as if eye contact were a dangerous thing.

As he ate, Dusty tried to come up with something to say that would break the tension. But every word, every thought, was second-guessed, then discarded as useless—or worse.

Patty was the first to crack. "What's *wrong* with everybody?" she demanded in that tone common to teenaged girls.

The three adults glanced her way.

"*Well?* Why doesn't somebody ask Karen what she's gonna do? Is she staying or going?"

Sophia set down her fork. "Patty's right. What *is* wrong with us?" She turned toward Karen. "Have you decided what you're going to tell Mr. Gleason?"

"No." Karen shook her head slowly.

Dusty felt a spark of hope. Did that mean she might stay?

She pushed her plate back from the edge of the table and lifted her gaze to meet Sophia's. "Tell me about my real grandmother."

Dusty thought he'd misunderstood her.

"Why did Mother never tell me about her?" she continued in a near whisper.

"Because she never knew," Sophia answered.

"She never knew. Then tell me why she came to live with you? Why didn't she stay with her parents in Denmark?"

Sophia answered with a question of her own. "How far have you read?"

"The day of her birth."

"Then you have a ways to go yet." Sophia paused before saying, "I'd rather you wait to ask me more until you've finished reading the last journal. Esther should tell you as much as she is able in her own words."

Dusty was totally confused. It was like coming into a theater in the middle of a movie.

"My dear girl." Sophia covered Karen's hand with her own. "Esther loved her daughter very much. You know it's true. When Maggie came to live with Bradley and me, we loved her as our own daughter. But I didn't show it as I should have, and as time passed, Maggie came to resent me because of it." She closed her eyes. A sigh escaped her. "God alone really knows why things happen the way they do. What I do know is, Esther had an unshakable faith in Jesus, and He was the guiding factor in all she did. She was a true woman of God." She looked at Karen again. "She would have delighted in you, as I do. Knowing you, loving you, has been my greatest blessing this summer. And you *are* my granddaughter and forever will be."

Without a word, Karen rose from her chair. She gave Sophia a wistful smile, then walked across the kitchen, grabbed her coat from the rack, and headed outside.

Dusty stared at the closed door. "Do you want me to go after her?"

"No. Leave her be. She has much to consider."

❦

Karen shrugged deeper inside her coat as she walked. She had no particular destination. She simply needed to move rather than to sit still.

It doesn't matter if she isn't really my grandmother. I don't need her any longer. I don't have to stay. I've got options. For the first time in a long time, I've got options. I can decide for myself what's best for me. I don't have to depend on anyone else.

She turned up her collar to protect her ears.

Why am I confused? The money's mine. Of course I want it. Of course I should go back with Mac. It's a no-brainer. Three hundred thousand dollars isn't something I can walk away from.

She tried to envision herself beside some crystal blue swimming pool, basking in the California sun and sipping a piña colada. Strangely, it was no longer a tempting daydream.

The memory of yesterday returned to her. Riding beside Dusty, watching an eagle as it soared above the high canyon walls, rounding up a small herd of stray cattle for the Basterras, sitting at a neighbor's kitchen table and talking, eating, laughing. All of it seemed so much more appealing to her.

She stopped, drew in a deep breath, and let it out slowly.

She knew now what she was going to do.

❧

"I'm not going back with you, Mac," Karen told her friend as they stood together on the front porch.

"But, Karen—"

"No. I've made up my mind." She touched his arm. "My presence isn't required, and we both know it. You thought you were doing me a favor by saying I had to go back. I understand that. But whatever forms and documents I need to sign can be signed in Idaho as well as in California. The postman stops at our mailbox every day of the week, and Federal Express and UPS deliver even way out here."

"I don't think you—"

"Mac, you are the one true friend I had when my life fell

apart. Don't think I don't know it. I understand what you see when you look around this place." She let her gaze roam over the yard and outbuildings. Then she looked beyond the rolling, sage-covered desert to the rugged mountain peaks. "I felt the same when I first got here. But there's so much more. So much more. Beautiful, really, if you look deep enough."

"Well, I'll be," he whispered.

She smiled. "Don't think it didn't surprise me, too." She looked at him. "It still does. A little."

"I like your grandmother."

"She's wonderful, isn't she?"

Mac raised an eyebrow. "And Mr. Stoddard?"

"He's wonderful too."

"Ahh."

"So you'll send me whatever papers I need to sign?"

"I will." He leaned forward and kissed her cheek. "Stay happy, Karen." His smile was warm. "I'm betting you will."

Friday, June 5, 1942

Dear Diary,

Today is our fifth wedding anniversary. Where is the young girl who married Mikkel Christiansen? Who was she? I see no sign of her. What innocence she possessed. How sheltered her life. There are times when I miss her.

Mikkel refuses to carry a weapon as he performs his work for the resistance. He says he could never take the life of another human being. And, he asks, for what other reason would he carry a weapon than to harm or to kill? I do not know if he is right. If a German soldier were to enter our home and threaten Margaret Rose, would I not do anything to save her? Even fire a gun?

Ah, my little Rose. How beautiful she is. She sat up, unassisted, today. I think her hair, still as fair as her father's, will be curly, lucky girl. She is such a good baby, happy and smiling, her pale blue eyes sparkling with merriment. She has no understanding of the world outside the walls of this house.

God in heaven, protect us. Save my child from the enemy without.

Esther

....

Sunday, July 19, 1942

Dear Diary,

It is nearly midnight, and I have slipped from our bedroom while Mikkel sleeps, to write, my mind too active to find rest.

When we retired for the night, Mikkel drew me to him, his need strong. As we lay nestled in each other's arms, he reminded me it was six years ago today that we met one another. It was his first Sunday to preach at our little church in Oregon, and I was a girl of only seventeen. He told me he began to fall in love with me on that morning. Then he said his love has multiplied a hundredfold in the years since. He called me beautiful in face and in spirit and quoted Proverbs 31 to me, saying the verses described me. He thanked me for little Sophie and for our Rose, for being his wife and their mother. He thanked me for seeking the Lord's will and setting an example for him and for our children. He called me courageous.

I had the horrible feeling he was telling me good-bye. He never said the word. It was only a feeling, but one I cannot shake.

This morning, in his sermon, Mikkel said we cannot halt for long between two opinions, that we must stop hesitating and step out for the Lord. He said as Christians we must choose to turn over our free will to the future God has in mind for us. If we remain stubborn, if we are afraid to step out for Him, then He will use someone else. But God's work will be done, even if we miss the blessing of being used by Him because of our own selfishness.

Was Mikkel speaking to us, the members of the congregation, or to himself?

Father God, keep me from halting between two opinions. Help me to step out for You. Keep me from being double-minded. Let me ask in faith, nothing wavering. For she that wavereth is like a wave of the sea driven with the wind and tossed. For let not that woman think she shall receive anything of the Lord. A double-minded woman is unstable in all her ways.

And protect Mikkel, Lord God. Keep him in the safety of Your arms. Amen.

Twenty-Eight

Dusty waited a full month to say what he wanted to say to Karen. Perhaps it was because he kept expecting her to change her mind, to announce she was going back to Los Angeles after all. But she didn't. She remained at the Golden T, caring for her grandmother, befriending Patty in countless ways, working beside Dusty wherever she was needed.

On that frosty October evening, with a full harvest moon to light their way and a dusting of the year's first snow covering the ground, Dusty and Karen went for a horseback ride. He led the way to the same bluff where he'd taken her back in June, shortly after she'd arrived at the ranch. Another lifetime ago, it seemed. So much had changed since then.

They rode in silence, except for snow-muffled hoofbeats, both of them lost in private thoughts.

Karen was the first to speak when they reached their destination. "Oh, Dusty. It's glorious."

Before them stretched the desert, glowing frosty white in the moonlight, a glittering wonderland.

"I thought you'd like it." He dismounted, then stepped over to her horse.

"I do." She slipped from the saddle. "It's more beautiful than anything I've ever seen."

He took her hand and drew her toward the edge of the bluff. When they stopped, he put his arm around her shoulders and stared at the wintry scene below while searching for the right words to say.

But he knew the words. He merely had to speak them.

"Karen?"

She leaned her head against his shoulder. "Hmm."

"I love you."

She straightened, turned toward him, and gazed upward with wide eyes.

"I love you. I don't have much to offer you, except my heart."

"Oh, Dusty," she whispered. "That's a great deal to offer a woman."

He cradled her face between his gloved hands and bent down to kiss her. She leaned into him. The kiss was even sweeter than the last one they'd shared, perhaps because of all that had happened in the weeks between.

When their lips parted, he whispered, "Will you marry me, Karen?"

"I can't."

It wasn't the response he'd hoped for, and his expression must have revealed it.

She pressed one hand against his chest. "I love you, too. Far more than I thought possible. But I can't marry you. Not yet. Not until I can be the wife you need me to be."

"You *are* the wife I need."

"No." Tears glittered in her eyes. "I'm not. Not yet anyway." She stepped out of his embrace, out of his reach. "Grandmother told me once that none of the differences between you and me mattered except for the matter of faith. She said what you believe and what I believe had to be the same or it would keep us apart. She was right."

"But I've watched you. You've changed. You *do* believe what I believe."

She smiled, but it was a sad smile. "I'm *trying* to believe it, Dusty. But something is still missing. Something I see in you and in Grandmother. Something I see in the people at church. Something I saw in Billy when he was with us. I can't explain it. I only know it hasn't happened inside of me."

Dusty didn't need her to explain. He knew. Deep in his heart, he knew. And he knew she was right to want them to wait.

"I don't want to lose you," she said softly.

"I'm not going anywhere."

"I've asked you to be patient before. I have no right to expect—"

"You have every right, even if patience isn't my strong suit." He chuckled, though he didn't feel like it.

She tipped her face skyward, staring up at the moon. "I was a stranger to love all my life. I never received it. I never gave it. But ever since I got here, I've been surrounded by it. I've seen love in action in the things you do. I've heard it in the things you say. And no matter how undeserving I've been..." She let her words trail into silence.

"We love because He first loved us."

"That's from the Bible, isn't it?"

"First John. It's in the New Testament."

She looked at him. "Say the verse again."

"We love because He first loved us."

"Is that why you fell in love with me?"

"At first, it was the only way I *could* love you." He smiled tenderly. "With His love. Then it became something more." His voice lowered. "Much more."

❦

As happened all too frequently of late, Sophia fell asleep in her chair while reading. When she awakened, she heard music playing on the clock radio in the kitchen. She set the book aside, then rose and walked from the parlor into the adjoining room.

Patty stood at the door, her back toward Sophia, staring through the glass at the moonlit night.

"Have they returned?" Sophia asked.

Patty glanced over her shoulder, then quickly turned back to the window. But not before Sophia saw her tear-stained cheeks.

"My dear." She went straightaway to the girl. "Whatever's the matter?"

"Everything."

Sophia placed her hands on Patty's shoulders. "Surely not *everything*."

"Daddy didn't even call me for my birthday." She choked back a sob. "He hates me."

"Oh no. He doesn't hate you. He's confused and he's angry. But I'm quite sure he doesn't hate you."

The girl turned suddenly toward Sophia. "Why'd I have to do something so dumb? Why'd I let Junkman talk me into it? He never loved me." She fell into Sophia's arms and wept in earnest now.

Sophia let Patty cry herself out, all the while stroking her back and her hair and murmuring soft words of encouragement. After a time, the girl's sobs turned to small hiccups and, finally, to an occasional sigh. Then Sophia guided her to the kitchen table and urged her to sit on a chair.

"I'll make some hot cocoa," she said. "And then you should go to bed and get some rest."

Patty was silent as Sophia moved about the kitchen, pouring milk into a pan and warming it on the stove, measuring cocoa from its container and stirring it into the milk until it was precisely the right color, then pouring the hot chocolate into two large mugs. Only after Sophia had set a mug in front of Patty and had settled herself onto a second chair did the girl speak.

"Am I as awful as my dad says?"

"Oh, Patty."

"I know what we did was wrong." She stared into the mug, held between two hands. "I knew it all along. But Junkman was so persuasive, and I thought I loved him. I thought he loved me, too." She squeezed her eyes shut. "But he didn't. Not even after I gave in."

Sophia touched the back of Patty's hand, causing her to look up. "Listen to me, dear. God meant for such intimacy to be something special shared between a husband and wife. When we break the laws of God, when we covet and lust and act willfully, we pay a price. But God is merciful, and He's forgiving. All we need do is confess our sins and ask His forgiveness. He won't refuse you." She paused a moment, then continued, "You'll get through this, Patty. After the baby comes, you'll go back to school and grow up and graduate. And someday you'll meet the man God intends for you, and you'll marry. Then you'll know the beauty of married love." She stroked the girl's cheek. "In its proper time."

Patty nodded, as if accepting what had been said.

"Drink your cocoa, dear."

The girl glanced toward the window. "Do you think Dusty and Karen will get married?"

"I don't know," Sophia answered softly. "I hope so. They love each other. Of that I'm sure."

❧

Karen wondered if she was making the worst mistake of her life. Everything inside her screamed she was. Everything told her to hurl herself back into Dusty's arms and accept his proposal, to ask him to save her from her own decision.

Except she knew it wasn't his job to save her. She'd even told him so, months ago—although she hadn't been talking about herself at the time; she's been talking about the boys at the ranch.

"You're shivering," he said, interrupting her thoughts. "We'd better start back."

"Could I ask a favor first?"

"Sure. Anything."

"Kiss me again before we go."

His soft laughter warmed her as much as his embrace could. "My pleasure, Miss Butler."

Her senses were on full alert as he drew her close and covered her mouth with his. She wanted to memorize every detail, in case it never happened again, in case she had thrown away her one chance for real happiness.

His skin smelled faintly of cologne, warm and woodsy. His mouth tasted of mint-flavored mouthwash. His cheek felt scratchy from his five o'clock shadow. She could hear the beat of his heart. Or was that her own pulse pounding in her ears?

This is crazy. His love should be enough.

But it wasn't enough. She wanted God's love, too. She wanted to *know* God's love, not simply be told about it. Somehow she had to find it.

Before it was too late.

Tuesday, September 1, 1942

Dear Diary,

Hannah has tried to hide it, but she is expecting another baby in the spring. She is much too thin because she gives her food to the children. There is great terror in her eyes. Isaac is working with Mikkel in the resistance, but unlike my husband, Isaac carries a weapon. I think he is helping in assaults on German officers. Of course, we never speak of this. There is a wall of pretense between us now that did not used to be there.

What of Mama and Papa and Sophia? Are they well? Are they safe? Did Papa sell the farm? Do they still live in Oregon? It has been a long time since I heard from them. Mikkel says getting a letter from them would be as dangerous as sending one. He has not allowed me to try to smuggle a letter out to them via the resistance. He says we must wait until the war is over.

Will it ever be over? Sometimes I think not.

Esther

Friday, November 6, 1942

Dear Diary,

I feel old. I am not yet twenty-four, but I feel as old as Grandfather Fritz must have felt before he died.

I am hungry. I long to be in one of the orchards near the farm, up in the arms of a leafy-green tree, cradled by the branches while I shake salt onto an apple, then take a big bite. I can close my eyes and almost savor the taste, can almost feel the juice as it trickles down my chin. I would thin apples for many hours for free just for a chance to do that once again. Or to eat a steak. Imagine eating beef from a cow Papa raised and butchered. Or the beans or sweet peas raised in Mama's garden. Wouldn't they taste heavenly?

I am cold, too. I wish it were summer again. I long for a hot dry August day with dirt whirling off the fields. I long to hear Mama complaining as she tries to keep dust from settling on her furniture. I wish I could jump onto the back of an old plow horse, maybe ride down to the pond and go for a swim.

I am sometimes lonely. I wish I could be with Sophia, the two of us seated at the piano, playing a duet. I wish I could hug her and whisper my deepest secrets in her ear.

Help me, Jesus, to remember that by Your grace I'm an overcomer rather than being overcome. I'm a conqueror rather than being conquered.

Esther

Saturday, November 21, 1942

Dear Diary,

The Germans have sent a new general, Hermann von Hanneken, to Denmark to secure the country against invasion. They are afraid, and it has emboldened the resistance. Mikkel thinks the tide has turned in favor of the Allies. But tension grows, and I fear we have not yet seen the darkest hour.

                              Esther

Twenty-Nine

Early November brought with it bitter winds. They whistled across the rolling desert and buffeted the small ranch house relentlessly. Sophia felt the cold more than ever before, and she spent much of her time in her chair near the small wood stove in the parlor.

The house was quiet on this Wednesday morning. Dusty had taken a job doing carpentry work for a family who lived about twenty-five miles east of the Golden T. Karen had driven Patty into Caldwell for her monthly obstetrics exam.

Sophia looked down at the shoe box resting on her lap. She'd retrieved it from the shelf in her closet about fifteen minutes before, but she had yet to open it. Now, with a soft sigh, she lifted the lid.

To the casual eye, there was nothing dramatic about the contents of the box. They were merely an odd assortment of keepsakes, reminders of a life gone by.

The first item she removed was a hair ribbon. At one time, it had been as bright as a peacock's tail feather. After lots of use and the passing of more than seventy years, it had faded to a nondescript color. Not quite blue. Not quite gray.

❦

"Stand still, Sophia. I'll never get your hair brushed if you continue to dance around."

"I can't help it. I'm going to school, Mama. Will I like it? Will the teacher like me?"

"Everyone will like you, my little angel."

"Esther has to stay home. She's still a baby. I'm six."

"That's unkind to your sister. Now don't move while I tie this ribbon in your hair. See. It's the same color as your dress."

"Oh, Mama. I've never had a satin ribbon for my hair before." *Despite her mother's command to stay still, Sophia turned and gave her a big hug. "Thank you, Mama."*

"You're welcome, darling."

❦

Sophia rubbed the ribbon against her cheek, her eyes closed. Was it her imagination or did the scent of lemon verbena linger in the air? It had been her mother's favorite toilet water.

How superior she'd felt because she got to go to school while Esther had to stay home. But the feeling hadn't lasted. She'd been lonely at school without her sister. She'd missed her.

"I still miss you, Esther," she whispered. "I'll be glad when I see you in heaven."

She set aside the ribbon, then reached into the box again, this time withdrawing an ivory hair comb.

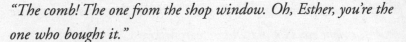

"The comb! The one from the shop window. Oh, Esther, you're the one who bought it."

"Do you like it then? Are you surprised?"

She hugged her sister. "Beyond words. I love it. I'll wear it because you gave it to me. You're my best friend, Esther, and my beloved sister."

"I love you too, Sophia."

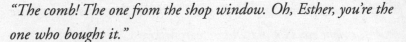

Sophia reached up and placed the comb in her hair, hair that was much thinner and totally white.

"I'll give it to Karen," she said. "It will look lovely with her blond curls."

She smiled when she saw the next item in the box. It was a

playbill, a program printed on one sheet of ivory paper and folded in half. *Pygmalion* was printed across the front.

Bradley had taken her to see the play on their first date, back in 1944.

***

"I hope you'll like it. The play, I mean. Shaw's my favorite playwright." Bradley took hold of Sophia's arm and escorted her toward the borrowed Ford.

She thought him handsome, even with the black patch he wore over his right eye. Not as handsome as Mikkel Christiansen, her first love, but handsome enough. He hadn't told her how he'd lost his eye. She only knew it had happened while he was serving in the Pacific.

But she didn't want to think about the war tonight, and she definitely didn't want to think about Mikkel. She just wanted to have a good time. There were few enough opportunities for fun these days. Besides, she liked the way Bradley Taylor looked at her, as if he thought she'd hung the moon.

He reached through the open window of the automobile and retrieved a small white box. He held it out to Sophia.

"This is for you."

She opened it. Inside was a single red rose.

"An American Beauty for an American beauty."

When she looked up, he kissed her.

"We were good together, Bradley, you and I. If only I'd realized it sooner than I did. I could have been a better wife to you."

She closed her eyes and allowed the memory of that evening to drift through her mind, savoring each and every moment. She'd begun to fall in love with him that night.

She sighed, opened her eyes, and looked once more into the shoe box. As she lifted out the crayon drawing, her eyes misted with tears.

"Dear, sweet Maggie."

She reached for a tissue. Then she smiled.

"That's you," Maggie said proudly, *"and that's Daddy and that's me and that's Pogo. See? I colored that black spot around her ear."*

"It's very nice, Maggie."

"Where's Daddy? I wanna show him, too."

"He'll be in for lunch soon. You can show him then."

Maggie slid onto a kitchen chair. "I love my daddy a whole bunch, and he loves me. I'm his honey bunny."

"And you're mine, too." Sophia kissed her on the cheek.

"Yours, too, Mama!"

Sophia sighed again. She wished those precious years could have been prolonged. Maggie hadn't doubted her love then. That had come later, when she was a teenager. If Sophia had only let go of that last seed of resentment, if she'd stopped feeling jealous because Maggie was Esther's child by birth, Esther and Mikkel's...

But she couldn't undo the past.

If she'd wanted proof of that, she only had to lift the final item from the shoe box. An envelope, smudged and made brittle by the passing years.

She opened the envelope and withdrew the letter inside. She didn't have to read it. She'd memorized it long ago.

12 March 1946
Copenhagen, Denmark

Dear Mrs. Taylor,

Pardon my poor English, but I write to tell you of your sister, Esther, and her husband, Mikkel. They were good friends to us before and during the war. Because of their goodness my husband Isaac, my children, and I are alive today.

I grieve greatly to learn of their deaths. I think you do not know perhaps, and it has taken much time to find you for Esther's sake.

We have living with us Margaret Rose Christiansen, daughter of Esther and Mikkel Christiansen. She was sent with us to Sweden to escape the Nazis. We hoped for long time to find Esther waiting for us in Copenhagen when we return, but know now she will not be here. We feel great love for little Rose, but she should be with family, as Esther wanted.

Mrs. Taylor, many horrors happened during war. I want you should know how Esther gave herself for others. Her heart was filled with love when many more were filled with hate. Even when she was afraid, she had great faith in her God. I will remember. I will never forget.

We await to hear from you.

Hannah Abrams

Sophia refolded the stationery and slipped the letter into the envelope. Then, with unshed tears blinding her, she placed it into the shoe box and closed the lid.

Saturday, January 9, 1943

Dear Diary,

Today is our little Rose's first birthday. We had a party for a few friends from church. Hannah and Isaac and their children were with us as well. It almost seemed an ordinary day. It took contributions from several families, but I managed to obtain the necessary ingredients to bake a cake. It was small, and no one got much more than a few bites. Still, it was good.

Ordinary. Normal.

How rare.

Esther

Tuesday, February 23, 1943

Dear Diary,

Hannah and I were stopped and searched today when we went to do our marketing. Rose was crying, and little Ashira was clinging to her mother's hand so hard and shaking. The soldiers made rude comments about Hannah's condition and her Jewish heritage. It was vile and ugly, and both frightened and enraged me.

Why must mankind be so cruel? Why, of all God's creations, are we the ones who mistreat and kill our own?

Esther

Monday, May 24, 1943

Dear Diary,

Mikkel and I had a horrible argument this morning before he left the house. I told him he is taking too many risks. I asked him to think about me and Rose for a change. He said he is thinking of us. He is thinking of our futures and the sort of world he wants our little girl to grow up in.

After he slammed the door behind him, I held Rose in my arms and wept. I wept for all we have lost and all we could lose. I tried to find comfort in prayer, but there was none to be found.

Mikkel has not returned yet, and it is nearly midnight.

Esther

Wednesday, May 26, 1943

They have arrested Mikkel. O God in heaven, have mercy.

Thirty

"There've been a few complications." Mac's voice sounded fuzzy across the telephone wires. "This is going to take longer than expected."

Karen smiled to herself. "It's okay, Mac. Whenever the money comes it'll be needed. You saw the ranch. You know there's a lot to be done."

"Are you sure you know what you're doing?"

"Not always."

"That property isn't worth investing in."

"It is to me."

He continued as if she hadn't spoken. "You can still come stay with us until this is settled. My wife and I—"

"Thanks, Mac, but I'm where I want to be. That's the honest truth. You know it is."

"That's what I thought when I was there. Still…well, you call if you change your mind."

"I won't change my mind, but thanks for asking. You're a good friend."

There was a brief silence from his end before he said, "I'll let you know as soon as I hear anything new."

They said their good-byes, and Karen hung up the phone.

"Mr. Gleason's trying to talk you into going back to California, isn't he?"

"Yes." Karen turned toward Sophia. "But it isn't working, Grandmother, so you needn't worry."

"Praise the Lord for that."

"Yes."

"I'd like to talk to you." Sophia walked to the table and set a shoe box in the center. "Would you mind getting Dusty? I already asked Patty to join us, and she'll be right out."

Karen felt a sting of alarm. "Are you feeling all right? Do you need a doctor?"

"I'm feeling fine, my dear." Sophia waved off Karen's concern. "But there are matters we need to discuss as a family."

"If you're sure you're okay."

"I'm quite sure."

Not convinced but not wanting to argue, Karen reached for her coat and slipped into it. Then after a glance over her shoulder at Sophia, she opened the door and headed for the bunkhouse.

A piercing wind cut through her down-filled coat as if it were nothing but fine linen. Shivering, she leaned into the wind and quickened her steps, wondering if it was possible for a person to freeze to death in the minute or so it took to walk across this barnyard. At the bunkhouse, she knocked on the door. A moment later, it opened.

"Grandmother wants to talk to you."

Dusty's welcoming smile vanished. "Is something wrong?"

"I don't know. She said she's feeling all right. She doesn't look sick."

"Step out of the wind. I'll be right with you."

Karen did as he said, stepping inside and closing the door behind her. While she waited for Dusty to return from his bedroom, she looked around the bunkhouse, thinking how empty it seemed without the boys there to mess it up.

Who will Dusty's boys be next summer? Could they be my boys too? Could I become a real part of this place?

Dusty paused in the doorway to his bedroom, watching Karen while putting on his coat. There was something wistful about her expression, something yearning and hungry.

He'd been aware of her diligent search for truth in the days that had passed since he'd asked her to marry him. She read the Bible her grandmother had given her almost as much as Dusty read his own. He knew because he'd seen her at it. He knew because she asked so many questions. She was trying hard.

What continued to hold her back? he wondered. What caused her to hesitate, even now?

As if suddenly sensing his perusal, she glanced in his direction.

He longed to kiss her, to hold her, to tell her he loved her. But he didn't. He hadn't let any of those things happen again since the night of his proposal. Perhaps he could wear her down, get her to agree to marry him by the sheer force of his will, but that wasn't the way he wanted her.

"Ready?" she asked, her voice cracking slightly.

"Ready."

✻

A short while later, Sophia looked at her loved ones seated around the kitchen table. They were all watching her with ill-concealed concern, despite her assurances to each of them that nothing was wrong.

"I'm not feeling poorly," she insisted. "I'm old but not sick." She reached for the shoe box, drawing it toward her. "But I've put off this discussion for too long. I meant to do it when I was released from the hospital. Time got away from me."

She saw Dusty and Karen exchange glances. It was apparent their anxiety was unchanged.

"Karen, dear." She waited for her granddaughter to look at her, then continued, "I spent much of today thinking about the past. The older one gets, I've found, the more enjoyable that pastime becomes."

She smiled to herself, knowing the young rarely understood the elderly until they became old themselves.

"In fact, that's what I was doing the day you arrived at the Golden T. My, but that seems a long time ago, doesn't it? I was thinking that day how I was ready to go home to the Father whenever He chose to call me."

"Grandmother!"

"Shh." She raised a hand to halt Karen's protest. "I'm not saying I'm eager to die. I'm simply saying I'm ready. My stay in the hospital served as a reminder that none of us know when our allotted time on earth will be finished."

She opened the box and touched the items inside.

"Karen, this is my keepsake box. I've written down what each of these items is and what it represents to me. After I'm gone, whenever that is, these things will be yours. I want you to put the box away until then." She picked up the letter from Hannah Abrams. "Except for this." She held the envelope toward Karen. "When you've read the last page of your Grandmother Esther's final journal, you may read this. Don't read it before. Please."

"All right," her granddaughter agreed softly as she took the envelope, turning it over in her hand to read the handwritten address on the front.

Sophia moved her gaze from Karen to Patty to Dusty and back to Karen again. Then she took a deep breath and continued. "In addition to these trinkets, I've a few other items to dispense with. I'd rather tell you myself what I want than leave it to some attorney after I'm gone."

She looked at Patty. "My dear, I don't know if your father will see how wrong he is. I hope and pray he will. More than that, however, I pray you won't let the mistakes of your youth ruin your whole life. You're a lovely girl, Patty Call, with a fine mind and a good heart. I don't know where God will lead you, but I know He has a plan for you. He will turn to good all things, if you let Him." She paused, collecting her thoughts, then continued. "I have a small life insurance policy, and I've named you as my beneficiary. When the time comes, you use it for your education. If I live long enough to see you graduate from college, then you take that money to help someone else in need. Agreed?"

Looking uncomfortable with the subject, Patty nodded.

"Dusty." Sophia turned toward him. "I've left you this land, what's left of the Golden T Ranch. I want to make —"

"You've *what?*"

"I'm leaving you the deed to the land. So you can continue your youth work."

"But, Sophia, you shouldn't—" He stopped, looked at Karen, then back at Sophia. "You can't do that. The ranch should stay in your family."

Sophia met her granddaughter's gaze. "I suspect, if you ask Karen, she'll tell you she wants you to have it. The house will be hers, of course, if she wants it and for as long as she wants it."

After a lengthy silence, Dusty said, "Karen?"

❧

It surprised her, more than a little, to discover how right her grandmother was. She much preferred the ranch go to Dusty. She supposed she should have felt cheated, rejected, by the decision. But she didn't. In truth, there was a serenity in knowing the land would go to someone who would use it to help others. There was a freedom to be found in lacking possessions.

What an amazing discovery.

And after she received the money Mac had found for her, she could help Dusty do even more with this place.

Excitement filled her heart.

Maybe she and Dusty could open a year-round home for troubled teens. They could hire several additional counselors. They could build more bunkhouses. Perhaps they could also help girls like Patty.

"Grandmother's right." She turned toward him, a smile curving her mouth. "I *do* want you to have the ranch. And once Mac—" The jangle of the telephone interrupted her.

Dusty was sitting the closest. He rose and answered it. Karen watched his expression darken as he listened to the voice on the other end. His responses were made in monosyllables.

"Yes," he said several minutes later. "Yes, I understand. I'll leave first thing tomorrow." He turned his back toward Karen and the others. "I'll let you know when to expect me. Thanks for the call." He hung up, then pressed the heels of his hands against the counter, his forehead against the cupboard above it.

Karen suspected he was praying, and her anxiety increased with each passing second.

Finally, he straightened and faced the room again. "It's Hal. He's in Seattle."

Karen glanced quickly at Patty, wondering what her reaction would be to the news. The girl's eyes were wide, her hands clasped tightly in front of her. Karen couldn't guess what she was thinking or feeling.

"He's in jail," Dusty finished.

"Oh no," Sophia whispered.

"I've got to go up there."

Karen turned to him. "Tomorrow?"

He nodded.

"Will you drive?" Karen asked.

Again he nodded. "No money for the airfare. I'll take the van. It's the most reliable. And I can sleep in it if I need to."

"I have a little of my mad money left," Sophia said as she rose from her chair. "I'll get it for you."

God, why don't You help these people? Why can't You give them a decent break?

"Karen?" Dusty said softly. "I don't know how long I'll be gone. You'll need to look after Sophia and Patty."

"I will."

He stepped toward her. "Take care of yourself, too."

She nodded.

With the tips of his fingers, he lifted her chin, forcing her to look up at him. "I believe this is a good thing that's happened. Hal asked for me. He's stopped running. Don't despair. God is sovereign—remember that when it all seems too much and you can't see the purpose. God is good, and He is sovereign."

Tuesday, June 1, 1943 ·

Dear Diary,

I was allowed to see Mikkel today. The Germans know now
that we are Americans, but because of when we came to
Denmark and the reason, they seem inclined to believe we are
not spies. Or maybe this is only a trap. Maybe they are waiting
for another mistake.

They did not leave us alone to talk, but I could see all the
warnings in Mikkel's eyes. Our home is sure to be searched. I
will no longer be careless with my journals. Except for when I
am writing, I will keep them in the secret hiding place Mikkel
built such a very long time ago, back when I thought it would
never be necessary. I will make certain there is no shred of
evidence that might link either of us to the resistance movement.

I begged Mikkel's forgiveness for the argument we had the last
time we were together. I did not care if the Germans heard that.
I told Mikkel how much I loved him and that he was not to
worry about Rose and me. We will be fine, with God's help.

He took my hands and held them tightly and reminded me
that I must not look at circumstances from man's point of view
but only from God's. He told me to look up Mark 8:33 when I

arrived home, which I did. In that verse, Jesus rebuked Peter, saying, "Get thee behind me, Satan: for thou savourest not the things that be of God, but the things that be of men."

I understand what he wanted to show me in this verse, that I must see everything against the backdrop of the cross, that I must view it all with an eternal perspective. But did Mikkel also realize Jesus said this because He knew He was about to suffer and die?

Esther

Monday, August 9, 1943

Dear Diary,

They would not allow me to visit Mikkel today. I am afraid of the reason.

Sabotage has been increasing throughout Denmark. The press has become a powerful instrument, and the Danes know the truth about the war from both it and the BBC broadcasts which we all listen to nightly, even though it is forbidden.

The Germans are losing ground. The tide has turned in favor of the Allies. But will the war end soon enough for Mikkel?

Esther

Sunday, August 29, 1943

Dear Diary,

The Danish government has resigned following the demands the Germans made as reprisal for the bombing of the Forum. A state of emergency has now been declared by the Nazis. Freedom fighters who are captured will be shot or deported to concentration camps.

I have not been allowed to see Mikkel for nearly a month.

Esther

It was three in the morning, one week before Thanksgiving, when Karen closed the last of Esther Christiansen's thirteen journals.

Tears flowed down her cheeks, but she made no effort to wipe them away. She hadn't the strength. She was emotionally drained, while at the same time feeling a strange lightness in her heart. She couldn't explain it. It simply *was*.

She wished Dusty were back from Seattle. He'd called to say he was on his way home, having done all he could for Hal. He'd sounded hopeful about the boy's future. "I think there's a good chance the court will give me custody. It'll be a few weeks before we'll know, but it looks like he'll avoid jail time." He'd said he would tell them more upon his return.

But that wouldn't be until late today. Karen wanted to talk to him now. She wanted to tell him what she was feeling. He would understand. He'd be able to explain what it all meant.

She closed her eyes, pressed her hands over her heart, and whispered, "What's going on, God? Maybe You should be the one to tell me anyway."

For a moment, it seemed all of heaven held its breath right along with her. It seemed she would get her answer. It seemed—

She sat up, listening. For just a moment, she'd thought she heard her name being whispered.

The wind playing tricks on her, no doubt.

"Karen..."

No. She wasn't mistaken. It was her name, but it wasn't the wind. It was Patty.

She jumped out of bed and hurried to Patty's bedroom, opening the door without knocking.

"Ohhh...Karen."

She flicked on the light.

"It hurts...it hurts." Patty lay on her bed, curled on her side, hugging her belly. Perspiration beaded her forehead and upper lip. "Something's wrong. I think...I think it's the baby." She groaned in pain.

"But the baby isn't due for weeks."

Another groan.

Karen hadn't a clue what to do. That line from *Gone with the Wind* popped into her head, the one about not knowing nothing about birthing babies. She almost laughed out loud at the absurdness of the thought. Of course, the impulse to laugh was from nerves; there was nothing funny about this. If Patty was in labor, then the baby could be in danger. And maybe Patty, too.

"Don't worry." She tried to sound confident. "It's probably false labor. Everybody talks about it. Happens all the time. Everything will be all right."

She spun around and hurried to the kitchen where she flicked on the light and began searching for the number of the ambulance service. She knew it was around there somewhere. Dusty had called it when Sophia was ill. Where had she seen that number? Where? *Where?*

She found it an instant before full-fledged panic overwhelmed her.

Muttering the number aloud to herself, she lifted the handset. The line was dead.

Panic won. She couldn't seem to move. She couldn't seem to think.

"Karen?"

There was no more welcome sound than that of her grandmother's calm voice speaking her name. She turned around.

"Are the phones out?" Sophia asked.

Karen nodded.

"You'll have to go for help. I don't think this is a false alarm."

"But what if there isn't time?"

"Then I'll deliver the baby, and you'll get back with help as soon as you can."

"Oh, Grandmother—"

"Take the truck and drive to the Basterra farm. Yuli has a shortwave radio for times like this." Sophia frowned. "Do you remember how to get there?"

"Yes," Karen answered. "Yes, I can find it." She hoped she was telling the truth.

"Then get going. God will go with you, dear. Don't be afraid." Her grandmother returned to Patty's room.

Karen hurriedly dressed, bundling herself in coat, knitted scarf, warm cap to cover her tousled hair, snow boots, and gloves. When she opened the front door a short while later, the icy wind nearly knocked her down. Blowing snow formed a blinding curtain before her. She couldn't see the barn or the bunkhouse. She had to find the truck by instinct rather than by sight.

How am I to see the road in this? O God, if You're really up there, watching and caring, then You'd better go with me. You'd better. If ever I've needed You, now's the time.

MY SON.

Dusty awakened with a start.

ARISE AND GO.

A shiver swept through him in response to the clear but silent command. He tossed off the covers on the motel bed and reached for his jeans.

What's wrong, Lord? What is it?

There'd been no bolt of lightning, no clear revelation of what was wrong. And yet he knew without a shred of doubt he'd heard the Lord's voice telling him to go. The exhaustion that had dogged him during his return trip from Seattle lifted as he tossed his few things into his duffel and left the room, moving quickly toward the van.

The temperature was near zero, and the night was black as pitch. Not a star in sight. He could smell snow in the air, although it wasn't falling there.

A hundred miles to go. Whatever's wrong, Jesus, be there in the midst. Keep Karen and Sophia and Patty safe.

❧

The drive to the Basterra farm was the most terrifying experience of Karen's lifetime. Blinded by the blizzard, she hadn't a clue how she stayed on the road, let alone found her way. Once there, it took what seemed an eternity of pounding on the farmhouse door before she was able to rouse the sleeping inhabitants. But once they did awaken and learned what was happening, they sprang into action.

"I'm going back to the ranch," Karen told Celia while Yuli headed for his radio.

"Wait for us to get dressed. We'll go with you."

She shook her head. "I don't want to wait. Grandmother may need help."

"It'll only take a few minutes."

"No." She opened the door. "I've got to go. I've been gone too long already."

Celia called something after her, but the wind swept the words away before they reached Karen's ears.

❧

Fear clogged Dusty's veins.

He'd come upon the blizzard suddenly. Heavy snow blew horizontally in front of the van, making the headlights virtually worthless. The road was little more than a sheet of ice. Dusty's van had to crawl along at a snail's pace or he risked ending up in the barrow pit.

If only he knew what was wrong at home. If only he knew why he was fearful.

God, protect them, he prayed silently. *Protect them.* Then aloud, "Strengthen Sophia's heart. I know she's lived a good long life, Jesus. But I'm greedy—I want to keep her here with me. With us. And Patty...she's just a girl, and she's pregnant and her body's going through all sorts of things I don't understand. Keep her and that unborn child safe and healthy. And, Father, if it's Karen..." His prayer faded to silence. He couldn't find the words to go on. He couldn't bear to consider losing her.

His fear multiplied.

I AM YOUR REFUGE AND STRENGTH, A VERY PRESENT HELP IN TROUBLE.

I love her, Lord. I love her more than I can say. If I were to lose her...

DO NOT FEAR, FOR I AM WITH YOU; DO NOT ANXIOUSLY LOOK ABOUT YOU, FOR I AM YOUR GOD.

"Make my way straight, Lord. Keep this old van on the highway. Get me there in time. Please, God. Please."

⁂

Karen felt a terrible sinking sensation. This wasn't right. The road shouldn't be climbing and twisting this way. She'd taken a wrong turn. She should have been at the ranch by now.

She carefully applied the brakes and brought the old truck to a halt. Even with the heater going full blast, she was cold.

Where am I?

She took a deep breath, mentally scolding herself. She didn't need to be afraid. She had only to turn the pickup around and drive back to the highway. That was all. How difficult could that be?

She squinted, trying to see beyond the snow, trying to see the surrounding terrain. It was pointless. There was only the snow.

If I'm careful I don't have to see. Even this old truck can be turned around by inches.

Taking a deep breath, she put the pickup in gear, twisted the steering wheel, and pressed gently on the gas. Little by little by little, she changed the direction of the vehicle. Finally, it was done. She was facing downhill. Now she could drive back to the highway, get her bearings, and find her way home.

"Thank God," she whispered.

She pressed gently on the gas pedal. The truck started forward. Suddenly the earth fell away.

Tuesday, September 14, 1943

Mikkel is dead. The news was brought to me today by the Gestapo. The man smiled as he told me, and I could see that he was warning me. No, not warning. Promising. He was making me a promise that I would not escape the wrath of the enemy.

Oh, my sweet, wonderful Mikkel. How I wish I could have held you in my arms one more time. Just to tell you how very much I have loved you. It was you who brought me to Christ. It was you who taught me to seek God in His word. You were a lamp to my feet, showing me the way to salvation. You were my husband, my lover, the father of our dear Rose.

But you are safe now, my darling. They cannot torture you again. You are in the arms of our Father and will never know pain or suffering or want. You will have only joy for the rest of eternity. As much as I hurt, as much as I mourn my loss, there is comfort in knowing you are safe again at last.

Esther

Thursday, September 30, 1943

Dear Diary,

   The Abrams family is in hiding in the secret room. The word came out that the Germans will begin rounding up Danish Jews at the start of <u>Rosh</u> <u>Hashanah</u>. None are safe in their homes because the membership lists and archives from the synagogue were seized and will surely be used to find all the Jews in the country.

   The greatest fear is that little Jacob, who is only five months old, will cry and be heard from the street. A baby's cry is different from a toddler's. But we hope, if Jacob cries and is heard, that we can fool others by saying it was Rose.

   We must get the Abrams out of Denmark to Sweden. It will have to be soon. Everyone knows the Germans will act quickly and with vengeance once they discover the Danes have thwarted their efforts to deport these innocent people.

                                                       Esther

Thirty-Two

Her head hurt.

Her body ached.

And she was cold. So very cold.

Karen opened her eyes, at first not remembering what had happened. Then it all came rushing back. The truck had gone off the road. She had no idea how long she'd been unconscious after striking her head, but it had been long enough for the battery to run down. The headlights cast a pitifully weak yellow glow into the silent night.

And it *was* silent. Absolutely silent. The wind had stopped blowing. The snow had ceased falling. There was only darkness and silence. Nothing more.

Be calm, she told herself. *There's nothing I can do until morning.*

There. She didn't have to be a Girl Scout to know that much. She simply had to wait for daylight. It couldn't be much longer. Maybe three hours. Maybe less. She could stand the cold for that long.

The winter emergency kit!

She should have thought of it immediately. Dusty had explained to her about the emergency supplies he kept in his vehicles during the winter in case of a breakdown. If this didn't qualify as an emergency, she didn't know what did.

It wasn't until she unfastened her seat belt and started to turn on the seat that she realized the truck had come to a rest at an angle. Perhaps as much as twenty-five degrees. The creaks and groans that accompanied her movements did nothing to inspire her confidence in the vehicle's stability.

She moved more slowly, rising to her knees and reaching behind the seat. The large duffel bag was easy enough to find, even in the dark, and with only a little effort, she managed to drag it from its narrow resting place.

Settling forward on the seat again, she released a breath she hadn't known she was holding. Then she unzipped the duffel. The first thing she withdrew was the thermal blanket. She wrapped her legs and lower body in it, hoping she would soon be warm enough to stop shivering. The next item she found was the flashlight. She hadn't known what a marvelous invention the flashlight was until she slid the switch and the cab was illuminated.

Better. Oh, so much better.

She pointed the beam of light into the bag. Matches and a couple of oversized candles. Flare gun and flares. A box of crackers, several canned food items with pull tab tops, and about a half-dozen candy bars. Several large bottles of water. Aspirin, bandages, ointment. There was even a small Bible.

She smiled, thinking of Dusty putting that Bible into an emergency kit. How like him. If he were in her shoes, he would probably find more comfort in those pages than from anything else in the duffel bag.

Maybe he was right.

She opened the Bible.

※

The stark white landscape was almost blinding.

Dusty stood on the front porch as the ambulance drove away, Patty and her newborn son inside it. The paramedics had assured him that both mother and child—a boy, weighing five pounds—would be fine, despite his early arrival. And in a few days, the baby's adoptive parents would take him home to a family who would love and nurture him.

Thank You, God, for Your mercy. Strengthen and keep them safe in the palm of Your hand. Thank You for giving Patty the courage to do what was best for that precious little life. And Karen... O Father, keep her safe too.

The past hours had been some of the longest of Dusty's life. When he'd arrived at the ranch and found Karen gone, everything inside him had screamed for him to go in search of her right then—even while it was still dark. But Patty had been in labor and he'd been needed. He hadn't been able to leave.

But now...

Hearing a sound behind him, he turned to find Sophia watching him from the doorway.

"The search-and-rescue team has been dispatched," she said. "They'll find her."

"I'm going out." He turned again, looking south, toward the mountains. "Up there."

"But there's no reason she would have taken that road. The Basterra farm is the other way."

"I know."

"The van would never make it with all this snow. You'll need a four-wheel drive."

"I'm taking the horses."

"Dusty, are you sure you—?"

"I can't explain it, Sophia. I just can't shake the feeling that's what I'm supposed to do."

She touched his arm. "Then do it. And God go with you."

When next Karen opened her eyes, it was day. But the light brought no comfort with it. For now she could see how truly precarious her situation was. Worse than she'd imagined.

The truck had slid down an incline and come to rest on a ledge. Beyond the ledge was a long drop to the canyon floor below. The driver's door couldn't be opened; it was wedged against something hard, and snow had piled up against the window. The passenger door was free, but even if she got out of the truck, there was no way she could climb back to the road without help. The mountainside was too steep.

She was trapped. Trapped and freezing.

Is this how I'm going to die?

She almost laughed. How ironic. She had tried to kill herself and failed. Failed miserably, just as she'd failed at much of her life. Now she wanted to live, now she'd found reasons to go on, and she might be about to die.

Cold and alone.

BELOVED, YOU ARE NOT ALONE.

She must be hallucinating. The hit on the head. The cold. She was delirious.

BELOVED, YOU ARE NEVER ALONE. I AM WITH YOU ALWAYS.

O God. Why couldn't I find You before? All these weeks, I've looked and looked.

I AM WITH YOU, BELOVED.

She closed her eyes against the stark white reality beyond the windshield. She was afraid, and despite the gentle Voice speaking in her heart, she *was* alone.

I HAVE LOVED YOU WITH AN EVERLASTING LOVE.

I'm so unlovable. Even my own parents couldn't love me.

I AM YOUR HEAVENLY FATHER, AND I DECLARE THAT YOU ARE LOVED. YOU ARE FEARFULLY AND WONDERFULLY MADE. NOTHING ABOUT YOU IS HIDDEN FROM ME FOR I FORMED YOUR INWARD PARTS AND WOVE YOU IN YOUR MOTHER'S WOMB. I WROTE THE DAYS THAT ARE ORDAINED FOR YOU IN MY BOOK WHEN AS YET THERE WAS NOT ONE OF THEM.

Karen opened her eyes, looking through the frosty windshield toward the wintry-blue sky. "So is this the day You wrote in Your book, God? Is *this* it? Is *that* what You mean by love?"

At that moment, the strangest thing happened. She stopped shivering. The cab grew warm.

And suddenly, she *knew*.

She wasn't alone.

She wasn't hallucinating.

He was with her.

"Jesus?" she whispered.

I AM HERE.

Tears flooded her eyes. "Why?"

She couldn't have explained what she was asking, even to herself. But Jesus—her Savior and her Lord—knew.

BELOVED, YOU WERE THE JOY SET BEFORE ME. FOR YOUR SAKE, I ENDURED THE CROSS, DESPISING THE SHAME. BECAUSE I SO LOVED KAREN BUTLER, I CAME.

Weeping, she covered her face with her hands. "You died for me. You died for *me*. Because You love me. O Jesus. Jesus. How could I not see?"

At last. At long last, she understood. This was what Grandmother Sophia knew. This was what Dusty knew. This was what Esther had known.

She remembered the final entry in the journal. Remembered the words and understood them as she hadn't before. When she'd closed the diary that morning, she'd cried but hadn't truly understood. Now she did.

A love like this could change the world. A love like this *had* changed the world.

And now it had changed Karen.

She stopped crying. She almost stopped breathing. She lowered her hands.

"I'm not afraid anymore." It was a statement of joyous wonder, a declaration of faith.

She was loved, and she was no longer afraid.

Not afraid to live.

Or to die.

Wednesday, October 6, 1943

Dear Diary,

It isn't dawn yet. The house is quiet. In another hour I will take food up to the Abrams and then I will tend to Rose's needs. But for now, this quiet time is mine alone.

I dreamed last night of Mikkel. It was one of those odd, disjointed dreams that make no sense in the light of day but seem so real at the time. I was running toward him, yet never reached him. There was fire all around us both. The heat of it seemed to be searing my skin.

Just before I awakened, I heard him say, "No matter what, Esther, we will praise the Lord. Remember that, my dear one."

My heart was hammering when I awakened. I prayed, asking God what the dream meant, asking Him to take away the fear and confusion. I picked up my Bible and began to read, seeking comfort therein. And He was ever faithful to provide it.

The first thing He told me was not to fear the fire. For when Shadrach, Meshach, and Abed-nego were thrown into the fiery furnace, not even their hair was singed nor did the smell of fire pass on them. Those men of God knew He could save them if such was His will, but even if He didn't, they chose to obey

Him, saying, "If it be so, our God whom we serve is able to deliver us from the burning fiery furnace, and he will deliver us out of thine hand, O king. But if not, be it known unto thee, O king, that we will not serve thy gods, nor worship the golden image which thou hast set up."

And Job said, "Though he slay me, yet will I trust in him."

Habakkuk says, "Although the fig tree shall not blossom, neither shall fruit be in the vines; the labour of the olive shall fail, and the fields shall yield no meat; the flock shall be cut off from the fold, and there shall be no herd in the stalls: Yet I will rejoice in the LORD, I will joy in the God of my salvation. The LORD God is my strength, and he will make my feet like hinds' feet, and he will make me to walk upon mine high places."

Yes, Lord God, I will praise You, no matter what. I will remember. I will choose You above all else.

Amen.

Thirty-Three

....

The gray lunged through another snowdrift as horse and rider continued their arduous climb up the mountain.

"Maybe the search-and-rescue team's already found her," Dusty said aloud, trying to reassure himself. "She's probably safe and sound at home."

But something drove him on. Some unrelenting force urging him forward.

"O God, help me."

BEHOLD, THE EYE OF THE LORD IS ON THOSE WHO FEAR HIM.

He drew back on the reins, stopping his horse. He swept the landscape with his gaze, his breathing erratic.

BUT AS FOR YOU, THE NEARNESS OF GOD IS YOUR GOOD.

"Lord, what are You trying to tell me? I can't see anything. There's nothing here but snow. What if I can't find her?"

YOU WILL BE HAPPY, AND IT WILL BE WELL WITH YOU.

Was it God's promise he heard or his own wishful thinking?
He dismounted, stumbling through the snow.

"The nearness of God is my good."

He squinted, as if doing so would change what he saw. He turned in a slow circle. Then, as he took another step forward, he tripped. Unable to catch his balance this time, he pitched forward toward the rim of the canyon. Despair washed over him as he lay in the snow.

"Help me, Jesus," he prayed softly. "I can't do this without You."

He pushed to his feet, and as he did so, something below caught his attention. It looked like nothing more than another snowdrift. Yet it seemed oddly out of place. He took a cautious step closer to the ridge. Reflected sunlight blinded him. Reflexively, he covered his eyes. When his vision cleared, he looked again. His heart nearly stopped.

It was his truck. Half buried in snow, but his truck all the same.

"Thank You, Father," he whispered. "Thank You."

❧

Karen dreamed of Dusty. She dreamed she could hear his voice calling her name. It was a sweet sound in her ears.

She wished she could have told him about Jesus. That she

had found Him. That she'd finally understood the love He had for her. That she'd been born again into the family of believers. She wished she'd had one more opportunity to tell Dusty she loved him.

"Karen! Karen, are you all right?"

His voice seemed so real to her. So close.

"Karen!"

Struggling to return from her half-conscious state, she managed at last to open her eyes.

"Karen, can you move? Are you hurt?"

"Dusty?"

She wasn't dreaming. It was him. He was here, right outside the truck.

"Dusty." She raised her arm, as if to touch him. She had so much to tell him.

"Don't be afraid," he called to her.

"I'm not."

"Are you hurt?"

"No. Just stiff and cold."

"Can you reach the handle and roll down the window?"

"I think so."

Dusty's gaze never wavered from hers. When the window was open, he said, "I've been looking for you." He sounded as if there was nothing more important happening than telling her that.

She smiled in response, loving him so. And then she saw how precarious was his own position, and her smile vanished. His feet were planted against the rocky side of the steep cliff. He held on to the end of a rope—the *very* end—with his bare left hand.

Her heart fluttered; her peace fractured. "Maybe you should go for help. You could fall. I'll be all right until you get back."

"No." His answer was firm. "I'm taking you home with me." He stretched out his right arm. "Take my hand, Karen."

It matters only that we obey, Esther had written in her diary, and Karen knew that was what the Lord was telling her now.

She reached up. Their fingertips met, then curled like two fishhooks snagged together. No, not like a fishhook. More like an anchor. They were anchored in Christ.

Those were the longest minutes of Dusty's life, those minutes it took them to work their way up the side of that cliff. If not for the promise God had spoken to his heart, he might have despaired. He might have given in to fear. Instead, he clung stubbornly to the promise that they would be happy and it would be well with them.

He wasn't letting go.

He wasn't giving up.

Because God was greater than the snow and ice. God was greater than the mountain. God was greater than anything and everything, and by His strength and His alone, Dusty knew they would prevail.

Finally, he dragged Karen over the lip of the canyon rim, and they collapsed side by side on the snowy ground, gasping for breath. For the longest time, they lay there, staring upward. Dusty silently thanked God, too winded to do so aloud.

At long last, Karen spoke. "Dusty."

"Yeah?"

"That was a crazy thing to do. You should have gone for more help."

"I had help."

"You could have fallen." She rolled onto her side, facing him. "You could have been killed."

He met her gaze. "Not this time," he said with quiet assurance.

Tears shimmered in her eyes.

He touched her cheek. "But I'd be willing to die for you, if that's what was asked of me."

"I learned something while I was down there."

"What, Karen?"

"Someone *did* die for me."

He pulled her into his arms, drawing her close, looking deep into her eyes.

"Jesus already died for me."

Rejoicing burst forth in his heart as understanding dawned.

"All you have to do is love me, Dusty." A tremulous smile curved her lips. "Just love me."

Wednesday, October 13, 1943

Dear Diary,

Tomorrow, the Abrams will leave my home, and I know now what I must do. I will send Rose with them to Sweden. I must stay and do what I can to help others.

It has been more than three years since Grandfather Fritz died, but I can still hear his last words to me. "Remember this. Esther never faltered. Esther fulfilled her destiny, serving where she was planted. Remember it always, Esther. Remember."

I could not imagine then what he meant. Now I know, for I have found it in God's Word. In the Old Testament, the book of Esther.

Like me, Esther was in captivity. God put her in a place where He could use her. And the day came when she had to defy the law of the land in order to save her people, the Jews, whom the wicked Haman sought to wipe out. And Esther's uncle Mordecai, who knew of the evil plan, said to her, "And who knoweth whether thou art come to the kingdom for such a time as this?"

And so I must do whatever I can to help. I am only one person, a woman, young, and a foreigner who speaks the language but poorly. Yet, God has shown me I am to do what He calls me to do, and whether it is a lofty deed or a lowly one, it matters only that I obey.

I cannot turn away and do nothing. If this is the destiny God has called me to, then I will follow Him wherever He takes me.

I do not know the reason God brought me to Denmark, but perhaps it was simply to be here, like Esther of the Bible, for such a time as this.

"And if I perish, I perish." (Esther 4:16)

Author's Note

....

Dear Readers:

Although I didn't go into detail regarding World War II and the Holocaust in *Whispers from Yesterday*, I would be remiss if I failed to explain why I chose to set the diary portion of the book in Denmark.

The Holocaust is only one in a long list of horrific examples of man's inhumanity to man. Nearly six million Jews (as well as others who did not meet Hitler's ideal Aryan specifications) died at the hands of the Nazis and their collaborators.

But in the midst of this unimaginable horror, acts of tremendous courage were performed by ordinary citizens throughout Europe. Some acted as individuals, some as part of an organized Resistance Movement. Some carefully planned the actions they would take, others acted spontaneously as opportunity presented itself. Regardless of the success of their acts, these people were and are heroes who should be remembered.

Several countries in Eastern Europe saw over 80 percent of their Jewish population exterminated. Such statistics make all the more noteworthy the rescue of approximately 95 percent of Danish Jews by the Danish citizenry while the country was occupied by the Germans.

The Danes have a history of religious tolerance, and the political leaders dismissed the idea of special treatment for Jews with, "We have no Jewish problem. We have only Danes." Popular legend says King Christian X, in protest, wore a yellow star while riding his horse on the streets of Copenhagen. While that may be only legend, the following is true:

On the eve of Rosh Hashanah (September 30) 1943, the Germans disconnected telephones and raided Jewish homes throughout Denmark. Thankfully, few Jewish families were in their homes. The Resistance Movement had obtained advance information and had passed the word. Danish citizens, indignant and determined, hid their Jewish friends and neighbors that night, and over the next few weeks, more than 7,200 Jews escaped across the Øresund to Sweden. Only 474 fell into Gestapo hands, and the majority of those captured survived the war in the German concentration camp Theresienstadt.

As I researched both this and other acts of courage from the Holocaust, I prayed that I would be prepared to behave with equal courage if it were required of me. I hope I will never have to find out.

But no matter what the future brings, I find comfort in the words of Jesus: "These things I have spoken to you, that in Me you may have peace. In the world you have tribulation, but take courage; I have overcome the world" (John 16:33).

Romans 8:37

Robin Lee Hatcher

To learn more about acts of courage during the Holocaust, I recommend the following:

Conscience & Courage: Rescuers of Jews During the Holocaust by Eva Fogelman. Anchor Books, a division of Bantam Doubleday Dell Publishing Group, ISBN 0-385-42028-5.

The Giant-Killers: The Story of the Danish Resistance Movement, 1940–1945 by John Oram Thomas. Taplinger Publishing Group, ISBN 0-8008-3258-2.

Heroes of the Holocaust: Extraordinary True Accounts of Triumph by Arnold Geier. Berkley Publishing Group, ISBN 0-425-16029-7.

The Hidden Children by Howard Greenfeld. Houghton Mifflin Company, ISBN 0-395-86138-1.

Miracle at Midnight, a true story of one Danish family's moral courage, starring Sam Waterston and Mia Farrow. Walt Disney Home Video, ISBN 0-7888-1350-1.

If you enjoyed *Whispers from Yesterday,* ask for Robin Lee Hatcher's next inspirational novel, *The Shepherd's Voice,* available May 2000.

Wandering child.
I am here.
I am near.
I speak.
Do you listen?

Arms open wide,
I wait,
I call,
I woo,
I weep.

No matter how far you run,
How high you climb,
How low you sink,
I do not change,
Nor does My love for you.

Return today.
Heed the Shepherd's voice.
Come home, My child.
Come home.

....

One

JULY 1934

Gabe Talmadge felt the backside of his navel rubbing against his spine. An interesting sensation, he thought before losing consciousness.

He ran from the darkness. He always ran, and it always followed him. There was no escaping it. There would never be. The darkness would always be with him, hovering nearby, waiting to encompass him, enfold him, devour him. It would be so easy to let it overtake him, to allow it to...

"Are you hurt?"

The soft, feminine voice came from a great distance.

"Mister?"

A hand slipped beneath his head. A small hand, with a touch as gentle as the voice.

"Can you hear me?"

Gabe opened his eyes. A shadowy form leaned forward, the bright light of midday glaring behind the woman, blinding him.

"Here. Take a drink."

His head was lifted slightly, and something cool touched his lips. Water trickled down his chin. Covering the woman's hand with his own, Gabe steadied the canteen, then drank deeply.

"Easy. Not too fast."

His thirst momentarily slaked, he closed his eyes. "Thanks."

"We should get you into the shade. It's powerful hot today. Can you stand?"

"Yes," he answered, although he wasn't as confident as he sounded.

Holding his arm, she helped him sit up. "Don't hurry. Take your time."

He thought he could feel the earth turning on its axis and gritted his teeth against the sensation.

"Ready?" his angel of mercy asked.

He opened his eyes a second time. "Ready." As he rose to his feet, the woman slipped beneath his arm, close against his side, taking his weight upon herself. It was humiliating to be this weak. His mind raged against the humiliation, as it had raged against countless degradations in the past, but rage changed nothing, then or now.

He glanced down. He could see little besides a floppy brimmed straw hat above a narrow set of shoulders.

"We're just goin' over there." She pointed with her free arm toward a good-sized birch tree. "Careful. We'll go slow. Take your time. Not too fast."

If he'd had the strength, he would have told her not to worry. He couldn't do anything fast. Except maybe fall to the ground in a dead faint.

Which he promptly did.

❧

Well, Lord. What do I do with him now?

Akira Macauley rolled the stranger onto his back. It was difficult to judge his age, given the shaggy black beard covering gaunt cheeks. There were holes in the bottoms of his boots, and the knees of his trousers were threadbare. Both he and his clothes needed a good washing, but she guessed cleanliness didn't mean much when you were going hungry.

I hope this hobo's not the one You sent, Lord. He's naught but a rack of bones. I could make better use of a man who knows sheep, if that wouldn't be too much to ask.

With a shake of her head, she said aloud, "He'll be even less use to me if he dies."

She stood, grabbed hold of his wrists, then walked backward, dragging him toward the shade. Despite his rawboned appearance, he weighed enough to make the going hard. Sweat rolled down her spine.

The stranger groaned.

"We're nearly there."

Reaching the shade beneath the leafy green tree, Akira dropped his arms with a sigh of relief.

He groaned again as his eyelids fluttered and eventually opened.

She dropped to her knees beside him and leaned forward, waiting for his vision to clear. When she thought he could see her, she said, "Give yourself a moment. You're weaker'n a newborn kitten." She glanced over her shoulder and pointed at the canteen where she'd left it. "Cam, fetch."

Her collie, who'd patiently observed all the goings on from a short distance, jumped up and raced to obey her mistress's command.

Akira returned her gaze to the stranger. "When was the last time you ate something?"

"I'm not sure."

"Days?"

He nodded.

How'd he get so lost, Lord? He's a far piece from the rails. And any man who could get that turned around would serve me no purpose. I'd spend all my time lookin' for him in the hills. You must see that I'm right about that. Surely You've got a better way of answerin' my prayers.

Cam delivered the canteen, and Akira offered it to the stranger.

"Thanks."

With her help, he sat up, then opened the canteen and lifted it to his mouth. He took small gulps this time, washing the water around inside his mouth before swallowing. Finally he lowered the canteen and met her watchful gaze.

Something twisted in her belly, a reaction to the stark emptiness in his pale blue eyes. She didn't think she'd seen anything so sad in all her born days.

Dear Jesus, he's lost in more ways than one, isn't he?

"How far am I from Ransom?" His voice sounded empty and hopeless too.

Still reeling from what she'd seen in his eyes, she couldn't think clearly enough to answer him.

"I'm on the right road, aren't I? For Ransom?"

She swallowed the lump in her throat. "Yes. Yes, you're on the right road. Ransom's a mite better'n fifteen miles to the north." She frowned. "But if you're lookin' for work at the mill, you needn't bother. There's no work to be had."

He turned his head, judging the short distance to the tree, then slowly inched himself closer to it, stopping when he could rest his back against the trunk. Then he closed his eyes again.

"No work at the mill," he whispered.

"No."

"But it's still there?"

"The mill? Yes, it's still there."

Silence fell between them. He kept his eyes closed, and she kept hers trained on him.

There's no work for him in these parts. He'll turn around and go back the way he came. As well he should. Look at him.

YEA, LOOK AT HIM.

But, Lord...

FOR I WAS HUNGRY, AND YE GAVE ME TO EAT; I WAS THIRSTY, AND YE GAVE ME DRINK; I WAS A STRANGER, AND YE TOOK ME IN.

"What's your name?" he asked, breaking into her thoughts.

"Akira. Akira Macauley."

He opened one eye, arching the brow above it. "Akira?"

"It's Scottish. Means anchor. My grandfather wanted me to have a strong name so I wouldn't be afraid of life, so I'd have a reminder of where to find my Anchor. He placed great store in the meaning of names, my grandfather."

"Mmm." The stranger's eyelid closed.

"And what's your name, if you don't mind me askin'?"

"You can call me Gabe."

"Gabe. Short for Gabriel?" She smiled. "Gabriel—a strong man of God."

Eyes wide open now, he gave her a look that was anything but friendly.

"That's the meaning of your name," she explained.

"You're mistaken, Miss Macauley. That's the last thing my name could mean."

She wasn't mistaken, but something in his dark countenance warned her not to argue.

"I'll fetch my horse and take you to my place. Get you something to eat." She stood up, brushing the grass and dirt from the knees of her overalls.

"You don't have to bother. I've troubled you enough. I can get to Ransom on my own."

Lord, I have a feeling the trouble's yet to begin. Why is that?

She turned toward the road. "Mister, you couldn't make it fifteen yards, let alone fifteen miles."

With a shake of her head, she strode away, away from the stranger whose blue eyes were filled with indescribable pain, away from the man who denied the meaning of his name.

&

Gabe watched her go, her dark red braids swaying against her back, her collie trotting at her heels. Her stride was long and easy, a sign of a person used to walking great distances. She was slender as a reed, but her build was deceiving; she possessed enough brawn to drag a grown man from the road to this tree.

Akira. As strange as her name more than likely.

A strong man of God indeed.

If he'd had the energy, he would have laughed aloud.

But he had no energy, no strength, no courage, no hope. So he closed his eyes and allowed the threatening darkness to move toward him once again.

If you enjoyed *Whispers from Yesterday*, look for…

THE FORGIVING HOUR

by Robin Lee Hatcher

IS HER SON'S ENGAGEMENT A
DREAM…OR A NIGHTMARE?

Though Claire Conway's life hasn't
turned out exactly as she'd
planned, she has much to be
thankful for: She has raised a fine
son, Dakota. Her career is going
well. And for the first time since
her divorce, she's met a man
who stirs romantic feelings in
her broken heart.

Then Dakota brings home
his fiancée, Sara Jennings,
and for the second time in
Claire's life, her world crumbles.
By what seems to be a cruel twist of fate, Dakota
has fallen in love with the woman who was involved in the destruction
of his parents' marriage. The ramifications of this discovery threaten to
destroy the lives of all involved. Claire wishes she could forgive Sara.
But this seems impossible. Yet only in that hour of forgiveness can the
three of them be truly set free…

Filled with real-life issues of bitterness and self-protection, this beauti-
fully written story of one woman's search for peace—*The Forgiving
Hour*—dramatically illustrates the power of supernatural healing,
revealing how God's love transforms lives when we allow Him to work
in our hearts.

"Break out the tissues. I loved *The Forgiving Hour*, and so will you.
Robin Lee Hatcher shows God's grace and mercy in bringing healing
into the most painful of circumstances. This book cuts through the
darkness of betrayal and brings in the miraculous light of Jesus Christ."
— FRANCINE RIVERS, best-selling author

ROBIN LEE HATCHER

Robin Lee Hatcher is the author of more than thirty novels with over four million books in print and is a past president of Romance Writers of America. Her books have won numerous awards, including the Heart of Romance Readers' Choice Award for Best Historical, a Career Achievement Award for Americana Romance from *Romantic Times,* and the Favorite Historical Author Award from *Affaire de Coeur.* She has also been a finalist several times for the prestigious Romance Writers of America RITA award. For her efforts on behalf of literacy, Laubach Literacy International named their romance award "The Robin." Robin and her husband, Jerry, live in Boise, Idaho, as do their two daughters and three young grandchildren.

Readers may write to her at
P.O. Box 4722, Boise, ID 83711-4722
or visit her Web site:
<http://www.robinleehatcher.com>